Introduction

Finishing Touches by Kelly Eileen Hake
In order for Libby Collier's father to keep his business solvent, he agrees to a marriage between his chief financial benefactor and his daughter Tabitha. But when Tabitha jilts her husband-to-be the day before the wedding, Libby is called upon to serve as Captain Gregory Royce's bride in her sister's stead. Can she fill the void in Captain Royce's broken heart as aptly as she transforms his sterile new house on Cranberry Hill into a home?

Beyond the Memories by DiAnn Mills
Miss Maime Bradford has lived in the house on Cranberry Hill since her husband, Clay, purchased the house when they married. World War I sent her beloved to Europe, but he never returned, and Miss Maime never remarried. No man could ever take Clay's place. The Depression hits hard, and Maime opens her doors to those who have not been able to mentally handle the effects. One of the new residents is a man by the name of Hank. He reminds her of Clay, but Clay is dead.

Finally Home by Deborah Raney
Brian Lowe is home from Vietnam in a wheelchair—returning to a nation that doesn't appreciate his sacrifice. Enter Kathy Nowlin, the physical therapist assigned to him. How can he accept help from this outspoken war protester? Dare he befriend someone like her? And can she risk losing her heart to a man so different from her dreams? Will they discover any common ground on which to cultivate the love blossoming unexpectedly between them?

The Pretend Family by Joyce Livingston
When successful entrepreneur and self-declared bachelor Tadd Winsted learns his parents are coming to America for a visit, he has to suddenly produce the family he'd lied about to please them and hires actress Sabrena Stewart and her daughter to play the roles. But when their farce is over will Sabrena and Tadd be able to walk away from one another, or will their role as a family take on a life of its own?

Missouri MEMORIES

The House on Cranberry Hill
Holds Love for
Four Generations of Couples

KELLY EILEEN HAKE • JOYCE LIVINGSTON
DIANN MILLS • DEBORAH RANEY

BARBOUR
PUBLISHING

Published by Barbour Publishing, Inc., P.O. Box 719, Uhrichsville, Ohio 44683, www.barbourbooks.com

Our mission is to publish and distribute inspirational products offering exceptional value and biblical encouragement to the masses.

ecpa Member of the
Evangelical Christian
Publishers Association

Printed in the United States of America.

FINISHING TOUCHES

by Kelly Eileen Hake

Dedication

To God, who gave me the desire to write;
the editorial team at Barbour that gave me the opportunity;
and my critique partners/readers,
Kathleen Y'Barbo, Julia Rich, and Cathy Hake,
who gave me their honest feedback!

Except the LORD build the house,
they labour in vain that build it:
except the LORD keep the city,
the watchman waketh but in vain.

PSALM 127:1

Chapter 1

Hannibal, Missouri, 1898

She's gone!" Pa rushed into Libby's room, his bellow waking her long before he roughly shook her shoulder.

"What?" Libby blinked the sleep from her eyes and pried her father's clenched fingers from her upper arm. Pa had been known to walk the halls in his sleep, but he seemed alert enough this time. . . .

"She's left on the eve of her wedding with Royce to elope with that Lyte chap." Sinking onto the edge of Libby's bed, he extended a piece of paper.

Fighting the sick fingers of dread snaking over her spine, Libby unfolded her sister's crooked creases.

Good-bye, the short note read. *I love Donald and have left to marry him. I know this wasn't the plan, but I have to follow my heart. Tabby*

No apology, no asking for forgiveness—the note of a girl

who'd been loved by all, forgiven her faults, and who saw no reason to expect her charmed existence to change simply because she'd humiliated those who loved her best.

"She won't be harmed. Donald Lyte is besotted with her, and he's well enough off to provide for her. You needn't worry on Tabby's account." Libby traced the swirling loops of her sister's flamboyant writing, as delicate and lovely as the woman who wrote it.

So lovely, Captain Royce never spared a glance for her older sister. The man I've admired for so long. . . Tabby throws his love aside as though it were nothing. Libby's fist crushed the fragile paper before she caught herself doing so. She carefully smoothed the missive on her knee before passing it back to Pa.

"We must inform Captain Royce, Papa." Libby slid from beneath the warmth of her covers and slipped into a dressing gown. "The wedding must be cancelled. The whole thing will be much the worse if the ceremony begins and Tabby doesn't show up."

"Yes," her father agreed dully, not stirring from his defeated slump. "No!" He stirred, his eyes filling with horror. "No, Libby, I can't cancel the wedding!"

"It cannot go on without Tabitha, Papa. We have no choice."

"No choice," he repeated. Suddenly, his hands clasped hers in a viselike grip. "I promised Gregory my daughter's hand, and so he shall have it!"

"Papa," Libby started slowly, fearing he might have slipped into the waking sleep, which had sometimes haunted his nights since Mama's death, "Tabitha has left. She will not marry

Captain Royce. You cannot change that."

"I know; I know that." Papa's eyes gleamed in the light of her bedside candle. "I have more than one eligible daughter, after all. You will take her place tomorrow."

"I—? Papa, that's impossible!" Libby tried to pull away, but his grip tightened painfully. "He's in love with Tabitha! He asked to marry her, not me!"

"Nevertheless, you will marry him, Libby." He gentled his crushing grasp. "You will wed him, or we'll all be destroyed."

"Oh, Papa." Libby knelt beside him and patted his arm. "I already told you, Tabby will be fine. It's true, we'll have to deal with the backlash of her reckless and foolish decision, but the Collier name won't be *destroyed* by a bit of scandal. And Captain Royce. . .well, he did care for Tabitha, but I daresay he'll find another bride easily enough. So long as we don't make him a cliché—left standing at the altar—it will all come out fine in the end."

"No." Papa shook his head with such force, Libby heard the faint *pop-pop* of bones moving unnaturally. "It's not our reputations that will be destroyed, Libby—though surely that will come of it all, too. Our very livelihood is at stake. If one of my daughters doesn't marry Captain Royce tomorrow morning, my business is ruined."

"What are you saying?" She drew a deep breath and held it, bracing herself for the sharp, daggerlike thrust of his next words.

"I've accepted money from him, Libby. Large amounts of money to keep the business afloat—literally." A ghost of a smile chased across his face, leaving it even bleaker as it faded. "The shipping business would have failed without his investment. With this marriage, we were to merge more than our families—our businesses, as well."

The breath whooshed out of her lungs as Libby realized the magnitude of the problem. They wouldn't just be dealing with a jilted groom, but a jilted groom to whom her father owed enough money to ruin them.

"Surely. . .surely Captain Royce wouldn't demand restitution to be vindictive. He's a good man." *A wonderful, handsome, honorable, hardworking man who has sat at our table, listened to our conversation, and all but become a member of our family. . . .*

"We both know he would be within his rights to seek that. He'll be humiliated before the entire town of Hannibal—not to mention the fact that he genuinely cared for Tabitha." Papa buried his head in his hands, fingers viciously combing through his sparse hair. "He'll be furious."

Unable to refute the truth of his assessment, Libby held her tongue. But nothing could chain her mind or lock up the ache inside her heart. She should know. She'd been trying to do just that since the moment Captain Royce proposed to her younger sister.

"You'll have to take your sister's place. It's the only way to save face and still unite our families." Papa straightened and loomed over her. "I will send a messenger notifying Royce of the issue—and my proposed solution. I expect he will agree for the sake of his pride."

Libby winced at her father's statement.

Lord, I've prayed for You to take away my feelings for Captain Royce, to help me reconcile myself to his marriage to my sister. I prayed that if their plans were not Your plans to make it so that Tabitha wouldn't be his bride. Anyone but my sister with the man I care for. . .I never dreamed You would make me that bride—or that I'd regret it so deeply. In my selfishness, have I spoiled things for everyone? Lord, please don't let it be so.

"Come in." The low, melodious voice grated harshly in Gregory Royce's ears. This was not the soft, breathy voice of his beloved, but rather the tones of an imposter. He pushed open the door to find the room empty, save the lone figure seated at the dressing table. He could see no evidence of Tabitha, no indication that this was a cruel trick designed to make him all the more grateful when she glided down the aisle into his waiting arms. His last spark of hope flickered and sputtered.

"So it's true." The words came out clipped, his displeasure evident. He shut his eyes for a moment, reminding himself this was no more Elizabeth's fault than his own, and doubtless she was as wary as he. *Is honor worth such a price? Ah, but if not, what does a man have? I certainly have no love, not with my bride eloping with another man. What do I say to this woman whom I never saw as more than a friend. . .a sister? How do I ensure she's willing when I know that I, for one, am not?*

"It is bad luck to see the bride on her wedding day." Elizabeth's bowed head reflected only brown curls, the pose concealing her face. "I'm sorry, Captain Royce." The apology was for more than her downcast visage, and he knew it instantly.

"I believe we are past that now." The words came out sounding gruff, his consonants razor sharp and cutting.

"True." She raised her head, presenting her face in the mirror. No thick fall of straight blond locks, green eyes tilted slightly at the corner, patrician nose, and rosebud mouth reflected back to him. Instead, he saw a softly rounded face, pert nose, hazel eyes fringed with thick lashes, lips turned down at the corners. Elizabeth couldn't compare with Tabby—and it seemed to Gregory that she knew it well. "We're far past the point where silly customs can ward off bad luck, aren't we?" She gave a brave, if tremulous, smile. It never reached her gaze.

"No." He cleared his throat and tried again. "I meant we're past the point where you call me Captain Royce. A bride should call her husband by his Christian name. I'm Gregory."

"I know." She turned so she faced him completely, rather than conversing through the flat plane of the mirror. "And you should call me by mine. Elizabeth to most, but Libby to family."

"Thank you, Libby." Gregory cast about for the right words to say when everything tumbled around as though intangible. "I wanted to see. . .I need to know. . .are you willing to go through with this? Commit yourself to a marriage of convenience only?"

He saw her wince and mentally kicked himself for being such a brute. "Are you quite sure you're not being forced into anything?" Stupid question. For one reason or another, they had both been forced into this situation.

"Yes." She met his gaze more steadily. "Quite sure. I will see you in the chapel, Gregory." She inclined her head toward the door, only slightly, but with a clear message.

"Until then." He gave a bow and left her to her preparations. What more could he possibly say? They'd be exchanging solemn vows in mere moments. Gregory walked about the grounds until the time of the ceremony, standing through it as though no more than a block of wood until it was his turn to speak.

Looking into her hazel eyes, glistening with unshed tears, Captain Gregory Alan Royce had the distinct sensation of someone slugging him in the gut. A man could be forgiven for such a thought when he was marrying the sister of the woman he loved.

"I, Gregory Alan Royce," he gritted from behind a forced smile on what should have been the happiest day of his life, "take thee," *Tabitha Bethany Collier*, he mentally vowed even as he substituted, "Elizabeth Anne Collier, to be my lawful wedded wife. . ."

The knot in his stomach clenched more tightly with every word he spoke until he got to "for better or for worse," when an irreverent thought offered some relief.

It can't possibly get any worse. Not when my bright little Tabby ran away with another man to avoid wedding me. Not when I've been publicly rejected and saddled with the spinster of the family. Not when the house I've labored to construct for my beloved bride will never feel Tabitha's soft footsteps, hear her tinkling laugh, or see her sparkling eyes.

"As long as we both shall live." The final words throbbed in his temples as he sealed his own fate. Elizabeth was now his wife, and Tabitha lost to him. Forever.

Chapter 2

Libby did not sit beside her husband as she imagined most newlyweds did. Rather she rode into their future across from Captain Gregory on the seat that made her face backward.

The seat that made her stomach churn.

Oh, well. It's been roiling all day, anyway. When I really think about it, it is fitting. . .this marriage is as backwards as this seat. All the same, I wish I wasn't stuck looking back at what I left behind. It seems I can't look forward no matter how hard I try. How do I face the uncertainties before me when my thoughts are troubled by the past? Tabitha couldn't have known the havoc she'd wreak.

She sneaked a peek at her husband—*her husband!*—to find him staring bleakly out the window, resignation dulling his gaze, tension tightening his strong jaw and forcing his posture to be rigid. He had the look of a man on his way to the gallows. And the same noose he faced threatened to strangle her, as well.

"Cap—Gregory?" she ventured, her voice sounding small and hesitant to her own ears. "I was wondering. . ." Her boldness abandoned her and left the question unspoken. Would he elect to have a wedding night, after all? And how could she tell him she'd had no motherly advice. . .that their aunt had passed down marital wisdom solely to Tabitha. Libby had no idea what she was supposed to say to her husband, and her heart broke at the thought he might bed her while wishing for her sister, instead—as he'd done during their wedding that day. Would she ever be more than a weak shadow of her sister to the man she loved?

"Yes?" He turned to her, inclining his head as though encouraging her to speak. As though grateful she was making an attempt to ease the horrible weight of their mutual silence.

"I wondered if. . ." Her courage fled immediately, leaving a spineless heap on the carriage seat. "If there was anything you wanted to tell me about the house. Servants' names, the way you want things run, your favorite dishes, and so on." She finished her question too brightly, striving to push aside her discomfort.

Of all the things. . .I know his favorite dishes. I ask Cook to make at least one of them whenever I know Captain Royce is coming to dinner. After all this time, it was a foolish question. Just look at that gleam in his eye. . .the faraway glint that says more clearly than words that he's drawing away. The regret painting his features as he sees the bride he's bought.

"Jenson is the butler, Mrs. Farley the housekeeper, Mrs. Rowins the cook. There are three maids—Daisy, Rachel, and

Grace." He rattled off the names by rote, obviously uninterested, while Libby struggled to remember them. It might not be important to him, but it was imperative she, as new mistress of the house, get on well with the staff. "Larken is the stable master, and Mr. Barnett is overseeing the construction of the additions. That should be about all you need to know."

"The additions?" She closed her eyes, suddenly remembering Gregory's long, enthusiastic descriptions of the house he was building for Tabitha. She'd forgotten in the press of the wedding and the prospect of marriage itself that she'd be living not only with a man who loved her sister, but also in the house he'd designed and built for her. She'd stepped into Tabitha's life.

"The house is not finished, yet." If his terse answer hadn't conveyed the message clearly enough, his pointed return to staring out the window of the carriage certainly did. The conversation was closed. . .and so, Libby imagined, was his heart.

Stop it, stop it, stop it! She chastened herself. *You decided to marry him so you could make his life as good as possible—to make up for Tabitha's desertion, to show your own love of him. You can't go thinking maudlin thoughts and being selfish. Someone has to be strong enough to work at this marriage, and it's only fair that that someone be you!*

Having given herself that encouraging, albeit silent, speech, Libby straightened her spine and resolved to make Gregory's house. . .no, *their* house—a showplace of her love. She would give it her time, her attention, her focus, and as she worked to make his life comfortable, he'd become comfortable with her. He'd come to appreciate her efforts, and in time, maybe he'd look on her with something more. . . .

Please, God, she prayed. *I know I've no reason to expect it, perhaps no right to ask that he return my feelings in some small measure as time passes, but I have to try. After my selfishness, my envy of my sister's fiancé, and the way it's all turned out, it's the least I can do.*

Gregory sucked in a breath as Cranberry Hill came into view, his chest tightening—not with pride, but regret. Tonight he brought his bride home. . .but it wasn't the bride he'd planned on, and without Tabitha, Cranberry Hill would never be the home he'd envisioned, either.

As they ascended the hill, Gregory's heart sank. There, its Greek Revival architecture silhouetted by the pale moon, Cranberry Hill waited. What had seemed full of promise—a foundation for the future—now seemed stark and bare, cold and forbidding. The glassless windows he'd planned to fill with stained glass chosen with Tabitha now gaped as blind eyes. The sharp corners of the house, which he'd hoped to soften with wraparound porches where he and his bride could sit together in the evening, now gleamed with warning. The house seemed exposed as no more than dangerous angles and barren edges by the lack of trees and flowers, hedges and garden paths he'd thought Tabitha would love to create.

Gregory turned away from the sight of the house he'd loved, seeking solace from the crowding thoughts of loss. He looked up only to be confronted once again with the visage of his bride. No matter where he looked, all he could see was what he was missing. Everything had become a dark reminder of Tabitha's betrayal, and the mockery she'd made of Cranberry Hill—of him.

Libby barely had time to nod at the servants assembled in the great hall before the housekeeper whisked her up to her suite of rooms. As she passed through the corridors, Libby managed to register how, though the house stood empty for the most part, its construction had been seen to with loving detail. Every glance showed luxurious spaces, large windows that would allow daylight to pour into the house. It was a house waiting for its mistress to fill it with warmth and family—waiting for her to make it a home.

And I will, she promised herself. *Carpets, furnishings, draperies, windows, trees outside. . .there's much to be done. And every project I accomplish, every little thing I add, will proclaim that this house belongs to Gregory and me. I will make my mark on this house, as I will make my mark in his life. With God's help and a little determination, I can make this marriage work.*

"This is the master bedroom," Mrs. Farley declared proudly, making a sweeping motion to encompass the impressive sight.

"Oh," Libby breathed. This room was a dream sprung to vivid life, and she was careful to take in only portions of it at once lest she be overwhelmed. Gregory had seen to every detail, from the silk wall hangings in rich cream to the plush carpeting in deep blue and the heavy oak armoire claiming the corner near a cozy stone fireplace. Before the fireplace sat two wingback chairs, turned toward one another as though inviting the master and lady of the house to relax beside the fire. Libby's gaze followed the graceful lines of the tall chairs and beyond. . .and she caught her breath. There, against the back wall, protruding into the middle of the room, stood the bed. Mammoth, hewn of the same beautiful oak as the armoire and sporting a carved headboard and four posters, it seemed to fill the entire room, though Libby could see a settee in the rounded corner beyond. The blue silk canopy matched the cream-and-blue patterned coverlet and plump pillows. Without a doubt, the bed was the focus of the room. . .and it rapidly became the focus of her thoughts, as well.

The master bedroom—his bedroom. The room I'm to share with him. Tonight. Libby closed her eyes against a surge of apprehension. When she opened them, she realized that Mrs. Farley had begun speaking once more.

"The master bath is through the door beside the armoire, here." She pushed open the door to give Libby a glimpse inside.

She caught the impression of sparkling white tiles and gold-finished fixtures as Mrs. Farley turned a knob and added fresh water to the already steaming claw-foot tub.

"We thought you might like a bath." The housekeeper's ears turned red. "A nice, warm soak to relax you and make you comfortable-like. Master Royce went to the study, so you'll have some time to yourself. . . ."

"Thank you." Libby gave a short nod, and the woman bustled out of the bathroom.

"Daisy put your things in the armoire and dresser when they was sent over, so you should have all you need. And if you want anything, just use the bellpull and one of us will come straightaway." The woman folded her hands in front of her apron. "And when you and the master ring for breakfast in the morning, we'll bring in a tray of fruit and muffins and eggs and such. Master Royce prefers coffee, but do you have a liking for chocolate, instead?"

"Yes, please." And with that, the woman left Libby to prepare for the night ahead.

Chapter 3

With nothing better to do, Libby gave in to the lure of the hot bath, luxuriating in the water until it finally began to cool. She pulled the drain, wrapped herself in a fluffy blue towel, and peeked around the door to see whether or not Gregory had come to her. What she'd do if he had, she couldn't say. He hadn't, so she tiptoed to the dresser, searching through the drawers until she came to one filled with familiar, soft flannel nightdresses. She donned one, dismayed to find it was not loose or comfortable, as a nightdress should be, but close fitting, stretched across her chest and hips in a way that left her feeling exposed. Libby drew it off, quickly grabbing another only to encounter the same problem. The truth of the situation hit her.

These aren't mine. Everything in the room belonged to Tabby. When Mrs. Farley said the maids had put away the clothes she'd sent over, she assumed her things had been brought. Instead, she found the garments she'd lovingly packed and sent for her sister two days ago—before everything changed.

Libby carefully folded the first nightgown and laid it back in the drawer before wandering toward the fire and collapsing into one of the overstuffed wingback chairs. *Here I am, in Tabby's nightdress, in the room Gregory decorated for my sister, in the home he built for her, and all I can do is wait.* And so, she sat and tried to distract her thoughts from why Gregory wasn't with her yet.

And she waited.

Gregory glowered at the ledger spread before him on the desk in his study. He stared, unseeing, but knowing what it said by memory alone. Neat columns listed dates, prices paid, and shipping arrangements for lumber, tile, railing, cement, windowpanes, shutters, columns, cornices, bricks, and stone—everything required to build the house in which he now sat. A record of how he'd spent his time and money for the past year, preparing for what would never be.

Lord, rage burns in my belly, the weight of betrayal presses upon my chest.

How could Tabitha have done this to him?

Worse still, how did he not see that she had not returned his regard? Had he been so blinded by her beauty that he missed her selfish nature? She had made a fool of him! A mockery of all he offered her—everything she accepted. Now Libby waited in his chamber—no, *their* chamber—where he should be on his wedding night. But he could not go to her. Not when he'd thought so long about marrying her sister! So here he sat, a prisoner in the jail he'd constructed for himself, bit by bit. Never had an architect constructed such a fine goal. Never had Gregory dreamed his dreams would fail.

What am I to do with this bride who should be no wife of mine? Father, I seek Your peace but find it obscured by the cloud of my new marriage. Help me know what to do, Lord.

No matter how hard he tried to find an avenue of escape, he found nothing. Tabitha had eloped with Donald Lyte, leaving Gregory to wed her sister or be made a laughingstock.

Maybe, he mused as he thought of the strange woman upstairs, *it would have been better to be a laughingstock.*

Gregory fisted his hands in the hair at his temples and groaned. *No.* More was at stake than just his pride. That would have ruined his business, too. Clients needed to know he was a man who delivered on his promises, who had everything under control. If they lost their belief in his ability to do that, it would all be over. And after the money he'd paid to help William Collier and to build Cranberry Hill. . .he couldn't afford that. None of them could.

That's it! Abruptly, Gregory knew what he'd do to avoid this sham of a marriage without losing face. Dipping his pen in an uncapped bottle of ink, he began to scratch out a message.

Libby awoke the next morning to find herself inside the enormous canopied bed, snuggled under the covers. Alone, she could find no memory of having left the chair before the fire.

I must have fallen asleep, she deduced. But she must have drifted off while sitting before the fire. There wasn't a chance Libby would have climbed into his bed to wait for him! She knew she hadn't.

Gregory wasn't in the room now—he must have come in and found her sleeping then carried her to the bed. Why must she be such a sound sleeper? Had he even tried to awaken her? She sat bolt upright at her next thought.

Did he think I was trying to avoid him? Did he spend the night beside me? She could feel the heat of her blush creep up her neck and into her cheeks.

Desperate to know, she looked at the pillow beside her, intending to search for anything that would show he'd slept there. An indentation in the pillow, something. . .but all she found was a folded sheet of paper with her name written on it, resting on a pristine and undisturbed pillowslip.

Libby, it read. Not, "Dear Libby," or "My Darling Bride," but simply her nickname. She bit back a sigh at the stark beginning and tried to focus on the few lines scrawled across the page. Maybe he'd tell her what he planned for the day, or how he hoped to make the marriage work. . .

Libby,

 I've been called away on business and will leave early this morning to oversee a paddleboat run. I should be able to return in a fortnight.

 I've already made arrangements with the bank, so you may furnish the place as you see fit. Mrs. Farley should be of great assistance.

Gregory Alan Royce

She flipped the paper over to make sure nothing more was written on the back. Blank. A few curt words, a handful of sentences, and no apology or endearment whatsoever. Libby felt her shoulders slump, and she drew her knees to her chest, scanning the lines once more to be sure. It was the letter of a man happy to get away.

From me. She pressed the back of her hand against her lips to suppress the powerful swell of emotion. Gregory had never wanted her before, and she'd been a fool to hope that a ceremony would change his feelings. How could she have ever thought he'd soften toward her so soon? Her husband was a strong man who had known what he wanted, but he had been cheated out of it. Expecting Tabitha and ending up with herself, instead. . .it wasn't too difficult to imagine his bitter disappointment.

When Tabitha became engaged, I feared I'd never be wed, that I'd be the lonely spinster for the rest of my days. All my prayers, all my dreams of having a love of my own, a home and family outside of my father's. . .and I inherit Tabitha's castoffs. Tears slid down her cheeks as she shut her eyes. *How was I to know that marriage to the man I wanted would leave me more alone than ever? At home I had Papa and the servants I've known my entire life. Here I have nothing.*

Wrong. A small but powerful voice shook her from her self-pity with its conviction. She considered for a moment, dropping her head in shame and relief.

Lord, how could I have thought for a moment I had nothing when I have You? You will neither leave me nor forsake me, and with the power of Your love and the force of Your will, anything is possible. Thank You. Her tears were of gratitude now.

How foolish of her to wallow in pity when she'd been given so much for which to be thankful. Papa's business was saved, Tabitha was safely wed to the man she loved, and, although it wasn't the way Libby had dreamt it, so was she. Of course, Gregory was struggling with the situation. Who could blame him?

It was up to Libby to be the best wife she could be, make his house a home and this marriage a family. She, for one, had meant every word of her marriage vows. Now was the time to live them out.

She pushed aside the covers and sank into the thick cushion of carpet beneath her bare feet. Libby rifled through the delicate dresses made for her petite sister until she found a shapeless brown piece that accommodated her more generous frame. One of the first things she needed to do was have her own things sent over. She cast another glance at the bursting wardrobe and reminded herself to have the maids pack up Tabitha's things and return them. They had no place here, and Tabitha, no doubt, needed them.

Fully dressed, her hair pulled back in a loose chignon, Libby threw open the door.

"Oh!" A startled maid, her hand raised as though to rap upon the door, quickly recovered and bobbed a curtsy. "Mrs. Royce is waiting in the parlor, ma'am. We tried to say you wasn't at home, but she insisted I fetch you immediately."

"Ah. I'll see her straightaway." Libby pushed her thoughts of exploring the house to the back of her mind and made her way to the parlor with a quick prayer for strength. Surely Gregory's mother would have questions about. . .everything.

Chapter 4

M rs. Royce." Libby stepped into the room and politely acknowledged her new mother-in-law.

"Elizabeth," the woman returned. As she perused Libby unabashedly, Libby did the same.

Mrs. Royce's black hair, so like her son's, bore streaks of white. Age had stolen none of her handsome looks, for hers was no soft prettiness, but rather the attraction of lively intelligence and inner strength.

"Daisy will bring us some refreshments shortly." Libby made small talk as she sat on the settee opposite the other woman. "I'd imagine it's a good time for us to get better acquainted. Gregory should be pleased to return and find us. . . companionable." She finished with a slight smile, hoping Mrs. Royce would feel the same way rather than blame Libby for the unfortunate situation they had to deal with.

"So he has left, then?" Mrs. Royce huffed in disbelief. "I could scarce credit it when I read his short note. Inexcusable behavior." Her gaze warmed as it rested on Libby. "I assure you I did raise him with manners, my dear." The warmth in her eyes fled as she set her jaw. "Though he's every right to his anger after the cruel trick your sister played upon him. My son deserves better than that type of treatment."

"Absolutely." Libby nodded. "Gregory has been coming to my father's house for many months and has always been a perfect gentleman. And no gentleman deserves to be thrown over on his wedding day." She leaned forward, encouraged by her mother-in-law's comments. "I don't blame him for needing a bit of time to himself after the...upset."

"You're a wise woman, Elizabeth." Mrs. Royce settled back as though ready for a long coze. "And, though I know Gregory fancied himself in love with Tabitha, I warned him she was a flighty chit who wouldn't be a match for him."

"I am fully aware of the repercussions of my sister's actions," Libby spoke more stiffly now, "but she is my sister and will make a fine wife."

"I didn't say she wouldn't, m'dear." Mrs. Royce patted her knee consolingly. "Simply that she wouldn't have made Gregory happy. Now, now, don't say anything at all. It's good that you're loyal to your sister, but Gregory needs more from a wife than a pretty smile and girlish charm."

Libby sat in silence, unsure how to respond to this pronouncement. It didn't seem to matter, as Gregory's mother plunged ahead.

"You see, Elizabeth, I'm of the opinion that this will be a much better marriage than the other would have been. After

Gregory gets over his wounded pride and realizes it, you'll do well together."

At this, Libby was so shocked—and pleased—she couldn't do more than gape at her new mother-in-law.

"Do close your mouth, Elizabeth." Mrs. Royce smiled and removed her gloves. "I've come to help you."

Gregory stood at the helm of his largest paddleboat the day after his wedding, looking out across the mighty Mississippi River. Usually the majestic sight soothed his nerves, reaffirmed his faith, and made him give thanks for the wonders God created. Today, glutted with the water from plentiful spring rain, the glorious river showed her less favorable side as the current did its best to push his vessel off course.

Bits of flotsam dotted the water, proving to be much larger and more threatening than they initially seemed, lurking beneath the hidden depths of the river's face. The mighty Mississippi, long his friend, had turned her power against him on this voyage. She, like his mother's hastily scribbled response to his notice, urged him to return to his unwanted bride.

"Women," Gregory growled to the breeze, "always contrary." *And formidable,* he added silently as the *Riverrider* narrowly avoided a large, mostly submerged patch of jagged rocks.

All the same. The river, with her smooth-flowing surface, turns to a churning threat at a moment's notice. *Tabitha fits the pattern, with her guileless gaze, showing only at the last moment her ruthless determination to leave. Ma, with her calm demeanor and steely resolve, hides her true strength until it is absolutely necessary to unleash it.*

Leaving charge of the boat to his first mate, Gregory made his way to his cabin. The more he thought about it, the more he knew he'd made the right decision. Better to have time to sort out the way he wanted to handle things than be blindsided by Elizabeth. There was no telling what she'd want to do.

As he sat at his desk to overlook the cargo log, Gregory couldn't concentrate as he pondered the mystery that was Woman.

No wonder Adam was undone by Eve—women always have the element of surprise!

"Help me with what, exactly?" Libby chose the words carefully, uncertain how this woman could help her make her marriage work, but somehow believing something wonderful lay ahead.

"Adjust to your new life, of course." Mrs. Royce beamed and gave a tiny wink before adding, "And show you how to make the adjustment easier for Gregory, too."

"Thank you, Mrs. Royce—"

"Sarah, please call me Sarah."

"Thank you, Sarah," Libby started again only to realize she'd forgotten what, precisely, she'd meant to say. "And friends and family call me Libby."

"Libby." The older woman tested it out and nodded. "That suits you far better. Fits your warmth and sparkle."

"Sparkle?" she echoed faintly. Tabitha was the one who sparkled.

"No one ever told you that?" Mrs. Roy—*Sarah* harrumphed. "That's what comes from losing your mother at such a young age. Men, my dear, tend to have difficulty looking beyond the superficial. However"—she pondered for a moment—"I think you'll find Gregory to be an exception, when given time enough. He always was a thinker—like his father."

"Oh." Libby had the feeling the conversation had moved along without her, since she was still marveling over being told she had sparkle.

"Yes. Now," Sarah squinted at her and questioned, "I suppose you've always heard that Tabitha was the pretty one? Heard more comments than you cared to about her loveliness, swiftly followed by some statement about what a good girl you were or some such thing?" She waited for Libby's nod, then kept on. "Well, Tabitha *is* pretty—"

Libby fought to keep the smile on her face. Would there be no end of comparisons between her and Tabby?

"—In an *obvious* sort of way." Sarah's tone caught Libby's attention once more. "But I think that makes it rather. . . commonplace. You have a loveliness that is far more than what meets the eye. I've been watching you girls for a while, you see. I know that you're the heart of your family, always putting your sister first, seeing to your father's comfort. . .it's easy to tell when one pays a moment's attention."

"We're a family," Libby protested. "We watch out for each other."

"And so you should. But you do the lion's share." Sarah sat back, satisfied with her point. "And that, dear Libby, is how you sparkle." She seemed to catch Libby's disbelief because she shook her head. "Let me put it this way, m'dear. Tabitha is like crystal—full of color to catch the eye. You, on the other hand, are like a window. You let the light of love shine through you and onto others. It's the best kind of sparkle there is!"

"I—" Libby blinked furiously to hold back what seemed a flood of tears. "No one's ever said anything half so wonderful to me." She took the handkerchief the other woman held out to her and soaked it through before regaining a semblance of dignity. "Thank you."

"It's nothing more than the truth." Sarah moved to kneel before her. "And I thought now, at a time when so much seems to have happened to throw you off-kilter, you might need to hear it from someone who's been around long enough to know."

"I'll never forget it."

"See that you don't, Libby. Now that you realize what it is you contribute to a household, let's get started."

"Yes!" Libby exclaimed. As Sarah rose to her feet, Libby stood to join her, determined to lavish love on this woman, her son, and their house. "Let's make this house into a home Gregory will be glad to come back to!"

Chapter 4

T elegram, Cap'n!" Mr. Bates thrust the paper toward him as Gregory oversaw the unloading of the cargo hold.

"Thank you." He took the message, absently tapping it against the side of his leg as two men almost dropped a crate. The telegram would wait, but it seemed his men might not be able to keep a grip on things.

"Cap'n?" His voice now hesitant, Mr. Bates wouldn't meet Gregory's gaze.

"Yes?" Gregory raised a brow, wondering what could be keeping the man from assisting his mates with the work at hand.

"Not that it's any of my concern, mind," he hedged, "but the telegraph operator made particular mention of the. . .wait, how did he put it? Said he'd never seen the likes of it before, and that. . ."

A growing sense of unease unfurled in Gregory's stomach.

Suddenly, the innocuous sheet of paper in his hand became a forbidding trap. Only one person would have sent such a remarkable telegram. . . .

"Your mam sounds a lot like his," Mr. Bates finished. "So. . .I thought you might like fair warning before you read the thing." With one look at Gregory's expression, the man scuttled away like a crab trying to outrun a vicious seagull.

Resigned to finding a lecture from his mother, Gregory unsealed the message and groaned at his first glimpse. The telegraph operator hadn't lied—who but his mother would send such a personal message through Morse code? He straightened his shoulders. Yes, he respected his mother, honored her as well he should, but he was a man grown. He'd make his own decisions, and that would be the end of it. But to decide how to respond, he'd have to read the thing.

Gregory Alan Royce–stop–Your hasty departure has reduced me to sending this telegram–stop–You didn't respond to my note–stop–Things went awry, but I have faith that God has plans for this marriage–stop– I've been getting to know your new bride–stop–She is a wonderful girl, and I think you're far luckier than you know–stop–I understand you have a business to maintain, but don't forget the important business left unfinished at Cranberry Hill–stop–There is much to do here, and we eagerly await your return which I'm certain will be as soon as you can manage–stop–God bless you, son–stop–Sarah Royce–stop

Gregory let out a snort of laughter. The message—so proper but underlined with steel—was so typical of his mother that a smile crept across his face. *She should teach politicians just what to say to make their comments unassailable but crystal clear.*

Here, again, was the proof of feminine trickery. Sweet words designed to elicit the desired response. Any man would have kept it short and simple: *Get back here, NOW.* But that wasn't his mother's style. Gregory shook his head ruefully.

Lord, I know You speak through Your Word, pastors, and the wise counsel of church elders. I just wonder how often the more subtle influence of our mothers is directly traced back to Your will.

Summons or no, he already intended to return. Leaving his bride—albeit the wrong one—with no more than a note on the morning after their wedding was a knee-jerk reaction to the death of his carefully laid plans.

"Mr. Bates!" Gregory strode toward his first mate. "I'll be in my cabin. As soon as the cargo is exchanged, we return to Hannibal." *And Cranberry Hill.*

"Isn't it perfect?" Libby breathed, surveying the newly renovated parlor. *Her* newly renovated parlor.

"To tell the truth, I can scarce believe the difference," her mother-in-law agreed. "Has it only been twelve days since we first sat in an empty room with bare floors and no more than a pair of settees thrown in the center?"

"I'm certain of it." Libby grinned. "Between this room and overseeing the main entry, I've needed every single minute!"

"And you've done a lovely job. When you showed me the color for those wall hangings, I had my doubts, but the primrose seems just right in here."

"Yellow was a bold choice, but with the circular windows the light pours in to make it bright and airy. The eggshell upholstery on the settees and new chairs softens it a little bit."

"Where on earth did you find this rug?" Sarah sank into the plush carpet, its muted tones of rose, gold, and cream centering the room.

"At the emporium, tucked away in a corner. When I saw it, I just knew I had to bring it home. And as soon as it was here, I realized the throw cushions and drapes needed gold trimming to match." Libby stepped around the room, eyeing the crystal-based lamp on an elegant end table, the porcelain mantle clock next to a vase of yellow roses. Not a thing stood out of place, all blended into a sense of inviting harmony she hoped would soon be the tone of her marriage, as well.

"The gold trimming really ties the cream and yellow together. You've a wonderful eye for color, Libby!" Sarah's approval widened Libby's grin.

"I thought the new marble tile in the entryway blended well." She cast a glance through the double parlor doors, thrown proudly open, to glimpse the entry beyond.

"Indeed. The sandy slate tiles from before were a poor choice," Sarah mused. "The white of the marble brightens the place, turns the attention to the grand stairway, as well it should. The slight golden veins through the tiles are what make it truly blend with the parlor. You have outdone yourself, my dear!"

"You helped pick out most of these things," Libby reminded her new friend. "It wouldn't have come together so quickly without the benefit of your expertise!"

"Pfft." Sarah waved away her gratitude. "I love shopping—any excuse will do. Though I must say"—she cast an admiring glance at her surroundings before continuing—"it's even more of a pleasure with results such as these. Gregory will be very surprised when he returns from his business trip."

"I hope he likes it," Libby fretted. "His note said I could put the house in order, and surely you would have mentioned it to me if he abhorred yellow, but it is a rather dramatic change." She stopped, considering how to phrase her next thought without abandoning diplomacy. "And he's had enough dramatic changes recently to last him a good long while."

"Ah." Sarah drew closer and reached for Libby's hands, giving them a reassuring squeeze. "But sometimes a dramatic change is precisely what's needed to show a man what's right in front of his nose. Speaking of which. . ." Her words trailed off.

"What?" Now Libby squeezed Sarah's hands, prodding her.

"I hope you take this in the spirit it is intended, my dear, but the house isn't the only beautiful thing here that could benefit from some attention and color." Her mother-in-law withdrew her hands from Libby's grasp and cupped her cheek. "It's time we showcased your loveliness. I daresay you'll be surprised by what you see when you put yourself in my hands."

"I've more than enough serviceable clothing," Libby hedged. "Though I could do with a few more aprons—getting this house into shape is surprisingly messy with all the construction!"

"Serviceable doesn't mean feminine," the older woman continued ruthlessly, "or flattering. Don't you think some lovely things, perhaps a new hairstyle, would put a spring into your step? Every woman should make the most of herself."

"Agreed. And I'm making the most out of my talents by making this house into the home where Gregory will want to spend his time." *I may not be able to make him want to share his life with me, but Cranberry Hill could prove an irresistible lure.* Libby left the thought unspoken but was certain Sarah knew, anyway.

"You're doing a wonderful job, that's true." The other woman's eyes gleamed with determination. "But I've a gift for knowing what will flatter the figure and bring a bloom to the cheeks of a young woman who never spent the time to experiment with such things before. Surely you wouldn't deny my gift?" Her eyes were widely incredulous now. "Not your mother-in-law!"

"It's not that I'm denying your gift, I'm just asking that you use it to help me with Cranberry Hill." Libby pasted on a smile.

"I'm already doing that, Libby." She strode—no, stalked—up to where Libby had retreated. "Behind your modesty there is a surprise waiting to be discovered. Let's make the most of it!"

"Now, Sarah," Libby admonished. "You can't turn a sow's ear into a silk purse." *And I'll never be the beauty Tabby is.* She forced cheer into her tone. "Let's just keep our focus on Cranberry Hill for now. Have I told you what I'm planning for the music room? With a little added elegance, it will do well as a ballroom, should we ever have need of one. Come with me."

Though Sarah frowned at Libby's obvious evasion, she followed her new daughter-in-law farther into the house. Libby was simply grateful Gregory's mother hadn't pressed the issue of her admittedly plain appearance. Lovely dresses couldn't conceal the fact that she wasn't the bride Gregory had wanted.

Chapter 6

"Good to have you home, Captain Royce." Jenson gave an angled bow at the waist before taking Gregory's coat.

"Mm? Oh, yes." Gregory looked up long enough to dismiss the butler before returning his attention to the floor beneath his feet.

The slate-grey tile he'd ordered and overseen as it was installed was no more. And he couldn't say he mourned the loss, not when its replacement was fit for a palace. In place of the grey lay the finest marble tile, golden streaks threading gracefully throughout the main entry. His footsteps clicked sharply as he moved toward the grand staircase, intent on a good bath and shave before he greeted his wife. *My wife.* He shook his head and kept moving.

Out of the corner of his eye, he caught a glimpse of the parlor to his left. He halted, making a measured turn to verify his first impression. It was correct—she'd decorated the room in a soft butter yellow turned sweetly vibrant by the afternoon sun. He detoured into the parlor to explore farther. Gregory moved toward the center of the room, halting as a feminine voice spoke from the doorway behind him.

"Welcome home, husband." Libby sounded warm, but hesitant.

"Thank you." Gregory moved to face her. "It's good to be home." The platitude escaped him before he had the chance to examine it. Was it good to be in the home where he'd brought the wrong bride? More importantly, was this even his home anymore?

He cast another glance around the room, taking in cream drapes with gold braid and fringe, settees and chairs furnished in the same eggshell, softening the yellow silk wall hangings. Even the rug beneath his feet, tempering the hardwood floors with luxurious depth, matched the décor.

"What do you think?" His wife sounded downright nervous now, and Gregory mentally kicked himself for his long silence. She'd obviously been hard at work.

"I like it." He made the decision aloud, surprised to find it true. "Yellow wouldn't have been something I would have chosen, but it's just right in here."

At his nod and words of praise, she beamed. Gregory stood stock-still for a moment, transfixed by his bride's sudden transformation. Libby's smile lit her face, brought a sparkle to her eyes, and almost seemed to make her taller.

I'll have to make her smile more often. The thought caught him off guard, and Gregory wondered why he'd never noticed

Libby's smile before. He'd known her for months, shared count-less meals with her. It was hard to believe she'd never smiled in front of him even once in all that time. He must have been distracted by Tabitha.

The thought brought him crashing back to the reality of his disappointment. Clearing his throat, Gregory excused himself from the room.

"I'll freshen up and see you at supper." The question came out sounding more like an order than a polite request.

"I look forward to it." Libby had raised her chin as though answering a challenge. "Though it will be served in the break-fast room tonight, as we began renovating the dining room yes-terday afternoon."

"Very well." He strode past her, boots clicking smartly on the new marble tile as he made his way to the staircase. The sound almost seemed to echo in the large space of the house.

When he reached the second floor he turned left by habit, only to be brought up short. The master bedroom was where Libby slept now. If he went there, it would be tantamount to announcing his intent to share the room—and its bed—with her. He made a sharp turn to the right, unwilling to make such a weighty decision before spending more time with his unex-pected bride.

Libby stood in the parlor, trying, as she had many times before, to see it as Gregory would. As Gregory had.

When the housekeeper informed her the master of the

house had returned, Libby hastily made her way downstairs to greet him. He'd already left the entryway, robbing her of his reaction to the new floor. She'd headed for the library, since that's where he'd disappeared on their wedding night, only to see him standing in the doorway of the parlor.

The light from the windows shone on his dark hair and illuminated the breadth of his shoulders beneath his jacket. His hands clasped behind him, legs spread for balance, he could easily have been on board one of his ships, surveying his domain. Which seemed to be precisely what he was doing here.

Libby opened her mouth but found herself reluctant to speak as her husband moved farther into the room as though drawn to its warmth. She bit her lip as his gaze swept the room, taking in the drapes, the newly refurbished settees, and even the carpet now beneath one of his black boots.

Still silent, Libby took in his every motion—the inquisitive tilt of his head, the measuring way he swept a hand along the back of the settee, and the way he compared the time displayed on the porcelain mantle clock to his own watch, nodding as he returned it to his pocket. When it seemed he'd fully assessed the room and would turn to find her gauging his reaction, Libby hurriedly said the first thing she could think of before he caught her watching him.

"Welcome home," she'd told him, as though it were her place to do so. And, strange though it felt, it was.

"Thank you. It's good to be home." His words sounded sincere, if awkward, before heavy silence fell between them. Gregory glanced around the room once more as though weighing his words before he gave his opinion. Still he re-mained quiet.

He hates it. Suddenly, she questioned her choices. Soft primrose and eggshell? What had possessed her? *I should have chosen what Tabitha would have—deep jewel tones vibrant enough to enhance her own beauty.* The bitter tang of failure clawed its way up Libby's stomach while she awaited his verdict, spilling out in a rush of blurted, desperate words.

"What do you think?" She winced as she heard herself demand that he share his thoughts with her. But she had to know.

When he praised her efforts, Libby locked her suddenly shaky knees, putting a hand to the doorframe to steady herself. She could feel herself smile, practically from ear to ear, know-ing that ladies gave tiny, polite, demure smiles, but unable to reign in her joy at the first hint of approval from her husband.

When he told her he'd go freshen up and see her later, at supper, she saw another opportunity to win his admiration. As he headed up the steps of the grand staircase, Libby rushed to the large kitchen hidden behind. She bypassed the cook for the moment, flinging open the door to the pantry and eyeing its contents. What would Gregory enjoy the most?

"I'd like to change tonight's menu," she informed Mrs. Rowins, who merely nodded. "As the captain is home now, we'll have more than a simple supper. Instead, we'll need to serve multiple courses. Not seven," she hastily amended as the cook blanched, "but certainly a soup course and a main course and dessert."

"Oh, yes." The cook nodded, obviously relieved not to be called upon to prepare a feast at the eleventh hour.

Libby had taken to a bit of soup and some cold cuts with biscuits on a tray for her supper. Since the dining room wasn't useable and the master wasn't home, it had been a sensible arrangement. Now that Gregory was back, meal plans needed to change. She and the cook put their heads together, planning a simple but robust meal of his favorites.

When all was settled, Libby headed to the breakfast room with one of the maids, issuing last-minute instructions that it be dusted, scrubbed, polished, and set for supper. As she left another room in a flurry of activity, she smiled. She would pull off this mistress-of-a-grand-house thing yet. Gregory would have no cause to complain of her ability to manage Cranberry Hill.

Libby turned to the master suite, coming up short when she realized Gregory might well be using the water closet. After all, he was the master of the house, and this was his room. He didn't forfeit his rights because he had elected not to share it with her on their wedding night. Now that the shock of it all was further behind them, would he come to her?

Libby tentatively stepped into the room, both relieved and crestfallen to find the door to the restroom wide open, the room beyond completely empty. He'd chosen to use a different room for now, perhaps out of consideration for her. Perhaps out of his own discomfort. Libby firmly pushed the troubling thoughts away. Now was her time to prepare, not wallow in doubt.

She freshened up, re-pinned her hair into her customary chignon, and stood before the enormous armoire. She flicked through her dresses, suddenly wishing she had taken Sarah up on her offer to "make Libby over" or had, at least, ordered a few more stylish items.

No. I'll not become a pale imitation of Tabitha. When Gregory comes to accept me, it will be for who I am without any furbelows or gewgaws to mask me. Her decision made, Libby changed into her best dress, a pale mauve with lace edging, and slid her feet into delicate leather slippers in a slightly darker shade. She may not look as though she'd stepped from the pages of *Peterson's Magazine*, but it was a vast improvement over the dowdy gray dress and walking boots she'd worn earlier.

So Libby went downstairs to meet her husband, a prayer on her lips and hope in her heart.

Chapter 7

Gregory came back to find the feminine touches that would make Cranberry Hill a home—furnishings and decorations and whatnot. Even better, he'd discovered a delightful supper companion for what might just be the best meal he'd eaten in the past year.

Beef and barley soup was made warmer still by Libby's earnest inquires about the *Riverrider* and her crew. No idle conversation, here. He got the impression she really wanted to know about his day-to-day life.

Thick-cut pork chops and buttered baked potatoes served alongside her generous smile went down a treat. Amazing the way her smile transformed her face from somewhat ordinary to riveting. Gregory almost found himself regretting his much-prized electricity as he imagined what the soft flicker of candlelight would bring to their table.

Just when he was sure he couldn't swallow another bite, the maids brought out his favorite dessert—rhubarb pie.

"This is my favorite!" He accepted a large slice and tucked in with relish.

"I know." Libby's soft whisper had him putting down his fork to concentrate on her words. "I remembered from when you ate at my family home."

"It's wonderful." He realized he didn't just mean the delicious sweet—there was something touching about having a wife who remembered his favorite dish and arranged to serve it to him on his first night home. He savored the dark coffee as she shyly mentioned plans for Cranberry Hill, seeking his opinions about what he wanted their home to be. Incredible how her ideas so nearly matched his own.

For the first time, he'd felt the faint stirring of hope that this marriage could work. Despite Tabitha's betrayal and the destruction of his carefully laid plans, Gregory saw that his mother might be right—he was fortunate in his bride. A new confidence replaced his earlier misgiving, and it seemed only natural to take the next step when darkness fell.

❀

Gregory awoke the next morning with a navy blue canopy over his head and his wife by his side. Her head cushioned in the nook between his arm and chest, her glorious hair brushing over both their pillows.

He looked down to see the dark sweep of her lashes against the rosy bloom of her cheek, a faint smile toying at the corner of her mouth. The warmth of her breath fanned against his side while he remained still, loathe to waken her. In sleep, Libby was all sweet vulnerability and softness.

My bride. Strange how the thought no longer shot arrows of remorse through the center of his chest.

Now, he cautiously slid his arm from beneath her neck, fingering the silken strands of her hair as he withdrew. Angling himself on one elbow, Gregory pressed a gentle kiss on Libby's brow before leaving the warmth of their bed.

Lord, he prayed as he dressed quietly and slipped out the door and down the staircase, *thank You for watching over me. It could easily have been the end of everything when I chose my bride rather than listening to Your will. Libby may never be the bride I wanted, but I begin to wonder whether she's the bride You knew I needed. Bless us as we seek to make this marriage work, Lord. Amen.*

Gregory strode into the library, which doubled as his study, intent on getting to work. There was business to be done, after all. He banged his knees as he sat at the too-short desk, setting it to a dangerous wobble. Gregory had to move fast to keep the day's mail from sliding to the floor in an undignified heap.

He began to go through the pile, divvying the letters into categories as he went. *Bill, invitation, invoice, bill, shipment request, accounting information for last quarter, invitation. . .* He stopped as he came across a thick vellum envelope, which bore only the Cranberry Hill address. No return address, no name of sender, nothing to indicate whether the message was for him or Libby. Something about the looping curls of the writing tickled the edges of his memory. . . .

Tabitha. His throat seemed to close at the realization. What could she possibly say to him after she'd left him standing at the altar, humiliated and betrayed before the entire city? How dare she write now! But it must be important, or, at the very least, the heartfelt apology she owed him.

Gregory slashed open the missive with such force the letter opener jabbed him in the thumb. A drop of blood welled on the pad of the injured finger, smearing onto the envelope as he withdrew the paper inside.

I'm so sorry, the first line read. No introduction, no use of his name whatsoever. Gregory crushed his hand into a fist, ignoring the sharp pain from his thumb. He unfolded the rest of the paper to read the note in its entirety.

> *I'm so sorry. Please believe that I never intended things to happen as they did. I truly love Donald and know he adores me just the same. We're wed now, on a trip to Boston to meet some of his old friends from university. It will be weeks before I come back to see you. I've heard the news. . .how the wedding went on without me. Such a thing was beyond my imagination, please, please, please forgive me, Libby.*

Libby? The name pulled Gregory's attention away from the remainder of the letter. Tabitha's letter was to *Libby*? And she was asking her sister to forgive her for forcing *Libby* to marry *him*? Had she really thought he'd be such an awful husband?

Where's my apology? Where does she seek my forgiveness for forcing me into marriage with her sister? Surely it must be further in. . .

But I know you'll make the best of the situation—you always were the strong one. Besides, I've always secretly thought you might have feelings for Gregory. Don't worry. You've hidden it well, but a sister knows. . .perhaps this marriage will turn out to be the best thing for you both. You'll make him happier than I ever could, I'm sure of that much, at least.

All my love, Tabitha

Gregory read the letter three more times, turning the paper over and staring at the blank back side of it as though expecting a secret message to appear. None did. That being the case, he pawed through the other mail on his desk, seeking a twin letter meant for him. He found no such thing. Burying his head in his hands, he groaned aloud.

Libby has feelings for me? The notion knocked him off-kilter. *Is it better to have the sister I do not love, but who cares for me, than the one I do love, but who cares not for me? And now that I've consummated our marriage, will Libby come downstairs with stars in her eyes and the expectation of storybook romance?*

The thoughts swirled around his brain, pounding in his temples, until Gregory could take no more. Stalking into the entryway, he shouted for Jenson to fetch his coat. With that, he strode through the door and headed for the docks.

Libby snuggled in the warmth of the bed, unwilling to open her eyes and lose the memory of Gregory's tenderness to the challenge of a new day. Taking a deep breath, she peeked through her lashes to find an empty space on her husband's side of the bed.

He had awoken and been careful not to wake her, as well. Libby smiled as she pressed her hand into the indentation of her husband's pillow. Today they'd truly begin their life together as man and wife. In the eyes of God, they were joined forever.

Filled with sudden energy, Libby hopped from the bed, wincing only slightly at the soreness in her muscles as she made her way to the restroom. She hummed as she washed and readied herself for the day, eager to spend time with Gregory and seek his opinion on all the plans she had for Cranberry Hill.

She glided down the stairs, peeking into the study to see whether her husband had begun work for the day. Seeing only a stack of opened mail, she headed for the breakfast room. How wonderful it would be if they could start the day with a meal together.

But he wasn't in the breakfast room. Or the parlor, the music room, the dining room, any of the spare bedrooms, or the widow's walk atop the house. Libby felt the tension in her brow as she sought the housekeeper, thinking perhaps Gregory had left a message with Mrs. Farley.

She found the housekeeper enjoying some toast in the kitchen. "Excuse me, but did my husband go out this morning?"

"Yes, he did." The woman swiftly rose to her feet and dusted crumbs from her apron. "Left less than a quarter hour ago."

"And did he leave notice of where he was going?" At the woman's silent headshake, Libby tried again. "Did he say when he'd be returning? If there was anything in particular he'd like for dinner this afternoon?"

"Not to my knowledge, ma'am." The woman pulled a folded piece of paper from an apron pocket. "He did direct Jenson to see that you received this."

Libby turned away from the woman's curious gaze and unfolded the note to find a single line.

Gone on business. Will return.

Gregory Alan Royce.

"Very well." Libby straightened her shoulders, determined not to show her discomfort. She addressed the cook. "We'll have ham sandwiches with egg salad and fresh fruit for dinner this afternoon. Please have things ready at twelve thirty, sharp. We will, of course, be dining in the breakfast room again."

With that, Libby swept out of the kitchen and made her way into the dining room. Today the workers would begin installing the chestnut wall paneling she'd selected for the lower half of the walls. She'd also selected a decorative chair rail in matching wood to add polish and ease the transition from paneling to paint.

The workers had already painted the walls a deep shade of burgundy. The color would have been too dark, save for the electric lights unique to Cranberry Hill. Until Gregory returned, she would throw herself into remodeling the house. That should occupy her mind and make the time pass quickly.

The morning flew by in a whirl of hammering and noise.

Dinner came and went—Gregory had yet to return. Libby oversaw the installment of the furniture she'd purchased. The china cupboard stood at one end of the room, the buffet at the other, and the matching table with seating for twenty stretched between. The hours plodded more ominously as suppertime arrived but her husband had not.

As Libby sat at one end of her new dining room, her only companion an empty place serving, her appetite fled. After an entire day had passed, she could no longer deny the truth. Their night together hadn't meant to him what it had to her.

Gregory had left her. Again.

Chapter 8

A week passed, then another. Libby found constant reminders of her husband's desertion in almost every corner of Cranberry Hill. His half of the bed obviously had not been slept in, his clothing untouched in the armoire. No scratching of pens came from his study, no shared meals in the breakfast room or conversations enjoyed in the newly refurbished parlor.

Libby directed the cook to make simple trays once again. The dining room sat in darkness, never showcasing its new luxuries. Her footsteps echoed on the marble tile of the main entry. The staircases stretched to reach empty rooms, not the least of which was the nursery.

Lord, her heart cried as she stood in the doorway of the barren room. *I thought Gregory realized we could build a marriage together. He came to my bed, filled my heart with hope, and snatched away the dream once again with scarcely a word. I don't know where he is now or when he'll return. Even after he left, I prayed that You would bless me as You blessed Leah. But she bore her husband a son, and I carry no child beneath my heart. Will I have no family to love—no husband, no daughters, no sons—no laughter and joy?*

Tears slipped down her cheeks, dripping onto the collar of her serviceable brown dress. Drawing a shaky breath, she swiped at them with the back of her hand before heading downstairs. The workmen had finished the conservatory yesterday, and it was time she decide what she wanted to fill it with. Libby would be visiting another type of nursery later in the day.

She wouldn't go until that afternoon, which left her the entire morning to fill. Libby wandered around the floor level of the house, absently taking in the changes she'd already made and more determinedly taking note of what else she wanted. The dining room, parlor, and breakfast room were completed. The conservatory simply needed to be filled. She made her way to the music room.

Large and wide, with two sets of double doors leading outside, the room should have been welcoming. As it was, it simply seemed hollow. The floors lay rough and unfinished, snagging at her slippers. The walls bore nothing but bare paint, the only furniture a lonely pianoforte in the corner. Even the electric lights cast no warmth.

Libby walked the full length of the room, planning her changes. It wasn't long before she could practically see the room as it would be, newly laid parquet floors gleaming, a raised dais gracing one end of the room, large enough to hold a string quartet. Silk wall hangings in light green contrasted with heavier drapes in a darker shade, all highlighted by electric wall sconces.

Wanting to make a note reminding herself to consult the electrician, Libby realized she'd left her notepad in her room. It didn't take long to fetch it and quickly map out the décor for the music room. Done up as she planned, it would serve as a ballroom, too. They'd need whitewashed chairs with green cushions to line the walls. Libby wanted one more look at the dimensions of the room before she went to the shops.

As she descended the steps, the doorbell summoned Jenson from the pantry. She reached the main entry as he opened the door to reveal—

"Tabitha?"

"Libby!" Her sister rushed across the hall to envelop her in a crushing hug. "Oh, Libby, you have to forgive me!"

"We'll adjourn to the parlor, Jenson." Libby interrupted Tabitha before she could pour out the whole story in front of the butler, who couldn't quite hide his interest at the tableau.

Libby ushered Tabby into the parlor, closing the double doors behind them. The moment they sat down, Tabitha was off and bursting out with apologies once more.

"I had no idea Papa's finances were dependent upon my marrying Captain Royce," she babbled, her hands fluttering in distress. "That you'd have to take my place. . .I never thought. . ."

"Neither had I," Libby agreed. *Nor Gregory, for that matter.* "But what is done is done."

"If you're not happy, you can come live with Donald and me.

We have that lovely little house on Charter Street now—his father gave it to us as our wedding gift." Tabitha fair beamed with pride. "It's not half so grand as this." She gestured to encompass the surroundings Libby had put so much time and thought into.

"No, I can't." Libby shook her head. "We'll make the best of what we have. Gregory, so far, is rarely home. . ." She winced at the dull throbbing in the back of her throat, refusing to add that he stayed away because he didn't want her. "And it doesn't matter what the size of your house is." *More rooms mean more to be left empty and alone.*

"All the same, it's our home, and we'd be glad to have you." Tabitha tripped blithely along as one of the doors swung inward. "No one should be trapped in a loveless marriage, Libby. I wouldn't have fled my own if I knew I'd be condemning you to the same fate."

"Condemning?" Gregory's voice thundered from the doorway, his face folded in a forbidding scowl as he strode into the room.

He came to a halt at the side of Tabitha's settee, not allowing himself to look at her. Instead, he focused on Libby. She'd gone pale, then red as he made his way over, raising her chin.

"Is that the way you feel, Libby?" He lowered his voice and raised a brow. "Condemned?"

"No, of course not." Libby met his gaze, but he saw a shadow of doubt flicker in her darkening hazel eyes. "Tabitha was just being"—she glanced at her sister before finishing—"dramatic."

"She does have a flair for the dramatic," he agreed, rounding on the woman who'd jilted him. He refused to be distracted by the light blond of her hair, the wide blue eyes so filled with dismay at the sight of him. When she didn't respond, he prodded further.

"Leaving a man at the altar certainly qualifies as dramatic, wouldn't you say?" He loomed over her, turning his gaze back to Libby. *Did Tabitha really think I'd be so awful to her that marriage to me is a type of doom?* He felt the muscle in his jaw twitch, and he gritted his teeth.

"Oh, Gregory—" Tabitha began, but he wouldn't let her speak.

"No. I believe we've had enough drama in the past month." He held up a hand in dismissal. "Now, *my wife* and I have things to discuss. I trust you'll see yourself out." Gregory walked over to hold the door wide, refusing her the option of dawdling. Once she'd left the house, he slammed the parlor door shut, covering the distance between himself and Libby at a rapid pace.

"Gregory, that was rude," she chided as she faced him.

"My apologies." He sat for a brief moment before bolting up again, his steps eating the length and breadth of the room as he paced. "I suppose I should have been more polite to my fiancé who eloped on the eve of our wedding."

"You've every right to be angry with Tabitha," Libby soothed, putting out a hand and laying it on his arm in an attempt to stop him. She closed her eyes for a moment when he shook her off.

"Good to know." He loosened his collar. "It's always nice

to have permission to be mad at the lying woman who betrayed you."

"She is my sister." Libby's voice hardened. "That hasn't changed."

"Everything else has." He strode toward her, drawing just short of standing on her toes. "You know that as well as I do."

"Yes." Instead of shrinking back into the settee, she tilted her chin to look up at him. "And with change must come compromise if things are to work out."

"Compromise? What am I to compromise on with Tabitha?" He raked his fingers through his hair and thumped onto a nearby chair. "If you'll recall, she dishonored the last deal we made."

"This is no longer about Tabitha." Libby leaned forward. "This is about the two of us reaching a compromise. She just happened to be visiting at the same time you came home."

"It's my house." He glowered. "I've every right to be here. She doesn't." *Not anymore.*

"She's my sister," Libby repeated slowly. "She'll always be welcome in my home. We have to find a way to reconcile that."

"No." Gregory got to his feet. "Tabitha will never be welcome here."

Chapter 9

I'm in love with...

Y ou're not thinking about leaving?" Libby stood up, hands clenched at her sides. "Because in a month of marriage, I've seen you for no more than three days— less, if you want to be particular." At her words, he'd stopped midstride. She pushed ahead. "So you can see why I'm certain you wouldn't walk out on our first disagreement after forbidding me to see my own sister. Such a thing would be. . ."

"Would be what?" He turned and stalked toward her, his voice low and deceptively soft. "My right as master of this house? Your duty to carry through with my wishes?"

"Unconscionable." Libby met his gaze, refusing to give an inch. "Walking out on your wife now would be unconscionable."

"Libby—" He drew a deep breath. "I'm not trying to punish you."

"What would you punish me for?" She furiously blinked back the tears that sprang to her eyes. *For not being the bride you wanted? For not reviling my own flesh and blood?*

"Nothing. But as my wife you must support my decisions."

"Not when your decision cuts me off from my family." She shook her head sadly. "I know Tabitha hurt you, Gregory—"

"She didn't hurt me!" The words exploded with incredible force. "Tabitha came close to humiliating me, it's true. But she made me furious—it's a mistake to confuse the two." His eyes sparked with a barely banked fire.

Recognizing her error, Libby sought to regain ground. "Of course she's provoked your ire."

"See that you don't forget it." With that, her husband headed toward the door once again.

"I'm the one who's hurt." Her whisper sighed in the deserted room as Gregory didn't even look back.

❦

"I've decided to take you up on your kind offer," Libby announced as she walked into Sarah's modest home.

"Excellent!" Sarah tugged on the bellpull, summoning a maid. "I'll need my cloak, Betsy. And please have the carriage pulled 'round. We'll have need of it today!"

Libby kept a smile on her face as the maid scurried away, but it didn't fool her friend.

"But why do you look as though you're preparing to do battle?" Gregory's mother narrowed her eyes. "What has my son done?"

"I've not come to bear tales, Sarah." Libby rubbed the back of her neck to ease the tension. "Suffice it to say that I'm not doing this for Gregory. I want new dresses and so forth to please myself."

"Very well." The older woman didn't probe. "I couldn't believe he came home for a single morning before going off on his third trip since your marriage. I'm beginning to think he needs a business partner."

Libby refrained from offering her opinion as to what, precisely, Gregory needed. She was, after all, a lady. Instead, she made an announcement.

"The study will be finished within a few days. I'll be sending out invitations for my first dinner party at Cranberry Hill."

"It's about time you entertain guests!" Sarah looked Libby over, a shrewd gleam in her eye. "I take it this means you know when Gregory will be back. What is the date to be?"

"A week from tomorrow." Libby couldn't help but add, "Though I do not know whether or not my husband will be in attendance."

"You're hosting a dinner party without Gregory?" Sarah's tone was flat, disapproving.

"Yes. I've scarce seen my husband for three days out of the past thirty-seven." Libby pleaded with Sarah to understand her unconventional decision. "I can't spend all my time alone in Cranberry Hill. Why am I working to make it beautiful if no one will ever see it?"

"Agreed." Her mother-in-law drew her brows together. "Gregory has always been one to go his own way, so let it be on his head that you're left to your own devices."

"Then I can count on your assistance?"

"Absolutely. I know the most charming soloist who should provide your guests with after-dinner entertainment in that lovely music room of yours. . ." And with that, they began planning the evening.

They ironed out the particulars during the carriage ride to Madame Celeste's shop, who, Sarah informed Libby, was the most talented hairdresser in these parts.

"Such lovely hair," Madame Celeste mused, combing through Libby's heavy locks. "Ze curl must be freed, no?"

"I keep it so long because the curls spring wild, otherwise," Libby explained. "It ends up looking like a dandelion when it's shorter."

"*Non, non.*" Madame protested. "You use ze pomade to tame ze pouff and is lovely."

"Exactly my thoughts," Sarah interrupted. "And a few locks cut shorter around the face to frame her eyes."

"*Exactamente.*" Madame nodded her approval and, at Libby's hesitant nod, rinsed her hair with a shampoo smelling of lemons. "Zis will lighten ze color," she promised. Then the woman set to her task with comb, shears, and an almost frightening enthusiasm.

Libby closed her eyes as, with the snip of the scissors, locks of her hair littered the floor. *It's time I took better care of myself, took more care with my appearance.* She cracked an eye open to see Madame's gleeful smile, and snapped it shut once more. *This will be worth it. It has to be!*

As the *Riverrider* pulled into the dock, Gregory argued with himself.

Should he spend the night in his cabin, as he'd done so often over the past six weeks, or go back to Cranberry Hill? Ah, but going back to Cranberry Hill would be perilous enough in the light of day.

Loath though he was to admit it, through much prayer and thought Gregory had to face the truth. He'd treated Libby horribly. She had every right to flay him with her words the moment he stepped over the threshold. After all, what kind of man deserts his bride directly after their wedding night—twice—before throwing her sister from their parlor?

Granted, Tabitha deserved far worse from him, but Libby did not. When it came right down to the bare bones of the matter, she'd had even less choice about this marriage than he had. He had faced humiliation and a heavy toll on his business image. She'd faced the betrayal of her sister and the financial destruction of her father should she refuse. And, to boot, she was saddled with a negligent, angry groom who disappeared when he should have been seeing to their marriage.

Father, I've made a mess of things. Part of me says I should go home immediately and apologize, try to compromise with Libby. The other part of me argues that it would be unfair to arrive at night, expecting her to welcome me when it would shortly be time to go to bed. I cannot expect that of her.

Ah, but I could sleep in one of the spare bedrooms so as not to pressure her. And it would be so good to be home. . .

No matter what difficulties lay between them, he knew Libby had made Cranberry Hill the warm, welcoming home he'd always intended it to be. His desire to be home, to begin patching things up with Libby, immediately won over.

A short carriage ride later, he pulled up to a house blazing with lights. He let himself in, drawn up short at the sight of a magnificent chandelier, crystal drops of all different sizes capturing the light over the grand staircase. The sight was breathtaking so as almost to distract him from the sweet notes coming from the music room. Almost.

He followed the sound of the pianoforte and a woman's breathy soprano to find the music room completely transformed—and filled with guests. He stood in the doorway, staring blankly for a moment as he struggled to process what was going on. Surely Libby wouldn't entertain without his presence? What wife would open her husband's home in his absence?

His wife. There was no denying the truth of what lay before him. Where was she? Libby had some explaining to do. He silently surveyed the crowd of no fewer than twenty people, scanning for the long, honey-brown locks of his wife.

Gregory recognized his mother first, his gaze slipping past the attractive woman seated beside her until a niggle of recognition made him focus more intently on. . .*Libby?*

Chapter 10

Libby's hair, much shorter now, tumbled from a loose knot in riotous curls. A few soft tendrils framed her lovely eyes, drew attention to the generous curve of her smile as she tapped her gloved fingers in time with the music. She easily outshone every other woman in the room. . .all save her sister. Tabitha reclined only a few seats away.

His good intentions forgotten, Gregory strode down the side of the room until he was level with his wife. He touched her bare shoulder, scarcely registering the softness of her skin as he jerked his head toward the door in silent command. Her eyes wide, she followed him into the hall.

"Just what do you think you're doing?" His hissed question garnered attention from a few of the guests, and Libby ushered him into the study.

For a brief moment, Gregory was nonplussed by his surroundings. A massive mahogany desk stood in one corner of the room, easily large enough for him to draw up a chair. Floor-to-ceiling bookshelves adorned two entire walls, filled with rich, leather-bound sets of volumes and folios. Electric lamps sat on thoughtfully placed tables to cast light in every corner.

Squashy chairs and a leather sofa curled near the cozy warmth of the gas fireplace, cushioned by a rug in shades of deep blue and crimson. The room bespoke a woman's thoughtfulness to meet her man's needs, evidence of the type of harmony their marriage should enjoy.

Harmony that didn't exist. Remembering the reason she stood before him now, Gregory nearly choked on his anger. How could the same woman who made Cranberry Hill the home he'd always wanted stand there so blithely after denying him the pleasure of seeing people's reactions to it? How could she cheat him of his role as master of the house? *How dare she announce to the world that she doesn't need me?*

"Well?" Gregory thundered this time, grinding his teeth. "What do you have to say for yourself?"

"It's good to see you, too, Gregory." Libby closed the door behind them, shutting out the strains of a lilting melody and ensuring their discussion would remain private.

"Good to—" His mouth opened and shut again, giving him an uncanny resemblance to a fish out of water. "What are you playing at?"

"I'm *playing* at nothing." She said no more. Let it rest on him to dredge up reasons to argue. Libby was tired of it.

"Then what do you call that"—he gestured toward the music

room while searching for the word—"spectacle?"

"A dinner party, of course." Libby watched as her husband pulled a thick cigar from his pocket. "I'll have to ask you not to light that in here."

"Excuse me?" As he shook out the flame of his match, the sparks in his eyes glowed. "Last I checked this was my house."

"And it still is," Libby agreed pleasantly. "But since last you checked, I did stock and refurbish this library. I won't allow Papa to smoke in here—it ruins the books, you see. Makes them musty." She watched as he looked at the room once more, unable to hide his admiration for the luxurious furnishing.

"Very well." He still managed to sound disgruntled even as he tucked the cigar back into his pocket, then returned to the more pressing matter. His eyes narrowed. "A dinner party?"

"Precisely." She inclined her head. "Albeit one you interrupted. It's rude to leave one's guests, you know."

"It's rude to throw a party in a man's house without informing him, much less inviting him." His rich baritone was silky smooth, a signal of danger she'd come to recognize. "Isn't it customary for the man of the house to be present at such proceedings?"

"Traditionally." Libby fought to keep her temper, but lost the fight when Gregory's chest puffed up in triumph, his gaze scornful and dismissive as he began to speak once more. She swiftly cut him off. "Though it is also customary for the man of the house to spend time at said house. With you absent almost continuously for the past two months, it would have been nigh impossible to coordinate a gathering according to your timetable."

"That would almost prove an acceptable explanation—a worthy argument, even, but for one fact." He moved forward, effectively trapping her against the end of the sofa. "You disobeyed my wishes. Tabitha is here."

"Yes." Libby raised her brows. "*My sister* kindly agreed to support me by attending my first party, even though she'd been unceremoniously ordered away when last she stepped foot in our home."

"A good wife obeys her husband's edicts," he countered.

"Marriage is supposed to be a partner-ship." Libby laid a hand on his arm. "We'll both be stronger when we stand together."

"Tonight you chose to stand beside your sister." He pinned her with his gaze. "Will you choose to stand beside me, instead?"

"I want to, Gregory." The tears worked past her defenses at last as she whispered, "You're my family, but I can't stand beside you when you're not here."

"Do you want me by your side, Libby?" His voice rumbled with doubt.

"Yes." Her heart hammering in her chest, Libby broached the subject that could well tear apart their newfound trust. "Gregory, I understand if you don't want Tabitha at Cranberry Hill—it was wrong of me to disregard your wishes and have her here—but I still love my sister."

"I see." He stiffened and pulled away his hand.

"I won't have her here again," she vowed, snatching his hand with both of hers, willing him to listen. "But I need to be able to see her other places."

"We'll see." His frown softened, and he laid his hand over hers, covering her with warmth. "It's not right for me to expect your support when I've withheld mine for so long." He cupped her cheek with his other hand. "We'll do better from now on, yes?"

"I hope so, but I need an answer about Tabitha. I don't ask you to spend time with her, but I do ask that you let me do so." She held her breath as she waited.

"I respect that." He finally agreed. A faint smile replaced his frown now. "But I'm going to have to exact a price, I'm afraid."

"Oh?" Libby sensed he was being more lighthearted. *Anything you want, Gregory.*

"You're going to have to follow this one final edict." His expression turned serious once again, making Libby's heart plummet.

"What edict?" She somehow dredged up the courage to ask.

"You will never"—he closed the distance between them, taking her into his arms—"under any circumstances, cut your hair without my permission again."

And as he smoothed his large hand over her curls, gently tugging them to watch as they sprang back into place, Libby could speak again.

"You don't like it?" She squeaked, full of remorse.

"No." He threaded his fingers through more of her curls and lowered his mouth to hers. "I love it." His whisper fanned across her lips as he kissed her. It was a goodly while before he drew back and touched his forehead to hers. "Do you agree to my terms?"

"Oh." Libby smiled at him, sliding her arms around his neck. "I think that can be arranged."

Chapter 11

The days and weeks slipped by, fluid as river water while Gregory worked to improve his marriage—and Cranberry Hill. He fell into a comfortable pattern with Libby. For the first time, the captain who set up his own business, set out on capitalist voyages, and never rested long enough for life to become mundane, had fallen into a rut. And he liked it.

He'd wake up to find the sun shining and Libby's head pillowed against his side. Together they shared a hearty meal in the breakfast room before separating until dinner. He spoke with the architects, raising a low stone wall around the property and seeing the roof of the carriage house installed. Libby, for her part, saw to the running of the tiny details that made Cranberry Hill run smoothly.

At dinner they discussed their plans for the rest of the day. After he took care of business and paperwork, they fell into the habit of meeting for a short ride or walk in the afternoon, discussing possible landscaping projects to best showcase Cranberry Hill. Typically they would attend a dinner given at a friend's house. Occasionally they hosted one at Cranberry Hill, but not since they had begun construction on the wraparound porches.

The days may have melded into one another, but each was full of partnership, encouragement, and progress. Their excitements were minor but made richer by their shared joy. Slowly, the relationship grew and prospered, colored by the nuances they lavished on Cranberry Hill and each other.

Only one thing troubled Gregory's thoughts, marring the happiness he'd found. Libby had been forced into this marriage. Granted, she'd made the best of things, and her sister's letter hinted that his wife might bear deeper feelings for him, but had he made up to her his horrible neglect during the first months of their marriage?

Libby loved their home, lavished attention upon it, and shone with satisfaction as she surveyed the house. No doubt about it, Libby was happy at Cranberry Hill. The question was, was she equally happy with him?

He could think of one way to find out. Gregory left the accounts in his study and stopped by the parlor, looking for Libby. He finally tracked her down in the sewing room upstairs, hemming some sheets.

"There you are," he greeted her as he crossed the room to drop into the chair beside her.

"Here I am," she agreed, teasing him with the soft smile he'd come to crave. "What did you need?"

"I've an important question to ask you." He leaned toward her as he spoke. "Think about it before you answer. I don't want to push you into anything, mind."

"Go on." She pushed on his arm to accompany her demand. "You're making me nervous with all the suspense!"

"I've another business trip to take." He paused, pleased by the way her eyes widened and smile faded. *She'll miss me*, a voice in his heart crowed. "I'd put it off so as to spend more time with you, but it can't be postponed any longer."

"Don't worry, dear." She set aside her sewing. "It's been wonderful having you here, but I understand you must run your business." A twinkle came to her eyes, made green by the rich shade of her dress that day. "So long as you come back and stay awhile without rushing away again."

"I wouldn't do that—" he vowed. "Again," he added, being completely honest. "We both know I already pushed my good fortune to have such a patient wife."

"If I recall, she pushed back when she had to." Libby gave him a peck on the cheek.

"She's an amazing woman," he confided. "In fact, I was hoping that amazing woman might consider going along with me on this trip. What do you say, Libby?"

"Absolutely!" She sprang out of her chair. "When are we leaving? Where are we going? What types of things will I need to pack?" She scooped the rest of the sewing into a basket in the corner and tapped her foot impatiently as she waited by the door. "Why are you sitting there when there's so much to do?"

"I'm just taking a moment to appreciate my beautiful wife,"

he assured her. A few steps and he had her in his arms. *She wants to spend her time with me. Me.* "We'll leave tomorrow, if you like. You pack a few dresses and such. I'll take care of everything else you need."

Thank You, Jesus! Gregory asked me to go with him on his next business trip! Things have been going so well since the night of that first dinner party, and I've been truly grateful. . .but You know my heart, Lord. You know I wondered whether it was the idea of having a home, the pastime of putting the finishing touches on Cranberry Hill that really captured his heart. Now I know his affection is for more than the house, lovely though it may be.

Libby practically skipped down the hall to the master bedroom, already planning what dresses to take. She would pack underskirts, chemises, pantaloons, silk stockings, and garters, of course. The dresses were more difficult. She threw open the doors of the great wardrobe and began flipping through her outfits, thinking aloud.

"I won't need a riding habit for a trip on a paddleboat," she decided easily. "And I suppose we won't be dressing for dinner. . . though perhaps once we've reached the city? I'll bring along the sapphire evening gown then. . ." She plucked the dress out of the wardrobe and laid it on the bed, along with the undergarments she'd chosen. A day dress in light green followed, accompanied by a similar frock in rich rose. She'd wear the cream-and-gold at the departure.

A few other dresses made the pile on the bed grow ever

higher, until Libby judged the selection complete. "Now...where did I put the trunks I'd brought over from Papa's house?" She thought for a moment before vaguely recalling the storage in the attic. She made her way to the small stairwell behind the master bath.

The stairs brought her up to the attic, beside the access to the widow's walk. She rummaged around the boxes until she found her trunks, carrying them one at a time back to her room. When she came back for the second, she spied a small door next to the maids' quarters. Curiosity getting the better of her, she put down the trunk and walked over, trying to open it.

The door wouldn't budge, though it appeared to have no lock. She grasped the knob more tightly and pushed, hearing the rattle of a lock on the other side. *Intriguing.* Libby went through the maids' quarters, searching for an entrance through the wall shared with the small chamber. Nothing.

Must be a construction mistake of some sort. Brow wrinkled at the mystery, she retrieved the other trunk and made her way back to her bedroom. She'd be sure to mention it to Gregory. After all, he'd been involved in designing the house and drawing the blueprints. He'd want to know about the mysterious sealed room with no access. Of course, it could be like the basement, an area taken up by the steam heater and electric wiring. It could have been sealed for safety.

Half an hour later, she'd packed everything into the trunks. Fighting the feeling she'd forgotten something important, Libby searched through her dresser drawers and bathroom cabinets. In a last-ditch effort to pin down what she'd forgotten, she opened the wardrobe once again. Pushing aside coats and dresses, she spotted her old black hooded cloak wedged in the back corner of the armoire. She tugged but couldn't pull it out.

Determined, she pushed her upper body between two dresses and tried again, pressing one hand against the back wall for better leverage. Libby swiftly found herself flat on her face, half sprawled in the wardrobe as the back wall of the armoire sprang back to reveal a secret staircase.

Chapter 12

Pressing her palms against the wardrobe bottom, Libby levered herself to her feet. She spent several moments staring in disbelief, unable to believe the sight before her.

What is a hidden staircase doing behind my wardrobe? More importantly, where did it go? Libby stepped through the clothing and into the small passage. Her hands encountered a light switch as she groped at the walls to gain a sense of her dark surroundings.

Instantly, the yellow glow of electric lights illuminated the way, almost beckoning her forward. Unable to resist, she followed the narrow passageway, up into a dark space. Squinting, Libby could see that she was in a small room. She groped about the walls, hoping for and finding another light switch.

She blinked for a moment before seeing that the room stood empty, not so much as a picture, rug, or old rickety chair gracing the barren space. *Why?* She moved farther into the room, searching for some clue as to why it even existed. Her eyes fell on the doorknob—and the lock beneath it.

The room in the attic that locks from inside. Elated that she'd made the connection, Libby unlocked the door and opened it, still not quite understanding why Gregory would have commissioned a third stairway to the attic. There was already one leading here from the second floor, which she'd used not long ago, and one that connected the attic to the pantry.

The second was to give the maids ease of movement as they bustled between the kitchen and their chambers—Libby's elated excitement died a swift death as she turned to see the maids' rooms just beside her.

It was suddenly so clear. There was only one reason why a man would construct a secret stairway from his bedroom to the attic, which held no more than the maids' quarters. And how brilliant of him to have hidden the passage at both ends—a spring-loaded wardrobe in the master suite below, a mysterious door above, locked from within. All to conceal the sordid truth from a wife's prying eyes.

Gregory thought of everything, Libby admitted even as she relocked the small chamber and returned to the bedroom she shared with him. Almost tripping over her just-packed trunks, she stopped for a moment before mechanically unpacking them. Her chest ached from the simple act of breathing, the daylight streaming in through the windows as sharp as daggers to her eyes.

Now what am I to do? Footsteps shook her from her reverie.

"Libby?" Gregory's excited voice floated up the stairs.

She looked around, wild for a way to avoid him. *Not now.*

I can't face him now! Inspiration struck with an ironic blow, as Libby opened the back of the wardrobe and darted inside the stairway she shouldn't have even known existed. Sinking onto the bottom step, cradling her knees against her chest, Libby listened as Gregory stomped into the room and back out.

She could have sneaked away, but what was the point unless she was ready to confront her husband? So Libby sat in the secret stairwell, in the dark, and prayed.

"Where are you?" The playful question lost its humor as Gregory checked room after room without finding Libby. Perhaps she'd been freshening up when he'd gone to their bedroom and hadn't wanted to draw attention to it? He loped back up the stairs.

No such luck. The room was empty save two trunks near the open wardrobe. He smiled at the evidence his wife had been packing for their trip together. The smile faded as he realized Libby was still missing. Gregory mentally ran through all the rooms of the house—parlor, dining room, breakfast room, kitchen, music room, spare bedrooms, sewing room, nursery. . . he'd checked them all.

She wouldn't have left without telling him, so where could she be? He circled their bedchamber, more restless than he should have been at his wife's sudden disappearance. Try as he might, he couldn't shake the feeling that something was wrong.

Think, Gregory. Where would she be? He rejected the basement. The only things down there were the steam heater and electrical wires. Libby would have no reason to venture there. *The attic?* He couldn't imagine why. Besides, she still should have heard him calling. *The widow's walk!* That had to be it. Libby was on the flat, railed walkway set atop the house.

He'd had it built following the sailor's tradition. During troubled times, a seaman's wife could stand atop her home, looking out over the water, and wait for her husband's safe return. Libby had never mentioned it to him, but the housekeeper had said Libby liked to venture up there on fine days.

This will be a good chance to try out the hidden stairwell. I've not seen it since its installation. Smiling broadly at the thought of showing Libby his secret staircase when they returned to their room, he pushed on the back panel of the wardrobe, feeling along the revealed wall for the light switch.

As light flooded the stairway, Gregory saw his wife huddled on the bottom step. He sank to his knees immediately, grasping her cold hands and chafing them between his own.

"Libby? Libby, what's wrong?"

"Don't." Her voice sounded dull as she jerked her hands from his grasp and scuttled away from him.

"Don't what?" He tried to catch her eye, but she'd turned her face from him. A sudden image of her falling down the dark staircase made his stomach roil. "Libby, are you hurt? Let me see."

"Can't you already see?" She gave a hollow bark of laughter. "It's obvious to me."

"What is?" He crooked a finger beneath her chin and turned her face toward his. He breathed a silent prayer of thanks when he saw no purple bruises or angry bumps. "What happened since we spoke in the sewing room?"

"This." She waved her arms to indicate the stairwell, knocking his hand away in the process. "I discovered your secret, Gregory. Stop acting as though it's nothing."

"You're upset because I hadn't shown you the staircase?" He tried to clarify things, but they seemed more muddied than ever.

"Oh, yes, I'm upset about the staircase." She drew a shaky breath before glaring at him. "How could you design such a thing in the house you built for your bride? I know I'm not the bride you had in mind, but that makes it no better! The *maids*, Gregory?"

"What are you—" In an instant, he understood. "You're talking about how the stairway leads to the attic, near the maid's room. You think. . ." He couldn't even bring himself to the words, instead recoiling from the very thought. *Is that what she thinks? After all the time we've spent together in the past weeks, she can believe such a thing of me?*

"Why else," she demanded fiercely, "would you construct a hidden passageway from your room—*our* room—to the attic?"

"I built it so my wife would have easy access to the widow's walk during bad weather." He spoke through stiff lips. "I didn't want you climbing the outside stairs when they were slippery with rain or ice. Forgive me for thinking my wife would be concerned and want to keep a lookout for my ship at such times."

"Why lock it from the inside at the attic door?" She questioned, her eyes showing the first faint gleam of hope.

"So no one could enter our room," he explained. *She was devastated at the thought I'd carry on with one of the maids—not because her pride was hurt, but because she cares for me.* The realization softened his outrage that she had believed the worst.

"Oh." The tiny sound melted the rest of his wounded pride.

"I'd never do something like that—no matter who my wife was." He scooted up to crowd beside her, nestling her in the crook of his arm.

"You're a better man than that." Libby wiped her eyes and gave a tremulous smile. "And I've always known it. I don't know why I jumped to such an awful conclusion. . . ."

"It made sense at the time." He squeezed her shoulder. "The important thing is you believe the truth, so we're ready to move on."

"I do." She nodded vehemently. "I overreacted, Gregory. I'm so sorry for that. You see"—she drew a deep breath before continuing—"I've always admired you, from the first night we met. And even now, when things are going so well, it's easy for me to believe that I'm not the wife you wanted."

"You weren't." At her gasp, he smiled. "You're far more than I ever wanted in a wife, and I know I'm blessed to have you, Libby. We may have started out on shaky ground, but I like to think we've found a solid path together."

"Me, too." Her hair tickled his cheek as she nodded.

"But even more than that"—he knew the time had come to speak the thoughts he'd hidden for too long now—"I love you, Elizabeth Anne Royce."

"I love you, too." Her words came out garbled as she wept all over his surcoat.

"Now then, that's enough." Gregory rubbed soft circles on her back as she composed herself.

"I'll never get enough of our life together," she murmured, looking up at him with love shining in her eyes. "It makes tears of joy keep springing up."

"I can think of a better way to celebrate." He smiled as he lowered his lips to hers. Neither one of them spoke for a long moment. When he caught his breath again, Gregory added the finishing touch. "Let's fill our nursery with beautiful babies."

"Mmm." She nestled closer. "I'd say that is a wonderful idea."

KELLY EILEEN HAKE

Kelly's dual careers as English teacher and author give her the opportunity explore and share her love of the written word. A CBA bestselling author and dedicated member of American Christian Fiction Writers, she's been privileged to earn numerous Heartsong Presents Readers' Choice Awards—including Favorite New Author 2005, Top 5 Favorite Historical Novel 2005, and Top 5 Favorite Author Overall 2006—in addition to winning the runner-up Favorite Historical Novel 2006. Currently she's pursuing a Master's Degree in Writing Popular Fiction and loves to hear from her readers. Visit KellyEileenHake.com for more information.

BEYOND THE MEMORIES

by DiAnn Mills

Dedication

In loving memory of Jane Orcutt

Let another man praise thee, and not thine own mouth;
a stranger, and not thine own lips.
PROVERBS 27:2

Chapter 1

June 1932

Miss Maime, why do you use your mama's best dishes on folks who don't even know what day it is?"

Maime touched her finger to the edge of the silver knife and nudged it to the exact position beside the gold-rimmed china plate. She eyed the crystal goblet to make sure it was positioned directly above the knife. "My dear Lucy, the residents here at Cranberry Hill may not remember their names or how to dress themselves, but I will not have them lose their dignity."

"Yes, ma'am." The tall young woman proceeded around the long wooden table, placing the threadbare napkins next to the salad forks.

"As long as the good Lord provides, we will continue the tradition here that my mama instilled in me."

"Yes, ma'am."

"Lucy, look at me."

The young woman's gaze widened, and Maime captured it with a smile. "I know you don't understand how I feel about this house and the residents who have suffered so much with the Great War and the Depression, but they are my life."

Lucy smiled. "Guess I'm just tired today." She shrugged. "No more than you, I 'spect. It's that—that—"

"Are your folks giving you a bad time about working for Maime Bradford, who has a house full of folks who seem to have lost their minds?"

"Yes, ma'am."

"Have they asked you to find work elsewhere?"

Lucy patted the top of her dark hair. "I refused. Besides, I care about you, and I know your heart. I'm a nurse, and I'll be here as long as you need me."

Maime chuckled. "And there aren't many jobs out there, even for a trained nurse."

Lucy flushed as red as the tomatoes ripening in the garden. "It doesn't matter. It's you I work for, and I will be here for as long as you'll have me."

Goodness knows we need more with your commitment. "Thank you. I appreciate your loyalty."

Something thumped on the second floor, sending the crystal drops of the chandelier into a shiver. Both women startled and stared up at the ceiling.

"Mr. and Mrs. Weaver's room," Maimed whispered. "Do you suppose Mr. Weaver is emptying the dresser drawers again?"

A crash sounded above them. This time the chandelier

swung back and forth like a pendulum.

"Come on, Lucy. We need to see about this before the ceiling caves in." Maime rushed into the main foyer and up the wide staircase to the landing, then she veered right where the stairway split.

For some reason, Asa Weaver had started dumping his dresser drawers onto the floor looking for his gun. He'd fought bravely through the Great War, but when he'd lost his furniture business after the stock market crashed, his mind failed him.

Mrs. Weaver leaned over the second-floor railing. She closed her eyes and touched her heart. "Oh, please help me," she said. "Asa believes we're surrounded by Germans."

Maime rushed past the sweet, gray-haired lady into the bedroom. Asa sat in the middle of the couple's bedroom floor, tossing clothing and personal items everywhere but where they belonged. Maime eased down beside the elderly man.

"What are you looking for, Asa? I can help you."

He frowned and his shoulders slumped. "I can't find my gun."

"The Germans are gone. You don't need it."

He gasped. "Are you sure? They're a sneaky bunch."

"I know, but the other soldiers apprehended them. Led them away. We're all safe now."

Asa nodded. Lines pulled across his forehead. "What about the next time? I need to find my gun so I can protect all of you."

Maime touched his wrinkled hand. "The soldiers said for us not to worry. They will be guarding the house from now on."

Asa grabbed the footboard of the bed and pulled himself

to his feet. He shuffled to the window. "I don't see the soldiers."

"That's because they're hiding."

"Good."

Mrs. Weaver stepped into the room. "Isn't it about time for dinner? Asa, you told me a few minutes ago that you were hungry."

"That I am," he said, still staring out the window. "I think I see one of our boys. He's hiding behind that tree." He pointed to a maple that shaded the front lawn like a huge umbrella.

Mrs. Weaver joined him and laid her head on his shoulder. "I always feel safe when I'm with you."

Asa wrapped his arm around her waist. "Don't worry. I'll always take care of you."

Maime blinked back the tears and ordered her heart to stop its senseless fluttering.

"Dignity," Lucy whispered then cleared her throat. "I'll let everyone know dinner is ready."

"And I'll help Emma get it on the table right away. After dinner, we'll have singing in the ballroom."

"And you will play for all of us?" Mrs. Weaver asked. Her face softened, and Maime could tell she was slipping into her girlhood again. "Oh, and we can dance."

"Yes, ma'am. You can sing and dance until you're ready for bed."

Failing minds Maime could handle. Men who still believed they were in the war was another matter. Some days tugged at every ounce of energy that flowed through her body.

Maime left Lucy to inform the other residents about the

upcoming meal. She massaged her shoulders and walked down the stairs to the kitchen. One creak. Another creak. She wished she knew how to fix those steps. One of the residents thought the house was haunted because of those squeaks.

Her nostrils detected chicken and dumplings, and her stomach growled in response.

"Sure smells good, Emma," she said as she entered the kitchen.

Maime's cook stood at the door with her arms crossed over her ample chest. A frown dipped to her chin.

"What's wrong?" Maime folded her hands at her waist and rubbed the golden band on her left hand.

"I've had enough." The older woman peered down her nose. "I'm afraid of all these crazy people living here, and my husband said we could make it without me working at a job where I'm afraid."

"Emma, I need you."

The woman grasped the doorknob that led to the back porch and away from Cranberry Hill. "This should be no surprise."

I should have been ready for this. "You're right." Maime refused to cry.

"I understand taking over the cooking for all these people won't be easy, but I can't do this anymore." She paused for a moment and glanced at her hand squeezing the knob. "I'm sure with times being hard, you'll find someone real soon. You have Lucy." Emma nodded at a huge pot on the stove. "The chicken and dumplings are done. Green beans, too, and fresh bread is in the oven."

Maime nodded. "Your money."

Emma shook her head. "I'll send my husband to get it tomorrow."

The door shut, rattling the lid on the chicken and dumplings. Maime swallowed a lump the size of Missouri. She'd find a new cook tomorrow. But tonight she'd have to manage on her own. Tonight she'd smile and serve up dinner for all the precious people who lived here. She'd play the out-of-tune piano and sing as loud as the rest of them. And when the residents of Cranberry Hill slept, she'd figure out what to do about a cook. Problem was, folks didn't like what she was doing here—housing those no one else wanted to help, nursing folks who had forgotten how to take care of themselves. And feeding those who would otherwise starve. Hannibal didn't like it?

Too bad.

Hank hobbled down the streets of Hannibal. Eighteen years had passed since he'd been here. Twilight cast a hazy amber and copper cloud over the lazy town as day held tightly onto the fainting light. He'd expected change. After all, he'd lived with it for what seemed like a lifetime. But he hadn't expected the trees to be so much bigger and the homes to look so shabby. Peeling paint, sagging porches, broken fences. What did that say for the townspeople? The Great War had taken its toll, and now the Great Depression beat on a nation struggling to rise from the dirt. Nothing *great* about any of it.

Hank stopped in front of the courthouse and leaned on

his crutch. Years ago, before the courthouse was built, he'd race through this part of town and beat anyone who tried to outrun him. Back then, he was filled with the ideals of a young man and the love of a girl who had yet to grow up. And when she did reach the proper age, Hank courted her proper until she said yes and her daddy agreed. Hank thought he had life by the tail, and he had grabbed Maime's hand and held on for the ride. If only. . .no, he would not drink the bitter cup of regret. He'd served his country proud; he just never dreamed the price would cost him his heart.

He shoved away the bittersweet memories and drank in the fragrant summer blossoms that filled the warm air: jasmine, lantana, and a hint of rose. On both sides of the concrete steps yellow petunias clustered together. Those were just like Maime used to plant, but she mixed blue petunias with them and sometimes a little red. She used to say that flower gardens were like painting a picture, and God held the brush.

"Mister, we don't allow vagrants to sleep on the courthouse lawn."

Hank swung his attention to a policeman, not much more than twenty years old, a good-looking lad. His dark eyes still held the light of hope.

"I wasn't thinking of sleeping here," Hank said. "That's disrespectful."

The young policeman smiled. "We feel that way, too. Are you passing through?"

Hank nodded. "I plan to be leaving tomorrow before noon."

"You needing a place to stay?"

"Possibly. My first thought was to wander to the outskirts of town."

"That would be fine."

This time Hank smiled. He knew his place, and his nose detected the days he'd gone without a bath. A river bath sounded good before making his way to Cranberry Hill. Why yes, he'd do that very thing.

"I'll be moving along now," Hank said. "Thanks for talking to me."

"You're welcome."

Hank leaned on his crutch and hobbled down the street. Maybe coming back to Hannibal had been a bad idea. This was where it all began. . .a place he once called home. But those days died in the Great War, when he realized he could never come back to Maime. But he had to see her one more time. He wanted to make sure she was happy. He didn't want to think about anything else, not her being married or having children that belonged to another man, or that she had lost her vibrancy for life.

Tonight he'd find a place to sleep, and tomorrow he'd venture to the House on Cranberry Hill and hope she still lived there. A glimpse of her sweet face, even to catch a sparkle in her blue eyes, was all he needed to give him peace for the remainder of his days.

Then he'd leave.

Chapter 2

Maime rose at three thirty the following morning to clean the kitchen from the night before. Had she slept at all? She'd fallen asleep remembering the stack of Mama's finest dishes and silver and the pots from dinner. And this morning, the formidable job made her tired before she even began.

Last night she'd played piano until the residents were hoarse and ceased to make requests. Sometimes they wanted hymns, and sometimes they wanted the latest Broadway hits. All of them dearly loved music. Perhaps she should have music night more than once a week. Then she'd be thoroughly exhausted two mornings a week instead of one. Of course, she craved sleep every morning, but things were not about to change soon.

As she scrubbed the floor on her hands and knees and pushed the cloth across each area of the linoleum to the rhythm of a waltz, her mind dwelled on the evening before. The two married couples—the Weavers and the Caldwells—danced while the others clapped and sighed, no doubt wishing they had someone to hold. Maime had learned a few years ago not to permit unmarried couples to dance. That incident had tested her own sanity.

Today, exhaustion laced her body like her grandmother's corset—and the more she fretted about a cook, the garden full of weeds, and the neighbors complaining about the residents of Cranberry House, the tighter that corset got around her middle.

Lord, You know I need help. Hope You don't mind me re-minding You. Please send me a cook, an angel who can whip up the best food from my scant pantry and weed-ridden garden.

Maime finished cleaning the floor and carried the dirty water to the backyard. The moon still lit up the dew-laden earth, and it was quiet, peaceful. For a moment, she allowed herself the luxury of no one tugging on her to do something. Glancing up at the clear sky, she marveled at the star-studded heavens. Just as God placed the universe in order, He had her life carefully planned. That comfort always placed a balm over her heart. She could face the good citizens of Hannibal with a sincere smile, knowing they despised what she'd done to Cranberry Hill. They simply didn't understand that folks were entitled to dignity, no matter what their lot in life.

God continued to bless her: Vegetables grew in abundance in her garden, and the hens laid enough eggs to feed her hungry group. Just when meat grew slack, someone would leave a smoked ham or beef on her doorstep. But she knew who provided that. James Arnold, a nearby farmer, wanted her desperately to marry him. Both his wife and only child had died years ago during child-birth, and, like Maime, he had never remarried. At times, she considered his proposal, and then other times, she couldn't fathom the thought of ever loving a man the way she'd loved Charles.

I'm wasting the day thinking about too many things. This morning everyone would have oatmeal for breakfast. That was the easiest meal to prepare, and Emma had baked several loaves of bread yesterday. Today was washday, too, but some of the residents were able to help with that. Thankfully those who could do chores pitched in with whatever was needed. *A cook.* She needed a cook, and not a woman who had to be told how much to cook for fifteen people plus Lucy.

She'd make a sign and place it in the front yard. That should bring fifty folks to her door, even though she just needed one.

The familiar creak of the screen door echoed across the shadows and urged Maime back to the present. "Miss Maime," Lucy stepped out into the darkness. "How long have you been up?"

Maime laughed. "Three thirty. All I could think about were the dishes I didn't wash last night—and the state of that pot where the chicken and dumplings almost burned."

"I would have helped you."

"You have enough to do." Maime climbed the steps and gave Lucy a hug. "I needed solitude. Everything's clean now."

"I was thinking oatmeal would be an easy breakfast, and we have honey to sweeten it a bit."

Maime laughed again. "I believe that is an excellent idea."

"I'll start it."

"And I'm going to make a sign to hang on the front gate

saying that we need a cook." She glanced into the kitchen. "But first I need another cup of coffee. How about you?"

Lucy nodded. No need for either of them to mention what the day would be like without Emma. Maime had beans soaking and enough ham and a good-size bone to make soup and corn bread for lunch, and she could add a few vegetables and serve it again tonight. They were low on meat. Perhaps the good Lord would nudge James. Goodness, had she resorted to begging?

As the sun started to make its ascent in a brilliant yellow, Maime affixed a large piece of paper advertising COOK NEEDED to the gate. Surely before the sun made its evening departure, someone would be working in the kitchen.

❀

For the first time in many days, Hank was able to shove away the hunger raging in his stomach. His anticipation of seeing Maime caused him to whistle all the while he bathed in the Mississippi—not exactly the cleanest river, but it was indeed wet. Hobbling down the riverbank and into a shallow enough spot was his biggest challenge, but he'd navigated enough riverbanks to maneuver down and back up successfully with his one leg. He pursed his lips for another song and kept a lookout for snakes. Experience had taught him to keep a knife between his ear and his head in moments like these.

Once he'd dried and slipped back into his clothes and before he headed down the dusty road to town, he paused to thank God for this chance to see his sweet girl. All the way to Cranberry Hill, he thought about days gone by. The good times settled on him like the warm sun moving across the sky. If Maime had remarried and was raising a family, then that would be his closure, his cue to move on and stop the senseless wandering.

All of a sudden, Hank looked up and saw the house. Unlike so many others in Hannibal, this one still looked as magnificent as he remembered. But he expected no less. However did she manage to live alone in such a monstrosity? At one time, he and Maime planned to fill it with children.

He limped closer. Something was stuck to the gate. COOK NEEDED. He held his breath. If Maime still lived here. . .and needed a cook, he could apply and talk to her. She'd never recognize him. He would thank her politely for taking the time to speak with him and make an excuse why he couldn't take the job. Hank chuckled. His worn and dirty clothing would disqualify him for the position. But seeing Maime! *Thank You, Lord.* What a glorious blessing.

He hesitated. What he planned was deceitful. For certain she'd long since gotten over his death. Yet he no longer resembled the agile, strong young man who kissed her good-bye and boarded the train for war. . .the war to end all wars. Hank recalled what the Bible said: "And ye shall hear of wars and rumors of wars." Not a soothing thought for a man who had lost his leg and countless friends. Was he entering another combat zone with what he contemplated?

Hank had never stepped away from a battle before, and he wasn't about to start now. He limped toward the back door of

Cranberry Hill. His pulse raced and a strange stirring swirled in his stomach. This couldn't be wrong. He just wanted to see Maime. . .talk to her. . .make sure she was fine.

The sight of his old home bred both comfort and sadness. The windows on the conservatory to his left fairly sparkled in the morning sun. Green plants flourished, and his thoughts trailed back to when he and Maime first set up housekeeping, and a neighbor had brought them an ivy. Maime placed it in the conservatory and christened the plant "Miss Ivy" with promises of many more to come. She'd kept her word. . .unlike her husband who failed to return to her as a whole man.

For a moment, he considered walking away, but a woman inside spotted him and came to the door. She swung it open.

"If you are hungry, sir, we have some oatmeal left from breakfast," said a tall young woman.

"That would be nice, ma'am, but I see you have a sign out front about needing a cook."

The woman tilted her head as though trying to decide if Hank was a beggar or indeed a cook. "Do you have experience?"

"Yes, ma'am. In the war. After I lost my leg, I cooked for the rest of the soldiers."

She nodded, but no smile. "I'll have the lady of the house speak with you."

Is it my Maime? Is she still here? "I appreciate that. I don't look like much, but I can cook."

"Have a seat on the steps while I fetch her. What is your name?"

"Hank Carter."

The long moments waiting for someone to speak to him reminded him of waiting for his commanders to issue orders. He wondered why Maime needed a cook. When he had about given up, she appeared. Hank knew it was her without turning around. The faint scent of roses gave her away before the screen door slammed shut. He removed his tattered hat, then stood and turned to face her while leaning on his crutch. Trembling like a schoolboy, he offered a shaky smile. The woman before him had haunted his dreams.

"Good mornin', Mr. Carter. Lucy says you wanted to see me."

"Morning, ma'am. I see you're looking for a cook. I have experience from the army."

The mere sight of Maime caused his insides to quiver. The years had only served to increase her loveliness. Her pecan-colored hair had not grayed, but there were a few lines fanning out from her sky blue eyes.

"Goodness, sir. Are you faint?" She hurried down the steps to where he sat. "I bet you haven't eaten. Lucy, please give this man a dish of oatmeal and a slice of bread." Lucy disappeared, and Maime focused her gaze on his. The girl he married wouldn't have been able to do this; she'd been rather shy back then.

"Thank you, ma'am. About the job—"

"What kinds of things do you cook?" She motioned for him to sit back down on the step. Once he'd made his awkward descent, she joined him.

Do you have a houseful of children? "I can cook the toughest meat up tender and juicy, and I know how to stretch a potato as well as a skinny chicken."

She smiled, and he realized that God could take him home this very instant. "I have an unusual house full of residents, Mr. Carter."

"As long as they are hungry folks, I'm fine."

"Perhaps I need to explain. Obviously you aren't from around here. My residents are those unfortunate folks who came back from the war with nightmares that ruined their minds. I also have folks who lost everything in the Depression. They can't take care of themselves and need gentle caring."

Emotion tumbled through him at the thought of how Maime was spending her life. She'd done well without him. She'd grown up and taken her love for people to those who needed her touch. Which was probably why she was talking to him now.

"Mr. Carter, you're not saying anything. Does the thought of working with my residents sound distasteful?"

He peered into her eyes. No malice laced her blue pools. All the love he'd felt for her since the day they first met seemed to bubble up inside him. "No, ma'am. I'm just moved at what you are doing here in this big house." He chuckled. "Look at me. I'm a tramp. How could I ever find the people here distasteful? It would be a blessing to cook for all of you. And if you have doubts, let me start this very day. Then you can choose whether you want me or not."

She startled, then paled.

"What's wrong, ma'am?"

Maime shook her head. "I'm sorry. You remind me of a man I knew a long time ago—a kind and dear man."

"That's a good thought." Hank saw she still wore the wedding band he'd given her. He had to know the truth. "Do you need to get permission from your husband?"

A sweet smile tugged at her lips. "My husband died in the war. And you do remind me of him. I'm sorry for not introducing myself. I'm Maime Bradbury." Instantly she reached out to shake his hand and then stood. "I can't pay you much more than room and board."

"Since I don't have either, that would be fine."

Her slender shoulders lifted and fell. "Here I am letting the morning pass with much to do. If you can cook up something for lunch with what I have, I think we might have a deal."

"How many folks?" Hank asked.

"Sixteen counting yourself."

He grasped his crutch and pushed himself to his feet. "I will do my best. Show me the way to the kitchen." If only the war hadn't stolen his leg and his dignity.

"I just started a pot of beans, but I haven't added any seasonings yet."

"You're making my job easy." He smiled.

Her shoulders lifted and fell. "I do hope this works out."

"Me, too, ma'am."

"You can stay in the cellar. It's really quite comfortable and clean."

Lucy stepped outside with the oatmeal and bread and handed it to Hank. It smelled like the porridge of heaven. "I think your cellar would suit me just fine."

Chapter 3

Hank had moved into the cellar before the sun went down. The room was a cool reprieve from the summer heat, and the cot, though small, suited him just fine. He even had a basket to hold his few belongings. His conscience picked at him for accepting the job, but he told himself that he was only there to help Maime until she found another cook. He hadn't asked her to keep looking for another more suitable person, but he would. . .soon.

Two weeks later he couldn't think of ever leaving. All the deep-rooted feelings he'd once held for his precious wife had grown by leaps and bounds, and regret washed over him for the missed years. He understood her heart for the residents of Cranberry Hill. Even now she talked to a woman in the backyard, touching the woman's face and letting her know she was loved. He quickly glanced away before a tear trickled down his cheek. One thing he had to continually guard against was the need to stare at her. He picked up a scrawny potato and a peeling knife.

"Hank, the garden looks wonderful since you've been tending to it," Maime said, entering the kitchen from the back door. "Look, I've even found flowers that I didn't know I had. Someday I want a huge flower garden again."

He glanced up at the fistful of bright pink petunias, doing his best to focus on the flowers and not the sparkle in her eyes. "They'd look real nice on the dining room table, even though their scent is not the most pleasant."

"That's one of the things I like about you." She smiled. "You treat the residents here with caring and respect as though nothing is wrong with them."

"Oh, Miss Maime, there are times in all of our lives when we wish we could shut out the ugliness of the world."

"You sound so much like my dear Charles. I guess God has decided to bless me with a cook and a reminder of my late husband." She stepped into the conservatory. "My husband never liked the scent of petunias, either."

"There are those flowers which do have a more favorable smell."

"You sound just like him. However, Charles may not have appreciated what I've done to the home he bought for us."

Hank's stomach churned. How long could he keep up the deceit? "Why do you say that?" The words dropped from his mouth, though he needed to keep things to himself.

"Well, this big house was once a mansion, and I've turned the nursery, study, extra attic space, the music room, cellar, every available space into a spot for someone to sleep."

"I admire what you're doing, and I imagine he does, too."

Maime stepped from the conservatory and leaned against the faded wallpaper on the kitchen wall. "Perhaps he does in his heavenly home."

"I'm surprised you've never remarried."

She laughed. "No one ever suited me. You would need to have known my Charles. A more honorable, more loving man never existed." She paused. "Like many widows, I remember all of his finer qualities and none of his less desirable traits. Of course, he didn't need much improving."

"I'm real glad you have fond memories." Something in the backyard under the maple tree caught his attention. "Miss Maime, I see Mr. and Mrs. Weaver are welcoming a gentleman inside the fence."

She walked to the door. "Oh, it's James." She threw a glance over her shoulder. "He's a farmer outside of town who just seems to know when I've almost run out of meat and vegetables."

"That's the mark of a Christian man."

"Oh, he's a godly man all right, but he'd also like for me to marry him." She shook her head. "Widowhood has left him very lonely."

A surge of something between panic and fear rose in Hank. "Then maybe you should consider his offer." What was he saying? Maime still belonged to him. They were married. But. . . oh, the mess he'd made of her life, a woman who deserved the finest God could give a person.

She laughed again, a sweet tinkling sound. "And who would take care of my dear friends?" Without waiting for Hank to respond, she opened the screen door and walked out into the sunshine. "Morning, James. How good of you to come by."

"I have some fresh beef, chickens, and a smoked ham in the back of my truck," a man's voice called. "My, but you sure look pretty, Miss Maime."

Hank dropped a half-peeled potato into the basin and grabbed his crutch. Maime might need help bringing in the food.

One look at the man, and jealousy rose in Hank like stew in a bubbling pot. It was James Arnold. He'd gone to school with Hank and even served in the war, but he'd returned a whole man. Hank wondered how long he'd been a widow. The couple had married shortly before Hank and Maime wed.

Judging from the amount of meat and potatoes on the bed of his truck, James practiced Christian charity. Either that or he was serious about courting Maime.

"I want you to meet my new cook." Maime's cheeks tinted pink, and she blushed like a girl.

Hank hobbled toward them, all the while telling himself that he'd brought this trouble on himself. No doubt the good Lord had seen fit to show Hank the error of deceit. A fine man now looked after Maime, when her own husband had abandoned her. Hank had no right to be jealous or angry. Instead, he should be down on his knees asking God for mercy.

Hank stuck out his hand while balancing the crutch under his right arm. "The name's Hank Carter. Pleasure to meet you, sir."

James gripped his hand and smiled. "Glad you're able to help Miss Maime. I hear you can cook anything."

"I try to please."

James released Hank's hand and waved at a couple of the

men sitting under the maple tree. "Mornin', fellas. Who's winning the checker game?"

"I am," both men echoed.

James laughed, not in a condescending manner but good-naturedly. He hadn't changed much from boyhood days. They'd been close back then.

The three carried the food inside to the kitchen. Neither Hank nor Maime searched out Lucy. She had her hands full tending to the folks there at Cranberry Hill. The young woman worked nearly as hard as Maime.

"We'll be eating like royalty for a long time," Hank said.

"I brought you some strawberries," James said. "I know how you enjoy strawberry-rhubarb pie."

"Are you trying to fatten me up?" Maime asked.

Flirting. Could he blame her? "I can whip up a couple of those for dinner tonight, Miss Maime."

For a moment she paled, then took a breath. "That would be real nice."

"Is something wrong?" James asked. "Are you ill? Shall I find Lucy?"

Maime laughed. "I'm fine. Just remembering something."

James pressed his lips together. "About Charles?"

"I'm sorry. It was his favorite pie, too."

Hank wanted to hobble out of the kitchen.

"You can't keep living in memories. Neither of us can."

Maime lifted her shoulders and smiled. "You're right. And all of this because of a pie. Won't you join us tonight for dinner?"

"I'd be happy to."

Maime tugged on the corner of a sheet and helped Claudia smooth out her bed. All of the residents were to complete the task every morning and tidy up their rooms. If some were not able, then others were to lend a hand. Maime believed every one of these dear people needed to feel worthwhile and understand the satisfaction of a job well done. So housework, yard work, simple painting, and sewing were a part of the requirements to live at Cranberry Hill. She used to have them help her keep the small garden in good order, but some of the residents couldn't distinguish a weed from a flower or vegetable. Praise God for Hank. He was teaching some of the men how to till the soil. Already he planned a much bigger garden for next spring. His soft-spoken mannerisms gave rise to patience with all of the residents. Maime loved them all, but it was too easy to do the task herself rather than take the time to teach them. What had she ever done without Hank?

A clap of thunder sounded in the distance. Good, they needed rain. She walked to the window.

"Is it raining?" Claudia wrung her hands. A flash of lightning streaked across the sky, and the woman shuddered.

Maime turned to the older woman and took her veined hand. "Don't be afraid. The thunder and lightning will bring cooler temperatures and rain to green up our garden."

Claudia's lips quivered, and she nodded.

"Would you like to go downstairs with me?"

"What about the children?"

Poor Claudia. She'd lost two sons in the Great War and her husband had died shortly afterward. "God will take care of your children."

"I hope so. He always has before."

Maime led her outside of the bedroom and into the hall. "Let's see what Mr. Hank is doing. I imagine he's bringing the men inside before the storm hits."

As much as she welcomed the rain, the anxiety among the residents was often difficult to manage. Lucy met her in the kitchen as Hank hurried the men up the back steps. Lucy gathered the residents together, much like a hen with her chicks.

"This looks like a great afternoon for storytelling," Hank said. "Why don't we make our way into the parlor, and I'll start. Then one of you can tell the rest of us a story."

Maime inwardly breathed relief. How ingenious of Hank to consider a diversion for these precious people. A few minutes later, as clouds darkened the house and the storm rumbled closer, he began a story about a little boy who wanted a dog but was given a chicken. Hank's clear voice spun a delightful tale about how the chicken helped the little boy's mother by providing eggs for them to eat. In the end, the little boy realized that God had provided a way for him and his mother to survive during the hard times. He hadn't received what he'd wanted, but God gave him what he needed.

"Do you know what the story means?" Hank asked.

"I like eggs," Mrs. Weaver said. "And you can't eat a dog."

"Yes, you can," another man said. "If you were hungry, you could eat anything."

"Let's ask Miss Maime," Hank said.

He had a way of making her feel special. "I think it means that we need to trust God for all our needs, even if we don't understand what He is doing."

"Like my boys in the war?" Claudia asked.

"Yes, your boys," Hank said. "Even though the storm outside is not pleasant, we understand God is taking care of us by bringing rain."

"It will wash away the German's tracks," Mr. Weaver said. "Our boys won't be able to find them."

"But God can." Hank's quiet voice calmed the whimpering of a few frightened residents. "He can find every man, woman, and child who is lost. Nothing escapes the eye of the Lord. All we need do is ask Him."

"Would you pray for us, Mr. Hank?" Claudia asked, her voice brimming with emotion.

"Sure. Let's all bow our heads and close our eyes."

Each person in the parlor did as Hank asked. "Heavenly Father, we come to You this afternoon a little uneasy with the storm and all the worries of our lives. Be with us. Comfort us, and give us peace. In Your precious Son's name, amen."

Maime lifted her gaze and stared into Hank's blue eyes. She shivered. *Nothing escapes the eye of the Lord.*

Charles had made that very statement the day he left for war.

Chapter 4

Hank had a passionate nature about the Fourth of July. He'd lost friends and fellow soldiers in the war. And that didn't include his missing leg, the deep scars on the right side of his face, and the deeper scars embedded in his heart. He'd seen homes destroyed and lives shattered. But he didn't regret his act of patriotism—only his lost relationship with Maime.

Stop it. You're feeling sorry for yourself. He'd made a choice at the close of the war and thought he understood the consequences, until he saw Maime four weeks ago. This morning all the grief of that decision beat down on him. She was the one love of his life, and every moment spent in her presence pressed doubts against that desperate decision made in 1918.

"You sure are planning a grand celebration for the Fourth." Lucy set several jars and bottles of herbal liniments onto a tray.

"Well, I want the holiday to be in honor of those men who

have given their lives for their country. And I'd like to see a worship time for the God who protects us all."

Lucy laughed. "I think you should have been a preacher."

"Actually, I thought about it at one time, but I didn't feel the call." He glanced over at her tray. "I see you're planning to massage some of the sore muscles of our residents. How about I brew a little peppermint tea to go with what you have there."

"Oh, Mr. Hank, that would be wonderful."

He heard the light tap of Maime's shoes across the dining room floor.

"I hear my favorite two people in the kitchen," she called. "And I hear laughing, which means fun."

"We're talking about the Fourth of July," Hank said. "And peppermint tea."

"That's an unusual combination." Maime tilted her head. "Actually iced peppermint tea would taste good."

"The tea is for the residents to drink while I massage liniment into their tired muscles. We hadn't gotten to Hank telling me all about the party," Lucy said.

Hank chuckled. He'd laughed more in the past four weeks than before the war. "Miss Lucy wants to know what's going on so she can be ready."

"I know all about his plans for the Fourth of July." Maime folded her arms over her chest and feigned a superior stance.

"I had a sergeant who looked a lot like you," Hank said. "He sure kept us in line." *But he wasn't as beautiful.*

Maime cleared her throat. "As I said, before Hank compared me to an army sergeant, our Fourth of July will be the grandest this town has seen in years. We'll have games, wonderful food with watermelon, fresh corn, and roast beef—all courtesy of James—and a cake."

"A cake?" Lucy's eyes widened. "With flour and sugar so dear?"

"Hank assures me that he can make a heavenly cake that will not take much flour. He'll sweeten it with honey and top it with fresh strawberries. And later we can watch the town's fireworks from the backyard. Let's all pray Mr. Weaver doesn't get so upset like he did last year."

Lucy stiffened. "I remember he jumped over a chair to get away from enemy fire. Mr. Grayson got upset, too. Both men were trembling like fall leaves. We had a difficult time calming them down. Later I cried, not because of how hard it was but because I felt so sorry for what they'd been through."

"I understand how they feel." Hank sighed. "At times I wish I could hide somewhere in my mind. War is harsh. A man wants to forget it, but he shouldn't so he can do his part to make sure all the killing never happens again."

"I have no idea what you went through, but those of us who waited on loved ones to come home will forever appreciate your sacrifice," Maime said.

"Thank you. I've run into many folks who simply want to put it all behind them and not understand the danger of over-looking why we were there."

"You're an insightful man, Hank. I'm proud to know you." Maime smiled. "Seems to me you ought to be teaching school or behind the pulpit."

"I already told him he ought to be a preacher," Lucy said.

"Oh, I'd look real peculiar hobbling up to the front of the church with a missing leg and a face full of hair." He turned his attention back to the stove. Did Maime remember how she used to tell him he ought to teach school or preach?

"Give it some thought," Maime said. "I'd hate to lose you, but your wisdom needs to be shared."

Hank picked up the salt and pepper to keep busy, anything to keep from spilling out the truth. "What can I do to help Mr. Weaver and Mr. Grayson through the fireworks tonight?"

Maime touched her finger to her chin, just as she used to do when she was a girl. "I don't want to put the burden on you. Sometimes James can talk to them when they are all worked up. He'll be here for the festivities."

"Have you said yes to James yet?" Lucy asked.

"No. And I'm not. At least I don't think so."

Hank poured boiling water onto the peppermint leaves. *I will not be jealous. What if she says yes and marries up with him? Dear God, what have I done?* His Maime would be guilty of bigamy, and it wouldn't be her fault.

Maime touched Hank's shoulders. "Never mind. As long as I have Hank here cooking and filling my head with worthy things to be thinking about, I don't need James or any other man." She took the pepper shaker from his hand and added a hint more. "With all of this fuss, I wonder what you have planned for Christmas."

I can't be here. I've got to leave before you learn the truth.

The sound of a truck alerted Hank to James's pulling up

next to the house. The man sure paid a lot of visits to Cranberry House. Not that Hank blamed him.

"My lands, looks like James is courtin' today," Lucy said.

"Hush." Maime waved her away, as though her words might disappear in the wind. "What if he hears you? Besides, I need to check on one of my plants."

"That made no sense, Miss Maime." Lucy picked up the tray with the liniments and fresh-brewed tea. "If you decide not to take him up on his offer, let me know. I think he's handsome. I could settle into being a farmer's wife quite easily."

"Lucy! I can't believe you're talking that way in front of Hank."

Hank laughed. "I'm rather enjoying it. Poor James. Sure hope he ends up with the right woman." He dried his hands on a towel. "I'll go meet him. He most likely has food for the celebration."

Without another word, he grabbed his crutch and limped out the screen door and down the steps. Maybe he could take care of business and spare Maime the trouble. Who was he fooling?

"Mornin', James. Looks like you're going to make sure the Fourth will be done in style."

"I'm doing my best. Miss Maime around?"

"She's in the conservatory. Probably nursing a plant. I'm sure she'll be right on out."

James leaned against the side of his truck. "You remind me of an old friend."

Hank's stomach did a flip. "I take that as a compliment."

"He was Maime's husband. Quiet spoken, caring, and my best friend. Before the war, when my wife was still alive, the four of us used to spend a lot of time together." James lifted his hat, and with his sleeve he swiped at the perspiration on his forehead. "Charles loved baseball. Every Saturday afternoon, we'd round up enough fellas to play, and our wives carried on like we were the best players in the state."

Hank hated himself. Selfishness had climbed into his heart and taken over any shred of decency that he had left. He took a deep breath. "I'm pleased that I remind you of an old friend. Odd how life never turns out like we expect." He tugged at his ear.

"My wife's smile could rival the sun," James said. "Not a day goes by that I don't miss her. You ever married?"

"Yes. A fine woman. I think about her all the time."

James glanced up at the house. "Maime helped me through my loss. Both of us hurt real bad from losing our spouses."

Hank needed to change the subject before he stepped into the realm of confession. "I haven't told Miss Maime yet, but I need to be heading on down the road soon."

"I thought you liked it here in Hannibal."

"Oh, I do. But I have a restless spirit."

James sighed. "Think real hard on staying. Maime speaks highly of you, and so do I. You're a big help to her."

"I appreciate that."

"So you'll think about it? Pray about it?"

Hank tasted the bile rising in his throat. Pray about deceit? "Yes, I'll pray."

James picked up a slab of beef, and Hank grabbed a small basket of potatoes.

"Do you like to fish?" James asked.

"Sure do. Sitting on the Mississippi riverbank has a way of relaxing a body."

"Ah, so in all your travels, the Mississippi stays close by."

"Pretty much." *Watch what you say.*

"Mr. Weaver and a few of the other men here are always after me to take them fishing. I thought we could go next Saturday. By then, everyone should have rested up from the celebration on Monday. Could you arrange coming along?"

A longing crept over him. He'd missed James. "Just say when. All I have to do is put on a pot of beans with one of your fine ham bones." They'd done a lot of talking back when they'd fished together. "What you're doing for the men and an old cripple like me is. . .well, it's a fine thing."

"Thanks, Hank. I feel the same about what you're doing for Maime." James chuckled. "I don't look at you as a cripple."

"Unless we're running a race."

"I don't do that anymore." James headed for the backdoor then swung his attention back to Hank. "Maime's husband and I used to run races. That man always beat me. He used to say he could outrun me on one leg."

"He must have been fast."

"He was. More importantly, he was the godliest man around. Sure hated it when he didn't come back from the war."

Hank thought he would throw up.

❖

Maime felt Mrs. Weaver's head. The fever had returned, draining every bit of the older woman's strength. She'd complained of a scratchy throat since Memorial Day, and now that the Fourth had arrived, her health had not improved. She complained of a headache and now this fever would not go away. With the rattling in her chest, Maime feared pneumonia. The doctor who normally tended to folks at Cranberry Hill had left for St. Louis on Friday and wouldn't be back until tomorrow.

"Can you give her anything?" Maime asked Lucy.

"Some ginger tea would make her feel better. Sometimes a tea made from rosemary will help a headache."

"Let's do that." Maime swallowed hard to keep her emotions intact. "Mr. Weaver will have a difficult time enjoying the festivities without his wife."

"Tell him to let me rest," Mrs. Weaver said through closed eyes. "I want him to have a good day."

"I'll talk to him." Maime touched the woman's cheek. Although Mrs. Weaver had her moments when her mind slipped a bit, most of the time she was all right.

The older woman laid her hand on her chest. "I think I have a bad chest cold."

I hope that's all the doctor finds. "We'll have the doctor here tomorrow," Maime said. "He'll have you feeling better in no time at all."

"Of course." Mrs. Weaver smiled, her pale face causing Maime to pray for her recovery.

"I'll stay with her," Lucy said.

"That's not fair. You've looked forward to today since you first heard about it."

"Nonsense. I'm a trained nurse, and you're needed to direct all the goings-on." Lucy gathered up Mrs. Weaver's hand. "However, you could put on some water for the tea. I'll slip downstairs in a minute."

"We'll take turns," Maime said. And when Lucy opened her mouth obviously to protest, Maime kissed her forehead. "It's not good to argue with the boss."

Once in the kitchen and the teakettle on its way to boiling, Maime told Hank about Mrs. Weaver.

"I'll take the tea up to her," he said. "You help James with the residents."

"I should tell Mr. Weaver that his wife is resting, and she wanted him to enjoy the day." The smells from the roasted beef, potatoes, and green beans tugged at her stomach. She hadn't taken the time to eat this morning with the holiday preparations weighing heavily on her mind.

"I'll have the food ready in an hour. If you can help James dish it up, I'll sit with Mrs. Weaver so Lucy can join in with the fun. Both of you women work too hard to miss the games and food."

Maime frowned. "And what about you?"

Hank lifted the lid on the green beans and added some fresh dill. The aroma sent her mouth watering. Charles used to add a toss of dill to the green beans. Praise God that He had sent Hank into her life. All the fond memories of Charles washed over her like fragrant flowers. Hank had a way of blessing her at every turn.

"Do I dare say that Charles used to put dill in my green

beans?" She laughed. "I'd slip away from the stove, and he'd lift the lid and sprinkle it in before I could say a word."

"You don't like it?" Hank asked. "I can pull it out."

"Oh, I love the taste. It was a game between us. And he'd do the same with potatoes. We had a little herb garden in the right-hand corner of the big garden. We used to add herbs to vegetables and meat, even bread."

Hank dried his hands on his apron. He trembled and leaned on his crutch.

"I'm sorry, Hank. I'm forever talking about Charles, and it has you uncomfortable. Please forgive me."

He quickly glanced up. "Miss Maime, you talk about whatever pleases you."

"I miss him."

"And I imagine he misses you."

"In heaven? Do you think he ever wonders how I'm doing?"

"I'm sure of it."

Her shoulders lifted and fell. "I'm such a silly goose. Someone needs to scold me for such goings on. It's been far too many years." She focused on the residents and James in the backyard. "I'll go help James with the horseshoes."

"Hurry along. I bet you have an eye for ringing them every time."

"More like, I need to get the corn in here so you can get it cooking." She laughed again, that sweet sound. "Thanks for making this day special for all of us at Cranberry Hill."

"It's the least I can do."

Chapter 5

Maime lifted the worn rug from the clothesline. She'd taken out all of her frustration about Mrs. Weaver's illness and her dilemma about marrying James by pounding every last speck of dust from the rug. But before she carried it back inside, she took a moment to catch her breath and allow the gentle breeze to bathe her face.

The doctor had come this morning and given Mrs. Weaver medicine for the pneumonia. Maime hated that dreadful disease; it had taken her daddy, and she knew how it drained a body of all its strength.

Lord, must she go now? Mr. Weaver won't last long without her, and she's such a dear soul.

Perhaps Maime had given into selfishness, especially if the good Lord wanted Mrs. Weaver home where the fever and chest pain would no longer be a part of her life. Six people had died since Maime had started taking in helpless folks at Cranberry Hill, nearly twelve years ago. Death was a fact of life, but it never made saying good-bye any easier.

Like saying good-bye to Charles, an impossible task. In the beginning she planted flowers so when he came home, he'd see how well she'd taken care of the spacious area around the house. But as the years crept by, she did less and less work outside. Now her garden contained vegetables for her residents, and lately she'd taken interest in maintaining the conservatory. If a rare flower appeared, it was a surprise, like an expected gift from a friend.

If she married James, and he was a dear man, he'd make sure the rest of her days would be filled with love and devotion. And he'd help her find someone to look after Cranberry Hill. The idea of building a life with James nudged at her. He wanted children, and she had a few more childbearing years left in her.

"Do you need some help?" Hank called from the back steps. "I may be one-legged, but I can grab an end of that rug."

"I'm fine. Just thinking."

He hobbled toward her. "From the frown on your face, it must not be pleasant."

She shrugged and forced a smile. "I'm amazed at the way you always think of others before yourself."

"If you knew me, you'd know that's not always the case." He moved toward her.

"You don't give yourself credit for your fine qualities." She continued to stare into his kind face. Something about his eyes always drew her to him.

He leaned on his crutch and grabbed a corner of the rug. "I thought we started talking about you."

"Ah, a sly one you are."

"If I can help you with something, you know I will."

She nodded. "You are so easy to talk to, as though I've known you all my life."

Hank glanced at the frayed corner of the rug but didn't respond.

"Anyway, I'm concerned about Mrs. Weaver's health, but that is in God's hands."

"And I know there's more."

She laughed to keep from crying. "Oh, James asked me to marry him again."

"He's a fine man."

"Indeed. I believe the time has come for me to leave Charles behind and step forward."

"I'm surprised you haven't done that already."

"Hope, I guess. You see, they never found Charles's body, and I wanted to believe that one day he'd return to me. Guess I've gone all these years believing in fairy tales."

Hank lifted his gaze. His eyes watered, and he blinked. "He'd have wanted you to be happy."

"I know. I've told myself a thousand times that it's wrong to linger on false hopes. The man is gone, and it's taken me all these years to accept it." She paused with a little sigh. "Charles made me complete. But he was not my savior. That role is for Jesus alone."

"Sounds like you're thinking it through."

"I'm trying. For certain, I'm not doing a thing until I hear from the Lord."

"I'll pray for you, Miss Maime."

The intensity of his words nearly startled her. "What would I ever do without you?"

"Oh, you'd get along just fine. I'm sure there's a two-legged cook out there who'd love to have my job. One of these days the Depression will be over, and then you can hire a proper cook."

They walked toward the door. "Hank, you dwell too much on what you've lost and not enough on what you give to others." She laughed. "I sound like Lucy lecturing me. But I am serious. You are a gift from God."

"Yes, ma'am."

"And don't you ever think of running off. I'd send the sheriff and the best huntin' dogs in the country to track you down."

Hank chuckled. "There's always the train for me to jump onboard. Besides, you'll be singing a different tune the next time I burn corn bread or add a tad too much salt to something."

Maime shook her head. "Please, I couldn't take another heartbreak. Make this town your home, Hank. We need you. I need you, even if my reasons are selfish."

She peered into his eyes, and her heart did a little dance. Ignoring the strange sensation, she glanced away, a little flustered. Together they brought the dining room rug into the house.

Lucy appeared at the backdoor. "You should have called for me, Maime. This rug weights a ton."

"Hank and I are doing fine, thank you."

Lucy grabbed part of Hank's end. "Mercy, how did you get this out here and on the line?"

"Mr. Weaver helped me—while watching for the enemy."

The threesome carried the rug into the dining room and placed it over the polished wooden floors in the center of the room. Moments later the table and chairs sat perfectly beneath the chandelier. A white crocheted tablecloth spread over the ends of the table, and a pair of candlesticks stood like guards saluting the ceiling. Between the candles, Maime set a bowl that James had given her. He'd gotten it by purchasing gas for his truck. Actually, he'd given her several pieces of the inexpensive glassware.

"If you ladies don't mind, I'm going upstairs to speak with Mr. Weaver. Mrs. Weaver doesn't need him pestering her with nonsense. I'll bring him outside into the fresh air. Probably have him help me pick a few cucumbers and tomatoes."

"Thanks, Hank. Good luck with it, though," Maime said. "I tried earlier to have him help me beat the rug after we carried it out, but he insisted upon staying right by his wife's side."

Hank grinned. "I'll tell him I need a guard." He hesitated. "Don't ever think I'm mocking him. In his mind, he needs purpose, and still living the war accomplishes that."

"We understand," Maime said. "Hurry on. I sure hope he still plans to go fishing with you and James tomorrow."

"I'll do my best." With those words, Hank limped toward the stairway.

Maime watched him maneuver the stairs until he disappeared. She turned her attention to Lucy, who studied her in a most curious fashion.

"Is there something wrong?" Maime asked.

"Not sure." Lucy slipped a loose strand of dark hair behind

her ears. "Can we talk in the conservatory where we can have some privacy?"

Maime smiled. "Must be serious for you to want to move into my favorite room."

"Serious and reflective."

Had the young woman decided to quit after all? Maime trembled. The thought meant more than the loss of seeing her friend every day; it meant finding someone who loved the residents, and they loved her in turn. "All right."

In the conservatory, the two women scooted close together on an empty section of a plant-covered bench. Maime pulled a dead leaf from a vine and mentally noted that she should cut back a purple passion plant that had draped halfway across the floor.

"I saw something today," Lucy said.

Maime's mind flitted from one matter to another. "With the residents?"

"No, with you."

"Lucy, what do you mean? Have I offended you? Been negligent? Are your parents pressing you again? Is there a problem?"

Lucy shook her head and laughed lightly. "No, Maime. I made my decision to stay with you regardless of what anyone says. I watched you with Hank, and I saw a light in your eyes that's never been there before."

At the mention of Hank's name, her pulse raced. "What are you talking about?"

"I think you're falling in love with him."

Maime startled. "Surely you must be mistaken."

"Am I? Since Hank has started working here, you're happier, your cheeks are rosier, and you have more energy than two other women combined."

Maime allowed Lucy's words to settle. "He reminds me so much of Charles."

"But he's not your husband."

"I know. Hank is a kind man—but that doesn't mean I have a silly schoolgirl infatuation."

"My mama says love can come at any age."

"Well, I don't think this is true for me."

"What if you do love him? What if God has placed Hank in your life for this? To love again like you loved Charles?"

Maime glanced away. "I don't. . .know. I suppose it's possible."

"More probable than possible. I think you're fighting what he's doing to your heart. I've seen the way he looks at you, and I think his heart has been touched, too."

Maime didn't respond. "But what about James? How would he feel if I. . .you know, if you're right."

"The question is what about you? What does your heart say?"

Maime released a sigh. "Must you answer a question with a question?"

"When it calls for it." Lucy leaned in closer. "James is a fine man, and I daresay he'd not want you as his wife if you didn't love him. And if you're thinking this is all about my attraction to James, it isn't. This is all about you, my dear friend, whom I believe has found love in Hank Carter."

Maime rubbed her palms together. Could this be true? Her mind slipped back to the past several weeks with Hank. She did seek him out in the mornings and look for reasons to talk to him. His attentiveness to her and the other residents made him even more endearing. He prayed with them, and in the early mornings when she had her quiet time with the Lord, he brought her coffee and asked her what He had said to her. They talked about the Bible and its lessons.

"Lucy. . .if you are right, what am I to do?"

"Put Charles to rest. Cultivate the future, like you do these plants."

"Not sure I can." Maime repeated Lucy's words in her mind. *But I want to.*

Chapter 6

Hank listened to James talk about the afternoon's grand fishing.

"Now, how did you know this is the best fishing hole along this part of the Mississippi?" James pointed to Mr. Grayson's line. "Look, he has another bite. We're going to have to dig more worms. From the size of that line of stringed fish, we have enough to feed the whole town."

Hank grinned. "I had a feeling. That's all. Must be the cloudless sky, a good sign the fish are hungry."

James glanced skyward. "I never heard the sky had anything to do with fishing."

"Me either, but it sounds good."

"You got me there, Hank. I'll get even."

"Ya-hoo!" Mr. Grayson pulled on his pole. "You'd better get busy, Weaver. I'm one up on you."

Mr. Weaver ran his hand over his age-speckled head. "You forget I'm looking out for the Germans while you have a good time."

Mr. Grayson laughed. "I haven't seen any Germans. You must have scared them off with your complaining about me catching more fish than you."

Hank listened to the old men banter back and forth. Many times he envied their ability to leave the real world behind.

"James, the residents need to spend more time fishing. Even the women. I haven't seen these men this happy since I've been here."

"You're right. As long as I can get you to help me, we can do this on a regular basis. There's always work to do on the farm, but slipping away now and then is good for me, too."

Mr. Weaver grabbed Mr. Grayson's pole. Each man proceeded to tell the other how to bring in the fish—a huge catfish. But when the pole jerked with the weight of it, they worked together to land it. When the two sat exhausted on the riverbank and both claimed ownership of the catch, Hank laughed until his sides ached.

"Fellas, why not split that catfish in half?" Hank finally said. "It took both of you to hold the pole."

The two men stared at each other. Mr. Weaver reached out his hand, and Mr. Grayson grasped it.

"It's a deal," Mr. Weaver said. "Makes up for the fact you beat me in horseshoes."

"He remembered the Fourth," James whispered. "It still amazes me how he can forget his own name and then recall something."

Hank nodded. "Of course, the horseshoe game could have been twenty years ago with someone else."

"True." James studied him. "Have you decided to stay on at Cranberry Hill?"

Hank tugged on his ear. "I can't. Gotta be moving on."

"Why, Charles? Does it hurt that bad to be with us?"

Hank swallowed hard. His whole body chilled while heat flamed his face. "I believe you called me by the wrong name. It's an honor to remind—"

"I don't think I made a mistake. You're Charles Bradford as sure as I know my own name."

Hank attempted to shake off James's words with a nervous laugh. "I think you've been spending too many hours at Cranberry Hill. Or the sun's gotten to you."

James picked up a rock and sent it skimming across the water. "Charles, you were my best friend. I knew you long before you and Maime started making eyes at each other. I see it in your eyes, your mannerisms, especially in the way you pull on your ear when you're uncomfortable. And today you walked right to this spot, the one you and me used to come to when we went fishing together."

Hank didn't know if the right words were inside him to state what he truly felt. Over the years he'd twisted and turned everything he remembered about life before the war until he was certain his choices had been the best for his wife. A part of him feared the future because of the information James now had. A part of him sensed relief that the truth had surfaced.

"I don't know what to say except I'm convinced I did the right thing."

James nodded. "Let me say that I understand why you

couldn't come back to Maime. I served in the war, too. I lived the same nightmares. Still do." He gestured to Mr. Weaver and Mr. Grayson. "They haven't been able to hold on to their sanity with the war and the Depression, but you and I are different. We lived it and survived. I was afraid to come back to Ivy. Afraid I'd be a man she no longer recognized, a horrible killing monster who sent far too many men to their death."

The two sat in silence. Hank fought the sights and sounds of the war that still roared in his ears. He longed for hope like the catfish flopping on the riverbank ached to be back in the river.

Hank hadn't talked to another man about why he couldn't return home, only to God and now James. God responded in ways that often made him angry. *Go back to Maime. Live your life for Me in Hannibal.* James made him wish for Maime in his arms and not as his employer.

"I couldn't come back to Maime without a leg, with my face cut up, and with the things I'd done," Hank said. "She stood for all that was pure and good in my life. I'm dirty, vile, unworthy of her love. Strange, I believed God had forgiven me, but I couldn't ask my wife to do the same thing."

"Have you ever stopped to think how she felt?"

"Not until I came back and saw she hadn't married."

"And why did you come back?"

"Couldn't help myself. I had to make sure she was all right. I thought of her married to someone else, having a family. In the beginning I only wanted to see her, but the sign on the gate advertised for a cook. And one lie led to another. Every day I wake with the shame and guilt." He paused to maintain control. "I've got to leave. If you figured me out, she will, too. I prefer to let her live in my memory than to know the despicable man before you today."

"You aren't despicable, and I won't listen to that kind of talk. If you fall under that category, then so do I."

Hank shook his head, emotion welling inside him like floodwaters seeping over the banks of the Mississippi.

"I've asked her to marry me." James's words were soft, but they hurt nonetheless.

"She told me. You'd be good to her. I'd be content knowing she was safe with you."

"But Maime's your wife." James's voice rose. "How can you do that to her? How can you do that to me, your best friend? Would you let us sin that way?"

For the first time, Hank peered into his old friend's face. "It's best I leave and let life take its course."

"I think you're wrong, Charles. Tell Maime the truth. Let her decide the future, not you."

"She'd hate me. I've heard many times how she feels about Charles, her poor husband who died in the war. I've betrayed her. I deceived her. She's opened her heart to me—Hank, the cook—and look what I've done to her."

"Doesn't the Bible say something about the truth setting us free?"

"What's the point of being free, if I'm hated?" Hank flung the words like dirt.

"Maybe you need to choose what's the hardest to live with, hate or a lie."

Hank glanced down at the stump of his amputated leg. A lie had been his path for nearly two decades.

"Charles, was it concern for Maime that kept you from returning home or your pride?"

Hank sucked in a breath. *Pride?* How could James say such a thing? Unless it was true.

"No need to answer me," James said. "But I sure would like for you to think on it."

"Nothing better than batter-fried catfish," Maime said. For a moment, she started to say that Charles had fried fish as good as this, but that was in the past. "I'm going to send all of you fishing more often."

"Me and Grayson caught most of the fish," Mr. Weaver said.

She smiled. *He recalled the day. Is he getting better?*

Mr. Weaver poked a generous hunk in his mouth then pulled out a bone.

Maime gasped. She thought she'd done a better job filleting the fish. Perhaps she should go through what was on the residents' plates in case she'd missed more than one. As if reading her thoughts, Hank picked up the remaining pieces on Mr. Weaver's plate and began searching through them.

"I'll help, too." James grabbed a plate on both sides of him.

"I'm sorry." Maime picked up the plates nearest her. "If the rest of you would stop eating for a moment, I'd be grateful. I see Mr. Weaver found a bone, and I want to check your fish, too."

"Pshaw," the old man said. "A soldier like me can fight his way through a bone or two." He stared at the empty chair beside him. "Isn't someone supposed to be sitting here?"

"Your wife," Mr. Grayson said.

"I am married?"

Mr. Grayson blew out a sigh. "Yes, and she's sick. Pneumonia, I think."

"Where is she?" Mr. Weaver scooted back his chair.

"Mr. Weaver, Lucy is sitting with her while we eat."

"I will, too," he said.

Hank cleared his throat. "Tell you what. Let's both sit with your wife, and let Miss Lucy enjoy her dinner."

"And I'll finish checking the fish for bones," James said. "Thanks, Ch—Hank."

Chank? Maime picked up Hank's and Mr. Weaver's plates and walked toward the stairs. The other residents returned to talking. Praise God for Hank and James. Sometimes Mr. Weaver became very agitated when his mind teetered between reality and the dimness of his mind. Already Mr. Weaver stood at the stairs.

"Thank you," she whispered to Hank.

"You're quite welcome. There are times when only a wife can help a man through hard times." He motioned for her and Mr. Weaver to precede him up the stairs.

Maime heard a tone in Hank's voice that he'd not revealed before, as though he were in pain. . .or a deep hurt. She sighed. In all of this time together, she hadn't asked him if he wanted to talk, if there were things he needed to say. She'd been self-centered, always leaning on him and not offering a sympathetic ear.

At the top of the stairs, she turned to wait for him. "Hank, can I speak with you a few minutes this evening?"

He hesitated. Or perhaps he was out of breath from climbing the stairs. "Is there something wrong?"

"I've discovered a few things, and I need to discuss the matters with you."

"Miss Maime, can it wait until tomorrow? I'm really tired and wanted to get to bed early."

"Oh, yes. Tomorrow is fine."

"Good. Mr. Weaver, we'll have a fine time discussing the fishing this afternoon with your wife."

"What fishing?" Mr. Weaver frowned.

"This afternoon with several of the men from here," Maime said. Sometimes her residents' state of mind saddened her more than other times.

Mrs. Weaver was awake and talking to Lucy when the three entered the bedroom.

"Look who's here," Mrs. Weaver said. "My dear husband has come to visit me."

"Who's that? I don't know you." Mr. Weaver said.

"This woman is your wife." Hank led him to Mrs. Weaver's bedside. "That's all right. There were days I didn't recognize my wife, either."

Mrs. Weaver smiled at her husband. "We'll get reacquainted."

Hank clapped an arm on Mr. Weaver's shoulder. "I'll help you."

Maime smiled. Hank had definitely stolen her heart, just as Lucy had observed. The confusing revelation had to be sorted out. Later when she was in the solitude of her bed, she'd ask God for wisdom. Even if Hank didn't care for her in the same way, she'd need to decline James's offer. Would she have to give her old friend a reason? Mercy, how embarrassing.

Maime shoved her problems from her mind. Tonight was radio night, and as soon as supper had been cleared, she'd gather the residents together in the parlor to listen to the latest comedy from Ed Flynn.

She and Lucy descended to the lower level, one step at a time.

"Mrs. Weaver appears much more chipper," Maime said.

"She is rallying. I hated the thought of losing her."

"I don't know how she handles her husband's memory loss." Maime listened to the laughter from the dining room. "I'm afraid I'd not be so optimistic."

"Love covers a lot of faults." Lucy paused. "Have you considered what I said. . .about Hank?"

Maime sensed the heat enveloping her neck and face. "A little."

Lucy laughed. "From the pink in your cheeks, I'd say you were thinking about it a lot."

Maime forced a laugh. "At times I wish he wasn't so much like Charles. Makes me wonder if my feelings are really for him. Of course I don't know how he feels about me. Here I am again acting like a silly schoolgirl."

"Give yourself time."

"Oh, Lucy, I can't dally with this too long. James is anxious for an answer."

"Who says you have to choose between the two. James deserves his answer, which has nothing to do with your heart softening for Hank."

Maime touched her friend's arm. "So very true." She brightened. "I hadn't looked at it quite that way, but I will tell James soon that I must decline his proposal."

Chapter 7

James and Maime sat on the front porch swing and listened to the chorus of insects serenading the night. She sighed and allowed her thoughts to sweep over the evening and how one fishing trip had perked everyone up. The residents were all sleeping, or nearly asleep, with full stomachs, giving Maime a brief reprieve from the day—until a nightmare or illness woke one of them. Many a night she and Lucy held the hand of a frightened resident until sleep calmed them.

A faint candlelight flickered through the window from the parlor. Electricity was too costly, and candles were much less expensive. When the country recovered from the stock market crash, she'd not have to make such concessions. At least she hoped not.

"I should be heading home soon." James toyed with the brim of his hat on his lap. "Church is tomorrow, and I don't want to be late. I sure enjoyed today, even if it cut into the never-ending work on the farm."

"I think the men had as good a time today as on the Fourth. You and Hank are spoiling them. But they deserve it. All of us were partial to that delicious fish."

James chuckled. "Hank deserves more credit than I do. He led us to a great fishing hole."

She nodded. Guilt weighed on her for the way her thoughts focused on Hank. . .and the dilemma of James's proposal.

"You're quiet tonight. Are you tired?"

"A little."

"I'll head on home. Whose turn is it for church tomorrow?"

"Mine. Lucy went last week."

"Would you like for me to pick you up?"

Maime smiled. "I rather enjoy the walk, especially when it's warm. But thanks anyway."

James stood. Usually he held her hand. At times he kissed her cheek but not tonight. Could he tell she was confused?

"Maime, I've been thinking." In the cloak of darkness, James's tall form blended with the shadows.

Oh no. Does he want an answer now? What do I say when I don't know myself? "What is it?"

"My marriage proposal. . .I've been pressing you about it for a long time. That's not right, and I apologize. Let's wait awhile on this, and when the time is right, we'll talk about it again."

Relief swept through her—and guilt. "Have I hurt you?"

"Not at all. But I've worried you for an answer until I'm surprised that you haven't run me off. We're friends, Maime, and that may be all God intends for us." His voice rang soft through the night air.

"Thank you, James. I appreciate this more than you know. I treasure our friendship, and yet I'm not sure if it's meant for marriage. You are so good to me. While others would let the residents here go hungry, you make sure we have plenty of food. When the house needs repairs or I need a listening ear, you stop what you're doing at the farm and make a path to my door. Seems like the moment I lift a prayer, you're here as though God summons you. Makes me wonder when you get all of your farming done."

He chuckled. "Oh, there's not much to do at home but work. I try to take care of things for you as though Ivy and Charles were directing me."

"I know and I appreciate it."

He plopped on his hat. "Good night, Maime. I'll see you in the morning. Take some time to rest up tomorrow. I'm sure Hank would do anything you asked."

"He's a big help, but I don't want to put unnecessary burdens on him. I wonder if the strain of leaning on his crutch is painful. When I think of him having to use the cellar stairs, I'm afraid he might fall."

"Don't imagine he'd complain about anything."

She smiled. "I suppose not."

She sat on the swing until James's taillights disappeared down the road. Tears sprang from her eyes, and she buried her face in her hands. The reason for the outburst of emotion was as vast as the confusion about James and Hank—and all the responsibilities of maintaining Cranberry Hill. Her life was slipping by, and what did she have to show for it? She believed she had a purpose with her residents, but did God have more for her to do? The Depression had made it difficult to survive from one day to the next, and any future plans required money. Fortunately, none of them went hungry, unlike many folks in the cities. Even when things did get better for the nation, she'd still need to find resources to care for the physical and mental needs of the residents.

Had she turned to Hank in desperation to find a replacement for Charles? And in the process, had she hurt James, even though he denied it?

Dear God, am I just feeling sorry for myself? I'm tired, and I don't see much of an end in sight. But You do. Help me to live each moment for others and not myself.

She'd envisioned a much longer prayer, one that would include each resident and that person's special need. The problem with James didn't seem as critical now. But what of Hank? If they'd indeed begun to care for each other, then time and God's blessing would cause the relationship to grow.

Maime wiped her dampened cheeks and blinked back the remaining tears. Things always looked better in the morning. Spending time fretting over herself was not what God required of her, especially when those under her care needed so much of her attention.

Hank heard James's engine start up and the truck back out onto the street. A few moments later he heard Maime walk through the house and up the stairs. The sixth step creaked, and he knew she was on her way to the attic where she and Lucy shared a room. Maime and Hank's old bedroom had been given to a married couple a long time ago.

The time had come for him to leave, and he couldn't tell Maime good-bye except in a letter that sat atop the feed sack containing his meager belongings. He'd printed it rather sloppily so she wouldn't recognize his handwriting. The words burned in his mind, the ones he wanted to say.

> *Maime,*
>
> *Thank you for taking me in and giving me such a fine job as your cook. It was an honor to work for you, and I will never forget the fine woman who gave her heart and her time to those less fortunate. I will always pray for you.*
>
> *Next spring, plant that flower garden that you keep talking about. When I think back on Cranberry Hill, I'll see it full of color.*
>
> *I have to move on, and tonight is as good a time as any. I'm sure you'll find a good cook as quickly as you found me. Please thank James for his friendship. Tell him how much I enjoyed the Fourth of July and today's fishing. I hope you two will be very happy together.*
>
> *Fondly,*
> *Hank*

The train to St. Louis had left earlier today, which would have helped to add miles between him and Maime. The lonesome whistle had called to him, but with James still there and the possibility of Maime learning that he planned to leave. . . well, Hank couldn't risk it. So he had no choice but to hobble on down the road at night, the same path he'd been taking for years. The difference now was the past two months with his precious wife and the rekindling of love for her had given him fond memories that would sustain him until the good Lord summoned him home.

He refused to think about the lies and deceit that he left behind. Neither did he want to consider that James might tell Maime the truth. Hank trusted his old friend would keep the secret and let life go back to where it had been before Hank arrived in Hannibal.

Hank steadied himself with his crutch, hoisted the feed sack onto his back, and blew out the candle. He touched the note to his lips and kissed it lightly, then laid it on his bed. *Good-bye, my lovely Maime. May God bless you.*

He crept up the stairs and out the back door without summoning any attention. No one would realize he'd left until the morning. Maime had plans for church, and Lucy always tended to the patients before making her way to the kitchen. Hank had baked biscuits after dinner for their breakfast tomorrow, and he'd pulled out the oatmeal and a huge pot to cook it.

With a heavy heart, he set his sights on leaving Hannibal and all that it meant to him. Within the hour, the lights of the town had faded. He'd taken a dirt road off the main one just in case James got wind of what happened and came after him. Writing him a letter had crossed Hank's mind, but everything had been said today. How comforting to hear James's words of understanding. *Take good care of my Maime, my friend. I hate to leave you behind, too.*

Walking out into the inky blackness seemed fitting. But feeling sorry for himself didn't accompany each step anchored by his crutch, for now he had new fine memories to keep him smiling for a long time.

He would head south for St. Paul and then catch a train west, maybe to California. Years ago, stealing a ride had been a monstrous feat, but he'd learned a thing or two about the right moment to slip into an open boxcar. The need to survive did strange things to a man.

Chapter 8

The next morning, Maime rose to the sound of Lucy asking for help with Claudia. The older woman had not eaten much dinner last night, and this morning she was complaining of a sore throat and a headache. Then Mr. Weaver had seen Lucy up and proceeded to tell a story about a German soldier slipping through the night shadows, and he'd been up all night watching for more. While Maime assured Mr. Weaver that they were safe, Lucy administered Claudia's medicine. The hour quickly approached for church. As though reading her thoughts, Lucy appeared at the doorway of Mr. and Mrs. Weaver's bedroom.

"Go on to church," Lucy said. "I've got things here in fine order. Everyone is feeling better, and they are all able to dress themselves. If I have any problems, Hank will help me."

"I'll tell him I'm leaving." Maime adjusted her hat. Hank had been in her awake and sleeping world the night before, and she was anxious to see him.

"He isn't here," Mr. Weaver said. "I saw him leave in the night. Most likely chasing the enemy."

"If he's guarding us, then I'm sure we're all fine." Maime shook her head at Lucy. Poor Mr. Weaver. At times he tried the patience of them all.

She made her way down to the kitchen, but Hank was nowhere in sight. Normally the smell of coffee met her the moment she started down the stairs in the morning. The back door was slightly ajar, and she assumed he was having his Sunday devotions.

I'll leave him alone. Besides, she would be late for church if she didn't hurry. The walk was a good twenty minutes. James would have picked her up if she'd asked him last night, but she didn't want to burden him. At the back door she briefly searched the yard but saw no one. She pulled the door shut behind her and made her way to the street. The Sundays she was able to attend church were like a taste of freedom.

Birds sang a little sweeter this morning, and a cloudless sky seemed to usher forth a beautiful day. Instead of thinking about Cranberry Hill and the health conditions of her residents or dealing with her fledgling feelings for Hank, she chose to focus on worshiping God.

Inside the church, greeting friends and cousins helped her settle into the service. However, an aunt let her know one more time about the dangers of living with crazy people.

"One day we will learn you and Lucy have been murdered in your sleep." Aunt Flo cooled herself vigorously with a fan that had a picture of Jesus kneeling in the Garden of Gethsemane on one side and the Lord's Prayer on the other.

Maime smiled. "Aunt Flo, you should visit us sometime. The residents are very sweet and do help me with chores. Claudia crochets beautifully, and Mrs. Weaver embroiders better than my own mother."

Aunt Flo frowned. "You say the same thing every time I try to warn you about those people. I heard the other day that a one-legged man is living there. How many people does that make?"

"His name is Hank, and he's our cook."

"What happened to the woman you had—Emma?"

"Her husband wanted her at home."

The tiny gray-haired woman stuck out her lower lip. "Smart man."

Maime excused herself to find an empty pew near the front with James. The two had sat together in church for years.

"Did you get your chores finished?" she whispered.

"All of them. How's everything at home?"

"All right. Claudia and Mr. Weaver had a rough night, but things seemed fine this morning."

"How about Hank?"

"I didn't see him. The back door wasn't shut when I left. I assumed he was in the backyard. Sometimes he reads his Bible there. Odd, though, coffee hadn't been made." Then she remembered he hadn't wanted to talk the previous night. "I think yesterday wore him out. Maybe he needed to sleep."

James frowned.

"What's wrong?"

"Nothing." He reached for a hymnal.

The pianist began with "Onward Christian Soldiers," signaling to the congregation to prepare their hearts for church.

After the services, Maime hurried home. She didn't want Lucy and Hank stuck with all of the work. Under a cloudless sky, she contemplated this morning's sermon—Abram's lies about claiming Sarai was his sister when a powerful Egyptian king expressed interest in her. Abram was afraid of the truth. Maime wondered if she could have been forgiving if faced with the same circumstances. The preacher said the lesson was to show us that even though Abram was known for his faith, he failed to trust God to take care of him and his wife when danger threatened.

A good sermon for everyone who ever doubted God's providence. She'd spent a lot of years wrestling with trust, and although she'd made steady progress, it was still a struggle at times.

At the front gate, she stopped and admired the home she loved so dearly. Many folks during these hard times weren't able to maintain their homes, but that had never been a problem with her.

The front door opened, and Lucy stepped out. From the gate, Maime saw her friend trembling. A dozen scenarios darted into her mind.

"Oh, Maime, I'm so glad you're home."

"What's wrong?"

"Hank's gone."

Maime's heart pounded against her chest. "What do you mean he's gone?"

"Just that. I couldn't find him. So finally I looked in the cellar and found this note addressed to you." Lucy pulled a folded piece of paper from her dress pocket and walked down the front steps. "I'm so sorry."

Now Maime trembled. She lifted the latch on the gate and walked inside. She took the letter from Lucy and quickly read it. Blinking, she read it again and pondered over every word.

"I don't understand. I thought he was happy here."

"I did, too."

Maime blinked back the tears and refolded the note. If only she'd had an opportunity to talk with Hank like she wanted to do last night. "Goodness, you had your hands full this morning."

"I managed just fine."

"I. . .I need to be thinking about lunch for the residents."

"First of all, you need to talk about what has happened. I know this must hurt something fierce."

Maime shook her head. "It was pure foolishness on my part. Besides—"

The sound of a truck caused her to whirl around. James pulled up next to the house. A moment later, he was at her side.

"I couldn't go home without stopping by. Can I talk to Hank?" The solemn look on James's face made her wonder if he possibly knew Hank had left.

"He's gone." She held up the note. "Not sure when he left. My guess early this morning."

"Unless Mr. Weaver was right when he said he saw Hank last night." Lucy crossed her arms over her chest.

James studied Maime for a moment. "Do you have a few minutes? There's something I need to tell you, and now that Hank is gone, well, I think it's important."

"I need to help Lucy put together something for lunch, first."

"I have it all taken care of," Lucy said. "There's plenty of fish and green beans left from last night. You talk to James, and I'll come looking for you if things get out of hand."

Maime ordered her pulse to slow down. Anger bubbled in her veins. "You knew something about Hank that you kept to yourself? Has he been in prison? Has he robbed me of what little I have, and I don't know it yet? Why else would he leave without so much as a good-bye?"

Lines deepened around James's eyes. "No. He hasn't been in prison. Not to my knowledge anyway. But he's been in a prison of his soul. Let's sit on the swing, and let me tell you about Hank."

He placed his hand in the small of her back and gently guided her up the brick sidewalk toward the front porch. From the pained expression in his eyes, whatever James had to tell her must be heart wrenching.

Maime took a deep breath and eased onto the swing. "I'm sorry I blurted out those things about Hank. I'm simply. . .hurt that he's gone."

"You have a good reason to be hurt." James seated himself beside her. "Do you mind if I pray first?"

She nodded.

"Heavenly Father, guide me in what I need to tell Maime. Give her an open mind to hear the truth and a heart for forgiveness." He lifted his head and took her hand.

"You're scaring me." She hadn't seen James this upset since before Ivy died.

"I want to start with asking you to remember how much you and Charles were in love. Remember how caring and full of life he was?"

"Yes. But what does that have to do with Hank?"

"I'll get to that. The war changed all of us who fought— all of us who lived the horror of seeing people killed and the duties required of soldiers. I'm still reliving those nightmares when I labeled myself a murderer, or when a buddy was blown to pieces. Many times I've asked God why I was spared. And many times I wished I had been taken. What kept me going was knowing Ivy waited for me. When I came home, I feared she'd not recognize me because of the things I'd done."

Maime's stomach churned. She wanted to know the truth about Hank now, but an urging in her spirit held her back.

James squeezed her hand. "Charles did not die in the war."

She snatched back her hand. Her heart hammered against her chest until she thought it would burst. Could it be?

"Hank," she whispered. "My Charles is Hank?"

"Yes, Maime. I figured it out yesterday."

"But how could he do this to me?" She held her breath, sensing the anger raging through her body. "Why?"

"Because of what I just told you. When I returned home, I worried that I had forgotten how to be a good man. My mind and heart had been affected by the war. Charles not only had those fears, but he'd also lost his leg. In his eyes, he was worse than dead. He had nothing to offer you. He believed you were better off as a widow and free to have a life without him."

She stood on weak legs. "How dare he make such a decision? All these years I've loved and cared for a man who was so selfish that he chose to deceive me." Realization of her and James's relationship settled on her. "What if I had remarried? Look at the sin that would have caused." She whirled around. "I'm glad he's gone. He's vile, cruel—"

"Maime, I understand your anger, but I'm asking you to consider his side of the story. Do you have any idea how hard it was for him to come back?"

Tears trickled down her cheeks, and she swiped them away. Now she knew why she'd fallen in love with Hank; he was her first and only love—her precious Charles.

"Listen to me, please," James said. "He's wandered all over trying to forget the war and you. Neither has left his mind. When he came to Hannibal, his desire was to see Cranberry Hill and hopefully get a glimpse of you. But he saw a chance to help and be a part of your life in a small way. Don't you understand? He had to leave. He realized that if I could see the truth, you would, too. He begged me not to tell you, but since he's left, I couldn't let you go on believing a lie. We need Charles as much as he needs us. Help me find him, Maime. Let's bring him home where he belongs."

"No! I can't. How can I forgive him for the empty years? He betrayed me." She swallowed hard and flung open the front door, not knowing where to go for comfort, but she had to flee the truth. She hated what Charles had done. How selfish. How incredibly selfish. Let him get as far away from Hannibal as possible. She wanted no part of him in her life. Charles had died in the war. Her Charles would never have done such a despicable thing. Her Charles would have allowed her to help him rebuild his life. They would have done it together. They'd have raised a family.

Maime blinked. She brushed past Lucy in the kitchen and stepped into the conservatory.

"What is it?" Lucy hurried to her side. "Sit down, Maime. Are you ill? You're ghastly pale."

She turned to her friend. "Hank is really Charles. All these years. . .and I believed he was dead."

Lucy gasped. "You poor dear." She opened her arms for Maime, and she stepped into them. Lucy held her tightly. "Cry. Just cry until there are no more tears." And Maime did.

Some time later, Maime lifted her head from Lucy's shoulder. Exhaustion had left her weak, and she thought she might be physically sick.

"Tell me what is going on," Lucy said. "We can sit on the bench here."

In the next few minutes, Maime retold the story as James had done for her. "I am so hurt and angry," she finally said. "And James. . .how could he ask me to find Charles and bring him home? Does he think I can forget and forgive what Charles has done to me?"

Lucy pulled a handkerchief from her pocket and wiped Maime's face as though she were a child. "You have every right to be angry."

"Thank you." She sniffed.

"But I do have a question."

Maime nodded.

"Didn't you feel love for Hank?"

"I did. Even that was a lie."

"How many times have you wished that Charles was still alive? Do you think this might be an answer to prayer?"

"I've been deceived, Lucy. I've lived with memories of a man who didn't care enough to come home to me."

"I can see he couldn't. I can see that a man could love a woman so much that he'd rather she believe he was dead than face her with what had happened to him." Lucy grasped Maime's shoulders. "I'm going to leave you in here so you can pray about what God would have you do."

"Are you saying I should do what James asked?"

"I don't know, but God does." Lucy smiled and walked back into the kitchen. "James is still here. I'll enlist his help for lunch."

"Oh no, you can't—"

"Hush. You have an important task to do." Lucy turned her attention to pulling plates from the cabinet.

Maime thought her body could not contain a single tear, yet more fell from her eyes. Bitterness, rage, and a hurt that cut so deeply that she thought she would bleed. How could Charles do this to her? Had he ever loved her at all? They'd been closer than most couples were. Best friends. Did he think she was weak and unable to handle his missing limb or to understand his role in the war?

Question after question swelled in her mind. No answers.

Last night James had called him "Chank." He knew the truth then. Abruptly her tears gave way to prayer.

I have brought you together for My purpose.

Maime startled. *No, God.* Had He betrayed her, too? The One she trusted asked far too much of her. *No, God. It's impossible.*

Chapter 9

Hank had embraced sunrise hours ago, and its warmth had helped dry his tears while God eased his brokenness. Walking away from Maime had been harder this time than when he left for the war, for now all of his memories of her had been rekindled. The girl he'd married had blossomed into a mature woman with purpose. She'd fared well without him. His death had strengthened her, and for that he sensed a deep gratitude to the God they both followed.

Are you really following Me?

Where did that thought come from? He pushed aside the question and continued to hobble down the road. Sweat trickled down the side of his face.

His stomach rumbled. His body had grown accustomed to eating regularly, and it would take time for him to get used to going a day or more without food. He'd brought two biscuits and honey to eat this evening. Tomorrow was another day, and during this time of year wild berries were plentiful. As long as he put miles between him and Maime, he'd be fine.

Stop right here and turn around.

The heat must be getting to him. Twice his thoughts had been interrupted by strange comments. He spotted a maple tree ahead and decided to take a brief reprieve. With his typical awkward movements, he settled onto the soft grass and leaned his head back against the tree. The need for sleep seduced him into shutting his eyes. Soon he gave in to his body's weariness.

Dreams of Maime filled his mind, and he let himself live in a fantasy world.

They were happy at Cranberry Hill, and the home flourished for all the residents. Mr. Weaver and Mr. Grayson spent their days fishing, and the womenfolk helped Maime. Hank had both legs, and a Great War had never happened.

Hank woke with a start, recalling his delicious dream. Strange how the dream world mixed the past and the present, reality and fancy. The sun had started its descent; he'd slept too long. He grabbed his crutch and pulled himself up. The thought of eating one of the biscuits crossed his mind, but if he waited until tonight, he'd sleep better. He took a deep breath and started down the road. All the while, his mind and heart rested on his wife.

"Hank, you make the best biscuits," Maime had said. "They're better than pie or cake."

He remembered her compliments when he nursed a fledgling flower to grow through stubborn soil.

"I love color. Look what you've done for that poor plant," she'd said.

"God has done all the work," he'd said. "I'm simply making

the ground around it easier for it to grow."

"You have the touch." Her smile had spread wide, and he remembered the girl of fifteen who had captured his heart so many years ago. "When times get better, I'll have flowers blooming everywhere again."

Memory after memory rushed over him. The girl, the woman—his Maime, the love of his life.

The afternoon faded into the fiery hues of yellow and orange. His gaze scanned the horizon for a place to lay his head tonight. Incredible weariness settled over him, matched only by extreme loneliness. . .his oldest friend.

I have a better life waiting for you. Turn around.

Hank stopped in the middle of the road.

Turn around.

Turn around.

Maime is waiting.

What did he have to offer her? Could she ever forgive him for the years of deceit? But the whispers of God bid him to go back to her. Hank stood on the dirt road and stared back at Hannibal. The idea of walking back to Cranberry House and not revealing his identity entered his mind, but he understood what God wanted.

James's question about the truth setting a man free seemed to resound from every direction. Hank wanted to be happy, but he didn't deserve it for the wretched things he'd done. Yet the urging in his spirit called to him.

He realized what he'd known all along. Jesus had died for him so Hank could be free and live. God did not view Hank as wretched; that was the biggest lie of all. Hank needed to ask forgiveness from God and from Maime, and then with the help of Him, put the past to rest.

The truth seemed simple enough, but was he man enough to take the first step?

Oh, Lord, how I want to go back to her.

Lifting his shoulders, he took the first step back to God. For in making his heart right with Him, he had a chance at winning back his wife. He could stand before her as a whole man and confess his sins.

With every thump of his crutch against the road, his heart grew lighter. Charles Bradford was walking back to his wife.

❀

"It's nearly dark, Maime," James said. "Charles will be finding a place for the night."

"Just a little while longer." Maime searched both sides of the road. "I think you made a wise choice by staying off the main road."

"I want to find him as much as you do. But once the evening hides him, we'll have to stop looking until tomorrow."

Maime nodded, but she didn't agree. She understood that James had chores to do and even more in the morning. "I'll help you with chores tonight and in the morning. I don't think God would have convinced me to find him if we were forced to stop looking."

"Then pray it is soon." He slowed the truck and studied every direction.

She thought back through the day: the beautiful day, Aunt Flo's criticism of Cranberry Hill, discovering that Hank was missing, the heartbreaking knowledge of learning about Charles, and God's dealing with her selfish heart. They would find Charles tonight. She felt certain.

Maime startled. Was that a man limping toward them? Emotion choked her. "Look ahead. It's Charles. Pull over, please."

A few moments later, she ran to the man she'd loved for so many years. "Charles" was all she could utter.

The more she hurried, the faster he limped. She heard him call her name.

"Charles, I was afraid that I'd lost you again."

Once he was close enough for her to touch, she stopped and faced him. He didn't speak, but then, in the shadows, she saw the tears streaming down his face.

"I couldn't stay any longer," he said. "I guess James told you the truth."

"He did, but. . ." She swallowed the growing lump in her throat. "But. . .you're walking back to town."

"I was coming to you. To tell you the truth myself and ask for your forgiveness. I'm sorry for all the pain I've caused you. I know that sounds insignificant considering all the years I led you to believe I was dead. But I don't know what else to say."

She touched his shoulder. "You *are* forgiven. Please come home, Charles. I need you."

"I want to. I've loved you for as long as I can remember." Emotion ended any more words.

Maime waited. After all, she'd waited eighteen years.

"I have a lot of demons."

"We'll chase them away together."

"And I have only one leg."

"I fell back in love with your heart, not your legs."

"My face is scarred."

"Your face is not your heart."

He chuckled. "You are the most beautiful woman in the world."

"And I'm in love with the most handsome man in the world." She glanced about. "It's dark, Charles. We need to get home.

"Yes, I think it's time to go home. Our home."

Chapter 10

One year later

Daddy, your little girl wants to be held."

Charles reached up for his six-week-old daughter. "Oh, let me have my Kathryn Jane."

Maime laid the tiny pink bundle into his arms. He settled into the front porch swing, and Maime snuggled next to him. "She's such a good baby."

"That's because she's just like her mama."

Maime giggled. "She's more like you than me."

"God is so very good." He kissed his infant daughter. "I'm so blessed with my girls." He wrapped his arm around her shoulder.

"We're all blessed."

Mr. Weaver opened the front door. "Fishing sounds real good today. Can't find my pole or my gun."

Charles chuckled. "We went yesterday, but we can talk

about going today. Don't worry, Mr. Weaver. I'll protect you."

"I'm never afraid when I'm around you." The old man smiled.

"I think he's getting better," Charles said and peered into the deep blue eyes of his tiny daughter.

Maime kissed his whiskered cheek. "I believe I'm just like Mr. Weaver. I'm not afraid when you're here. Everything at Cranberry Hill is sweeter now that I have my husband." She laughed. "Besides a beautiful daughter, my flowers are blooming again."

"Just like our love."

DIANN MILLS

Award-winning author, DiAnn Mills, launched her career in 1998 with the publication of her first book. Currently she has over forty books in print and has sold more than a million copies.

DiAnn believes her readers should "Expect an Adventure." Her desire is to show characters solving real problems of today from a Christian perspective through a compelling story.

Six of her anthologies have appeared on the CBA Bestseller List. Three of her books have won the distinction of Best Historical of the Year by Heartsong Presents. Five of her books have won placements through American Christian Fiction Writer's Book of the Year Awards 2003–2007. She is the recipient of the Inspirational Reader's Choice award for 2005 and 2007.

DiAnn is a founding board member for American Christian Fiction Writers, a member of Inspirational Writers Alive, Romance Writers of America's Faith, Hope and Love, and Advanced Writers and Speakers Association. She speaks to various groups and teaches writing workshops around the country. DiAnn is also a mentor for Jerry B. Jenkins Christian Writer's Guild.

She lives in sunny Houston, Texas, the home of heat, humidity, and Harleys. In fact she'd own a Harley, but her legs are too short. DiAnn and her husband have four adult sons and are active members of Metropolitan Baptist Church. Visit her Web site at www.diannmills.com.

FINALLY
HOME

by Deborah Raney

Dedication

To Calvin William Layton,
who promises to be one of my favorite
Missouri memories.
With so much love,
Mimi

Chapter 1

June 1972

The acrid scent of burnt toast registered with Brian Lowe's nose a split second before he entered the kitchen. Through a haze of smoke, he propelled his wheelchair across the kitchen tile as if the hand rims were oars and his chair a heavy boat. He reached across the granite countertop and grabbed the toaster's electric cord, yanking the plug from the wall.

Flames shot from the toaster, and Brian wheeled his chair backward a few feet. But the smoke stung his throat and made his eyes water. He'd only been home six days since his dismissal from Walter Reed General, and this was the third time he'd made a burnt offering of breakfast. He was going to burn down his parents' house if he wasn't careful. He hoisted himself up in the seat of his wheelchair and gingerly pulled a blackened slice from the toaster. But it was still hot and he dropped it on the counter. The toast disintegrated, sending charred crumbs skittering across the tile.

Wheeling to the pantry to retrieve a broom and dustpan, the tires of his chair crunched the crumbs to dust. Working his way backwards toward the counter where the toaster sat, he lifted his mangled leg out of the way and flipped the footrest up, leaving a path for the broom to follow. He set the brake and bent at the waist, leaning to sweep up what he could reach.

He put the dustpan in his lap and rolled his chair backward another foot. But when he set the brake, the pan slid off his lap, spilling half the contents onto his last clean pair of sweatpants, and the rest onto the floor. He seized the dustpan by the handle and slammed it onto the tile, biting back a curse. He needed three hands.

No, he just needed his legs to work right.

By the time he'd cleaned up the worst of the mess, he was drenched in sweat and fuming with frustration. Mrs. Bennett would have the kitchen spotless again when she came to clean Friday, but that wasn't the point. He was worthless. A wave of nausea washed over him, and he wondered for the thousandth time if God could ever use this broken body, the broken pieces of his life.

Rocking his chair back and forth, he picked up his heavy leg with his hands and gave his best effort to kick the cabinet in front of him. He only succeeded in making pain shoot up his right leg from his knee. But pain was good. At least he felt something.

The doorbell started its protracted chime, and he blew out

another breath of frustration. He glanced at the schoolhouse clock hanging over the sink. Twenty till ten. The doorbell chimed again. If it was that physical therapist his mother had arranged for, she was plenty early.

He maneuvered the chair around the kitchen island and out to the entry hall. Rolling across the gold-shot marble tile, his mind scrambled to come up with an excuse to get rid of the woman as quickly as possible. Determination alone would get him out of this despised chair. A week of army boot camp had instilled that much in him. He didn't need anybody standing over him, telling him how to do it.

Since he'd come home from the hospital, he'd developed a workout on his own, lifting weights and doing as much of his boot camp routine as his body could tolerate. Because his upper body had been forced to do the work of his legs all these months, from the waist up he was solid, maybe in the best shape he'd ever been. But that didn't get him on his feet.

He slung open the front door to find a pretty brunette standing out at the edge of the porch steps, gawking up at the house. It was a familiar reaction—one the house always got from anyone who hadn't been up here before. The House on Cranberry Hill was impressive from the highway, but up close, it was downright imposing.

He cleared his throat loudly.

She whirled and almost tripped on the wide bell-bottoms of her blue jeans. "Oh. Hi. . . You must be Brian." She tossed her head, and a veil of long, shiny hair settled behind her shoulders. "This is quite the place you've got here." She looked east to the wide snake of the Mississippi River in the distance. "What a view!"

When he didn't respond, she stepped forward and held out a hand. "I'm Kathy. With Health Strategies."

She was *not* what he'd pictured when his mother informed him via long distance from Cartagena, Colombia, yesterday that a physical therapist—someone named Kathryn Nowlin—would be coming to the house to work with him this morning.

His vantage point from the chair made it hard not to stare at her slim figure and the embroidered peasant blouse that showed off smooth, tanned shoulders. He moved his gaze quickly to her face. Her smile revealed straight white teeth and lit a playful glimmer in her amber eyes. Okay. Maybe he could use some help with his exercises after all.

He wheeled his chair into reverse, holding the door open for her with his right hand. "Come on in."

She hoisted the duffel bag at her feet and slung it over one shoulder. She stepped through the door and her jaw sagged. "Wow!"

Brian followed her gaze to the wide stairway. She rocked back on the platform soles of her sandals, then pivoted three-sixty, taking in the view of the entry hall from bottom to top and back again. "Far out! What an amazing place. Did you grow up here?"

"Supposedly."

Cocking her head, she gave him a look that said she thought he might need a different kind of therapist.

"It was a joke. As in I never really grew up. . .you know,

like I'm still a kid at heart?" The bewildered expression on her face told him she still wasn't tracking. Did he have to draw the chick a picture? "Never mind," he muttered, glancing around. "And yes, I grew up here. I guess I sort of take it for granted."

"Well, you shouldn't. This place is incredible." She ran a hand over the polished wood on the banister. "I'd kill to live here."

Now it was his turn to give her that are-you-some-kind-of-psycho? look.

She smiled. "It was a joke." She mimicked his dry tone. "Don't worry. . .I didn't mean it literally. You're safe with me."

"Whew"—he gave an exaggerated swipe of his brow—"that's a relief. Now that we have that settled. . .what do you need from me?"

"Oh. . ." She shook her head as if she'd completely forgotten why she was here. She slid a clipboard from her bag and pulled a pen from under the clip. "Before I do the actual physical evaluation, I need to ask you a few questions about your medical history."

He blew a heavy breath through his teeth.

"I know, I know." Her smile held an apology. "You've probably answered these same questions a million times since you were injured."

"A million and a half."

Her laughter made him wish he were a comedian and she his audience. Well, the least he could do was humor her while she went down the list of medical questions.

"I'll need to do a physical evaluation, too—so we can figure out where you are. . ."

He looked pointedly around the entry. "I *know* where I am."

A wry smile touched her mouth. "Ha-ha. Your chart didn't mention that you were a comedian."

Aha! Success. "Did it mention anything about me being brilliant, dashingly handsome, and filthy rich?"

Her laughter was musical. "Um. . .I guess I haven't gotten that far yet." Her expression turned serious and she panned the large entry hall. "Where would be a good place for us to work?"

"We can use the parl—this room over here." He'd almost called it the parlor. That was what his mother always called the rarely used formal living room. Until now.

He'd come home from the hospital to find that all his bedroom furniture had been moved down to the study, and in the parlor next door, his father had pulled up the practically new shag carpets and laid tile. They'd stored the fancy antiques on the third floor and set up a weight bench, treadmill, and parallel bars in their place. Brian had a ways to go before he'd be ready to use anything but the weight bench, but just seeing the equipment in there each day inspired him to do a few more repetitions, lift a little more weight.

Just yesterday a plumber had come to install a whirlpool limb tub like the rehab center had used. Even from halfway around the world, Jerry Lowe was determined his son would walk again.

If money could buy a miracle, he was home free.

The girl—he still had trouble thinking of her as a professional, a physical therapist—stepped out of her clunky sandals beside the front door and padded barefoot to where his chair was parked.

Her braid-trimmed jeans dusted the hardwood floor in her wake. "Okay," she said, "lead the way."

He wheeled over to the double doors, leaning to push them open before she could do it for him. Strains of Don McLean's "American Pie" came from the radio in the corner. He'd forgotten to turn it off after his workout early this morning. He held the door open. "After you."

"Thanks." She looked down at his chair. "You get around pretty well in that thing."

He shook his head. His father had wanted to buy him an expensive motorized chair. But he hadn't allowed it. He didn't plan to be chair-bound for long. And he'd never get his strength back if all he had to do was push a button to get around.

As if she'd read his mind she asked, "Have you thought about getting a motorized chariot? One of those scooters they make now?"

He shook his head and opened his mouth to explain, but she saved him from it.

"That's okay," she said. "You're probably better off with this. Looks like you've got it mastered, too."

He wished everybody would treat him in the same straightforward manner she did. Since he'd been home, the people who'd come to visit had tried to pretend his wheelchair wasn't there. Instead, it ended up being the elephant in the room, with everybody scared to death they'd slip up and mention its floppy gray ears or its muddy toenails.

He tipped his head back to look at her. "I've had lots of practice. I've been living in a hospital for a while. I aced door-opening 101 at the rehab center."

She smiled. "So I see." She walked through the doorway and looked around the parlor. Her face lit up when she spotted the equipment. "This is outta sight. Good grief. . .you've got a better setup here than the rehab clinic where I did my internship."

She plopped down cross-legged on the end of a thick exercise mat, her hair hanging in a curtain over half her face, everything about her demeanor erasing the image he'd had when his mother referred to Kathryn Nowlin, PT.

For the next few minutes, she rattled off a list of questions that he answered with one-word replies. While she carefully copied down his responses on the forms she'd brought with her, he did his best not to stare. No small feat.

Finally, she put the clipboard away and hopped to her feet. "Okay. Let's see what you've got." She knelt beside his chair and looked at the thong sandals on his feet. "Can you slide those off for me? And. . .let's see, the biggest concern is your left knee, right?" She giggled. "I mean, correct?"

"Right." He winked. "Left."

Her mouth twisted to match his grin. "Will those pant legs slide up over your knee?"

He demonstrated, tugging the stretchy sweat pants up past his knee. "That good enough?"

"Perfect." She was all business as she knelt closer, but he watched her face, waiting for the telltale revulsion when she saw his injury. He didn't remember much from that day on the Mekong River—and what remained in his memory he'd worked hard to forget. The roadside bomb, pain searing through his left leg, his kneecap giving way. . .he shuddered. Muscle, ligaments, tendons, and arteries had been severed, leaving his kneecap hanging somewhere in the vicinity of his shin.

He was one of the lucky ones. He'd spent only ten days in a tented field hospital before being airlifted out. That had probably saved him from losing his leg to infection. His other knee had fared only slightly better. But it healed more quickly and now offered his best hope of getting back on his feet.

If she was grossed out, her expression didn't give her away. She put one hand under his knee and knelt beside his chair. "I want to do some strength tests so I can get an idea of where you are. I'm going to have you push against me as hard as you can, okay?"

For the next few minutes, she arranged his limbs—both arms and legs—in various positions, having him push against her as hard as he could. He gave her everything he had, and by the time she was finished, he felt like he'd done a second workout for the day.

"You're in good shape," she said matter-of-factly.

"Yeah, well, you can thank my old man for that." He looked pointedly at the roomful of equipment.

"You're blessed to have all this." She encompassed the room with a sweep of her hand. "Your parents must love you very much."

"Yeah. . .I guess so," he muttered.

If she only knew the truth.

Chapter 2

Kathy shifted the splintered picket to her left hand and hefted the poster into the air. "Make love not war! Make love not war!" She chanted in unison with the other tie-dye–clad protesters as they plodded single file in front of the Marion County Courthouse.

A cool rain spit on them and the spring air still seemed to hold reminders of the bleak winter barely behind them. She wanted nothing more right now than to be home in the warm bed in her loft apartment overlooking Broadway. But this was important.

The two dozen or so protesters started another chant. Kathy cringed at the profanity in the new slogan. She wished they wouldn't use the ugly words. She couldn't bring herself even to mouth the curses. But she understood why her friends did. People in this town, this nation, were dying of apathy as fast as the innocents in Vietnam. Somebody. . .*something* had to get their attention.

She took a sip of cold coffee from a Styrofoam cup. The bitter liquid slid down her throat, raw from hours of yelling. Sometimes she wondered if all their efforts did any good at all. This war had raged on for more years than she could remember. Every day it seemed new names were added to the list of the fallen—both the innocents and the soldiers, many of them drafted against their will. The cold metal of the POW bracelet on her wrist served as a bleak reminder.

She shifted her coffee to her left hand and twisted the bracelet, tracing the letters engraved in the nickel plating. *Lord, be with John. Give him strength and let him feel Your presence.* She'd come to feel she knew the stranger whose name she'd worn on her arm for over two years now.

"Murderers! Get out of Vietnam now!" She raised her voice louder as two businessmen approached the building, skirting the center of the wide steps that led to the courthouse. They walked with eyes downcast, trying to pretend they didn't see the protesters. Without discussion, the group shifted like an amoeba in their direction.

The men disappeared into the fortress of the courthouse, and the group resumed a quieter march. Kathy checked her watch. She had another appointment with Brian Lowe later this morning. They'd gotten off to a good start. He didn't seem bitter like so many of the men who came back from the war in wheelchairs, missing limbs, having lost wives or girlfriends to other men, sometimes having lost the ability to ever father a child. She shuddered. The horrors of this war were sickening.

Men like Brian were one of the reasons she gave her time

to the cause of peace. Of course, Brian was one of the lucky ones. He came from a family who had the money to pay for the best care. And though his injuries had disfigured him for life, he at least had hope he might someday walk again, live a normal life. She'd recognized his determination in the set of his jaw.

Her work as a physical therapist sought to accomplish that goal, to repair some of the less catastrophic damage of war. Her work as a war protester sought to ensure that what had happened to Brian and others like him—and most of all, to the men who came home in body bags—would never happen again.

An hour later she checked her watch again and gave a little gasp. She'd be late if she didn't leave right now. She eased out of her place in the picket line and caught up to march beside Charlie Morgan, the group's organizer and director of the Center for Peace. "I've got to run, Charlie. I have a client at three."

"I hear you, man." He held up two fingers in a V—the peace sign. Charlie had been arrested in the massive May Day protests in D.C. last year, and he wore the distinction like a badge of honor. "You go on. Do your good work, babe. We'll see you tomorrow."

She waved to a couple of other friends still marching, and carried her homemade sign to the parking lot where her red VW Beetle was parked. She stuffed the poster into the trunk in the front of the car. The sun had faded the words she'd painted red, to look like dripping blood: *BABY KILLERS*.

She drove too fast out to the mansion, not really wanting to explain why she was late. She wished every client she worked with had the kind of setup Brian Lowe had. With most of her patients she improvised, and she had been known to use canned goods for weights if that's all that was available. More than once, she'd paid for dumbbells out of her own pocket for long-term patients who could barely afford their next meal, let alone her services or equipment for therapy.

She wondered what Brian's story was. He'd no doubt been drafted, although surely his father's money could have bought him out of that situation somehow. She had to remind herself that even if he had enlisted, that didn't automatically make him a hawk. But she doubted he'd support the cause she and Charlie and the others from the Center for Peace were devoting their lives to. Few veterans of this war did. It was probably best to avoid the topic of the war with him—even though the war was exactly why Brian had need of her services.

Pulling into the driveway of the mansion, she felt the same tug-of-war she'd felt yesterday when she first saw the place up close. People called it the House on Cranberry Hill. Living here must be like living in a fairy tale.

She immediately checked the thought, feeling guilty for entertaining it for even a minute. The stately old home was the epitome of the American dream, life at its best and all that rot. But in too many important ways, this mansion represented everything that had led this nation into an immoral and unjust war. Its opulence represented a bloated, affluent establishment that based all its decisions on money and power and greed. The wraparound porches alone covered more square footage—and probably cost more—than the tract house she'd grown up in.

Some people just didn't get it. Money wasn't the be-all and end-all. If people could just get their priorities straight the country wouldn't be in the mess it was in. War was ugly. There were solutions to the problems the government was supposedly trying to solve that didn't snuff out innocent life.

She parked the Bug and snatched up her duffel bag. She didn't relish meeting Brian's parents, though from what Jerald Lowe had said, they were out of the country on an extended trip. Their travels often graced the society page of the *Hannibal Courier-Post*. But what overseas holiday could possibly take precedence over their only son?

Jerald Lowe had paid her for a full month of private physical therapy—no small change—and while she'd deposited the check, she'd done so with more than a twinge of guilt. It wasn't easy to weigh her need to make a living against her disgust with the well-known excesses of Lowe's lifestyle.

How ironic that the one thing their fortune couldn't ensure was their son's safety. Did Brian share his father's ideals?

She chided herself. It didn't matter. He was her client. She had to be objective.

Jogging up the wide stairs, it was hard not to compare the entrance to this mansion with the entrance to the courthouse she'd just left. She shook off the images that superimposed themselves in her brain. Brian Lowe was a client, and his politics or beliefs shouldn't make any difference in how she viewed him. *Easier said than done.*

The muted doorbell chimed only twice before the door opened. Brian sat there, smiling up at her, looking even more of a hunk than she remembered.

He rolled his wheelchair in reverse and held the door for her. "Hi. Come on in. Miss. . .Nowlin, isn't it?"

"Good morning. Sorry I'm late." She stepped inside. "And please, it's Kathy."

He nodded. "Okay. Kathy." A hank of straight, dark hair fell over his eyes. His hair still bore the contours of a military cut, but it was growing out.

He pivoted in his chair and led the way through the immense hall to the room that housed the workout equipment. She still couldn't get over the setup. And from the looks of his broad shoulders, he spent a lot of time in here.

Her evaluation yesterday had left her optimistic about Brian's recovery. The fact that he'd built up his upper body would make her job considerably easier. Being able to support his weight without taxing his injured knees would ensure faster healing, as well.

She rummaged in her bag for her clipboard. "I've got a plan pretty well mapped out for you, but I want to do a couple more evaluation activities before we walk through a core set of exercises I want you to do. Are you ready to get going?"

He shrugged. "I'm not going anywhere."

Something about the way he said those words struck a melancholy chord in her. Looking at him—only a year older than she was, just starting out in life—it jolted her to realize that Brian put a face on the American GIs she'd felt such ambivalence toward. She'd imagined what John, the POW whose bracelet she wore, might look like. If she were honest, when she'd first started wearing it, that bracelet had been as much for show as for the sake of the man whose name was engraved upon it. But as she'd prayed for John over the past two years, he'd become very real to her, and her reasons for wearing the bracelet had become more authentic.

But today, for perhaps the first time, she was starting to see that behind *every* U.S. soldier there was someone like John and like Brian Lowe. A young man with a story, with a family back home and a future that had been put on hold by the war. A man who risked his very life when he set foot on foreign soil.

The implications shook her more than she cared to admit. She thought of the homemade protest sign in the trunk of her Bug and was glad she hadn't propped it in the window of her car like she sometimes did.

❖

Miss Nowlin—Kathy—paused in the doorway to the parlor—exercise room—and looked around the space as if assessing what was next. Today she wore a tie-dyed T-shirt and a beaded headband tied around her forehead, its thin leather strings disappearing into her thick hair. He'd never been crazy about the hippie look. Too many connections to rebellion and the drug culture—and more recently with the hatred spewed at returning veterans by the antiestablishment, antiwar faction.

But Kathy Nowlin's sweet smile dispelled any such connections. And she did look cute in those hip-huggers.

"Okay. . .let's see. . ." Her gaze landed on the whirlpool tub. "Oh, this is great. . .you're already using hydrotherapy."

He shook his head. "They just put it in. My father heard it was supposed to be a cure-all. But I haven't tried it yet. . .not sure how the thing even works."

"Oh, you'll love it. We'll try it out tomorrow. I don't know if it's a cure-all, but I'll teach you some resistance exercises you can do in the water. And it does help to relax the muscles and keep them from atrophying."

She knelt in front of his chair and lifted his leg the way she had during the evaluation yesterday. She flexed his knee, pushing hard against his leg with the weight of her body. "You're really not too bad in that department. You have good strength and muscle hypertrophy—even in the damaged mus—"

"Whoa. . .speak English please. Hyper–what–y?"

She wrinkled her nose. "Sorry. Hypertrophy. It's sort of the opposite of atrophy. It just means you have good muscle bulk."

"Oh, you mean I'm a hunk."

She rolled her eyes. "Yeah. That." Gently, she lowered his leg and positioned his foot on the footrest, then rose and took a step back. "Can you transfer to a chair for me? I'd like to evaluate your balance."

"Not too bad in that department?" Feigning indignation, he wheeled himself closer to the chair she indicated and set the brakes. He tightened his fingers around the arms of his chair, feeling slightly self-conscious beneath her watchful eye. "I'll have you know that I am a very well-balanced individual."

She rolled her eyes. "You're also a very certifiable dork."

"Hey. . .now that doesn't seem very professional."

She shrugged. "You started it." She moved closer, no doubt to spot him in case he couldn't manage the feat.

He laughed. "Touché." He managed a textbook transfer to the waiting chair and looked up at her with a smug nod, grateful for the lean, strong muscles of his shoulders and back.

She nodded, obviously satisfied with the way he'd accomplished the transfer. "So, your upper torso isn't affected at all?"

"No, it's only my knees. And my left foot to some extent."

"Amazing how two joints can mess up your whole life, huh?"

The gleam in her eye made him wonder if she was making a pun about a different kind of joint. He'd learned more about marijuana in Nam than he ever wanted to know, but he'd managed to stay away from the stuff. Not that he hadn't been tempted by some of the "stress relievers"—wine, women, and drugs—that were readily available over there.

He pushed away the thoughts and shrugged in reply, opting to play dumb. He hoped she wasn't into the drug scene. She seemed like a nice girl.

She extended his arm and ran a finger up and down it. His skin puckered into gooseflesh. She eyed him. "You're feeling that, I take it?"

"Yes. I feel it."

"How about this?" She stroked a finger lightly along the inside of his arm. "You feel that?"

Did he ever. "Yeah. . .it tickles. I told you, I'm fine from the knees up." Realizing how that might sound, he quickly added, "You just get *these* joints working again." He put his hands on his knees, challenging her with his eyes.

She looked away and knelt beside his chair. She propped the right footrest up and lifted his leg, trailing a finger from the base of his toes to his heel.

"Hey, I'm serious. I'm ticklish!"

She laughed. "Sorry. But listen, that's a good sign. Be glad."

She took her same spot from yesterday, sitting cross-legged on the exercise mat on the floor.

"So. . .your surgeries were at Walter Reed General, right? That's what your records said. . ."

"Yeah. . .spent four months there."

"In Vietnam?"

"No. In the hospital. I was in Nam for two years."

"Oh." She bit her lip and looked away, no trace of her former playfulness lingering in her expression.

He wasn't sure how to interpret her sudden silence, but something changed in her demeanor, and for the rest of their session, Kathy Nowlin was all business.

Chapter 3

Kathy parked in the alley west of her apartment. Leaving everything but her purse in the car, she took the stairs two at a time to her tiny loft overlooking Broadway.

Inside, she parted the curtain of love beads hanging in the entryway and padded through the apartment, flipping on lights one by one. On her way through to the bathroom she switched on the television. The drone of the six o'clock news filled the silence as she showered and changed into her nightgown.

The days were growing longer, but rain clouds darkened the sky outside her wide windows, and the neon lights of the stores on the street below reflected off the painted walls. A flash of lightning zagged across the sky, and the TV added its intermittent flicker to the cacophony of light.

Kathy fixed a salad in the kitchen while rain splattered the roof and the broadcast catalogued the day's war fatalities as if they were a grocery list. Sprinkling homegrown bean sprouts and chunks of tofu over salad greens, she turned her full attention to the dispassionate voice of the newscaster. "Aided by U.S. Navy gunfire and B-52 bombardments, South Vietnamese troops began a counteroffensive to retake Quang Tri Province south of the DMZ."

No doubt reports of many more fatalities would follow. Not just U.S. military, but Vietnamese civilians. Women and children. The film footage that filled the TV screen made her sick to her stomach, and a black cloud of depression settled over her as thick as the one that hung over Broadway.

She took her salad and drink to the TV tray set up in front of the sofa. But after a few minutes, she got up and snapped off the TV. She put an album on the stereo, and soon Pete Seeger's mellow voice crooned to her. *Where have all the flowers gone?*

Sometimes she wished she could just stick her head in the sand and pretend the war didn't exist—the way her mother had ever since the day a military vehicle pulled into their drive to deliver the news that her father would never be coming home from Korea. Kathy had been an infant at the time, but she'd heard the story often enough she almost felt she remembered it.

She thought her mother would be proud of her efforts to fight against this war. Instead, Mom had withdrawn from her. These days, Betty Nowlin spent her time decorating and redecorating the same little house she and Dad had shared as newlyweds. And shopping for the perfect wardrobe she'd never been able to afford while she was struggling to raise a daughter alone.

Mom wanted to hear nothing about Kathy's activities outside of quick reports of her work as a physical therapist. Kathy thought her mother was proud of her accomplishments—a college degree, independence, a good career. But they didn't see eye to eye on much anymore.

Looking around her tiny loft, she tried to picture Brian Lowe alone in that huge, beautiful mansion on the hill. Something about the image tugged at her heart. If only she could help him to regain his strength, his ability to walk again.

She'd only worked with Brian for two days, but already he was challenging the stereotype she had of this war's veterans. There seemed to be a minimum of bitterness in him over what the war had done to him. She sensed his frustration with his limitations, sure. But she'd seen none of the hostility, none of the hawkishness so many returning soldiers expressed in TV interviews and in the counterprotests they sometimes staged.

The war had changed Brian's life more than most. Taken away things most men his age took for granted. It would be a miracle if he ever walked on his own again.

Surely he had regrets. Surely he was angry at the terrible price he'd paid for this unjust war. But if he was, he hadn't let her see it. But then, that was bound to change. She hadn't pushed Brian yet.

She smiled, remembering their playful banter this morning. But her smile faded as she thought of the work he would need to do to get back on his feet. She was proud of her reputation for getting the most from her patients. And if she was going to accomplish that with Brian, she'd have to push him to a point where he probably wouldn't like her very much.

That thought bothered her more than she wanted to admit, even to herself.

Brian made the nightly tour of the downstairs rooms of the house, turning out lights and locking doors. It seemed a waste for one man to be living in this huge house. Of course, his parents would be back in a few weeks, but he knew them well enough to know they would only stay long enough to be sure he was getting along okay. Then they'd be on their way back to Cartagena.

He tried to be happy for his parents. After chasing dreams of fortune—and being pretty successful at it with their construction business—they had grown restless and sought something to give their life deeper meaning. Two months after he shipped out to Vietnam, they turned the management of the business over to one of the vice presidents, closed up the mansion, and answered the tug of God's call on their lives. They'd spent the last two years building houses for the less fortunate with *Casas para Cartagena*.

Only recently his dad had told him, with tears welling in his eyes, that it was Brian's faith that had brought them to their senses, made them search their hearts and renew their faith in God. He was happy for them. He really was. But sometimes he had a hard time squaring Dad's teary confession with the image of his livid response the night Brian told them he'd enlisted. The weeks-long silent treatment Dad had given him still stung.

He knew much of his father's anger—and his mother's tears—had been from fear. One of Dad's managers in the construction company had sent a son off to war. Danny Brigmann had never come home. Not even his body. He was listed MIA—missing in action. Brian had little hope his body would ever be found, let alone that Danny would come home alive.

He understood their fear that the same fate might befall him. Still, it hurt to leave home, to hop on that bus to boot camp not knowing if he'd ever see them again. Not knowing if they'd ever forgive him. They had allowed him to cross that ocean without their blessing. And that was hard to take.

He looked at the clock. It was barely nine o'clock, but there was nothing good on TV. Besides, Kathy Nowlin had worn him out today. He'd thought he was rough on himself with his two-a-day workouts, but she'd pushed him past his limits. His dad would approve. He smiled. He had to admit, his physical therapy session hadn't been the drudgery he'd envisioned.

His time with Kathy helped relieve the boredom that had set in now that he was home and feeling more like himself. It had been nice having someone to laugh and joke with. Even though, at the same time, it reminded him how lonely he was. Maybe things would be better once he started working. Dad had reserved a place for him in the Hannibal office. As soon as he was finished with therapy.

He rolled through the converted study to the private bath where he washed up and brushed his teeth. Back in his bedroom, he looked around the former study. Mom had tried to recreate his boyhood room in this space.

She'd never been crazy about his Grateful Dead posters, and those had stayed upstairs—or gone in the trash? He wasn't sure. There wasn't room for them here anyway with bookcases covering almost every inch of wall space. Anyplace there was bare wall space between the rows of books and knickknacks, Mom had pinned the college pennants from his old bedroom at jaunty angles. The pennants had never held any meaning for him. They were apparently what she'd deemed appropriate décor for a teenage boy back then. On his nightstand, the bright blue lava lamp bubbled, just as it had a few years ago up in his old bedroom.

At his insistence, Dad had jerry-rigged his old dartboard on the bookcases to the left of the door. Brian plucked the darts out of the sisal bristles, wheeled backwards a few paces, and chucked a couple of throws. One bounced off the board and another pierced the wall. Even though the board hung a bit lower than regulation, being in this chair totally threw him off his game. He lobbed a third dart and managed to wire the double twenty.

Bored with the game, he wheeled one-eighty and rolled over to his bed. The navy and red-corded bedspread would have been made with hospital precision if his mom were home. Now it lay in a rumpled wad at the end of the bed. Mrs. Bennett would launder the sheets and make the bed when she came to clean Friday. And she wouldn't lecture him about the unmade bed, either.

He parked his chair beside the bed and set the brake. His parents had wanted to hire a full-time nurse to care for him, but he'd put his foot down about that. He wasn't an invalid. He'd learned how to fend for himself in rehab at Walter Reed.

He'd soon learned the agony of that personal challenge was

nothing compared to the pain of coming home to a nation that didn't seem to understand—or appreciate—the sacrifice he'd made for his country. Rehab might have taught him how to get around again in the world he'd come home to, but it hadn't taught him how to be alone in it.

He wound his alarm clock and set it for six a.m. Not that he had any real reason to get up, but army life had imprinted a regimen on him, and he did feel better keeping to a schedule. The clock's *tick-tick-tick* pounded like hammer blows on his nightstand in the dead quiet of the night. He twisted the dial on the radio until it caught a signal. As if on cue, the familiar chorus of Gilbert O'Sullivan's new song came on. *Alone again, naturally. . .*

He gave a humorless snort and clicked the radio off. With practiced ease, he transferred himself onto the edge of the mattress and lifted his legs onto the bed. He pulled up the covers and lay back on the pillows, hands behind his head. He tried to quiet his thoughts enough to pray. But as happened too often, his mind began to drift before two minutes had passed.

Jeff Porter, his old youth pastor, had offered to pick him up for church on Sunday. Most of his friends had left Hannibal for college or the military. He wasn't sure he'd even know anyone at First Community anymore. And he couldn't get too excited about parading in front of everybody in that stupid chair. Still, he thought he'd probably go. He looked forward to seeing Jeff and his wife, and it sure beat hanging around here all weekend.

He tossed off the blankets and fanned himself with the sheet for a minute before letting it settle down over him again. The June heat had left his room too warm, but the thought of getting out of bed and transferring to his chair to go adjust the thermostat made him weary. Besides, it cost a mint to cool even the first floor of this house.

Finally, after a few minutes, his eyelids grew heavy, and sleep began to settle over him. But instead of the relief he expected, he found himself trapped halfway between wakefulness and slumber. Some part of his consciousness was aware that his mind was transporting him where he didn't want to go, but he felt powerless to come back from the ledge.

The air hung heavy with moisture. He struggled to fill his lungs, but instead of fresh air, he breathed in the silt he'd trudged through in the soupy waters of the Mekong River. He lay perfectly still. Overhead, the *whup whup whup* of a helicopter grew closer. Medevac. *Dear God, let that Huey be coming for me. Please, God. Don't leave me here to die.* He tried to move, but he couldn't make his muscles work, couldn't feel his legs. Couldn't see them, either. He managed to lift one hand to his face. It came away sticky with sweat—or blood? He wiggled his fingers, but he couldn't see his hand in front of his face. All around him was pitch-black. He tried to move his legs. Nothing.

His prayer changed abruptly. *Lord, don't let me live if I can't be whole.* Like a machete hacking through a nipa palm swamp, his prayers cut through the panic. He forced his eyes open.

The ceiling fan whirred languidly above him. His heart stuttered and slowed. It was okay. He was at home on Cranberry Hill. He was safe. Life would never be the same. But he was safe.

Wide awake now, he sucked in a deep breath and threw off the sheets. He eased his legs over the side of the bed, transferred to the chair, and rolled out into the shadowed entrance hall.

He couldn't see the numbers on the thermostat from his eye level, but he reached up and turned the dial two clicks to the left, then two more, until he heard the air conditioner kick on. Satisfied, he wheeled his chair behind the grand stairway to the kitchen.

In the corner by the pantry, he pushed the button and waited for the elevator doors to glide open. Another fortune his father had spent on his behalf.

He rolled his chair inside, pushed the button, and rode to the second floor. He rarely came upstairs except for his weekly check of the property. The air up here had a musty, unused odor, and he made a mental note to open some windows before Mrs. Bennett came to clean.

He rolled his chair into his parents' room in the northeast corner of the second story. The shag carpet made navigating difficult, but he crossed the room and opened the drapes.

A full moon had risen, lighting the landscape and silhouetting the sweet bay magnolias that stood sentinel over the property. Through the eastern windows, he could just make out the silver snake of the Mississippi River winding through the hills below. There'd been a time when the view of the meandering river had calmed him, brought clarity to his thoughts. But staring at it now, it stirred a troubling chord in him.

He stretched to reach the thin cords and slowly pulled the heavy draperies closed again. Tonight the Mississippi looked too much like the Mekong River.

Chapter 4

"Okay, let's see if we can make this thing work." Kathy raised her voice over the drone of warm water running into the therapeutic whirlpool tub. A little smaller than a standard bathtub, this stainless steel model was nicer than anything she'd worked with since her internship at the children's hospital in St. Louis.

Brian sat forward in his wheelchair, looking a bit like a little boy in his swim trunks and white T-shirt. "You sure you know what you're doing there?"

She laughed. "I know at least as much as you do about it. Here. . ." She turned off the water. "Hop in."

He gave her a hesitant glance, then maneuvered his chair parallel to the low tub and locked the brake. He raised himself up in the chair, and she helped him lift his right leg over the side. He blew out a series of short breaths. "Hang on. . .that's hot. What are you trying to do? Boil me till I'm tender?"

She lifted his leg out, stifling a giggle. "I wanted to start out with the water a little on the warm side. It's going to cool down quickly."

"If this is on the warm side"—he grimaced, but teasing edged his tone—"I'd hate to see what you call hot!"

Feigning exasperation, she stuck her arm in the water up to her elbow. "Oh, you big baby. It's barely warm."

He pouted. "Yeah, but I have delicate feet."

She seized one of the size fourteen tennis shoes he'd left beside the tub. "These are not the shoes of a man with delicate feet."

Laughing along with him, she helped him ease his leg back into the water. He lowered it a few inches deeper into the tub but quickly pushed out of the water again, propelling himself with muscular arms. "I'm sorry, but this is going to have to cool down to a medium boil before I dive in."

She helped him back into his chair and handed him a towel. She twisted the faucet to cold and let it run for a minute, stirring the water with both hands, while Brian watched. Turning the water off, she flashed him a grin. "Okay, try that."

He let her lift his leg into the tub.

"Better?"

"Ah. . .much." Supporting his weight by bracing his arms on the side of the tub, he slid into the water up to his waist.

Kathy turned on the whirlpool jets, and warm water began to churn and circulate around him.

He slid down until the water covered his shoulders. "Mmm. . .That feels good." Closing his eyes, he lay back and rested his head on the steel rim of the tub.

She watched him, letting him enjoy the peaceful sensation

of floating. The roar of the water was hypnotizing, and she had to work to keep her eyelids from drooping.

After he'd been in the water for ten minutes, she touched his arm. "Hey you. . ."

He opened his eyes with a start.

She smiled. "You're not in there just to relax," she reminded him. "Sit and enjoy for another minute while I gather up some equipment, but then I have some exercises I want you to try."

He cocked his head, eyeing her. "Did anyone ever tell you that you are one bossy woman?"

She nodded. "Yep. . .right before they thanked me for helping them walk again."

"Ooh. . ." He thumped his chest with an imaginary dagger. "You really know how to make a guy feel lower than a snake."

"Mission accomplished." She snapped a salute then cringed inwardly, worrying he'd take offense. But he just laughed and flicked water on her.

"No siree." She shook a finger at him. "Rule Number One: The water stays in the tub. Every drop."

He splashed her again. "Oops."

"You!" She tried for her best stern-schoolteacher voice but ended up breaking into giggles. She was not being very professional. But she sure was having fun. She put a hand on his head and pushed, threatening to dunk him.

Instantly, his jaw tensed and his eyes went wild. He wrapped his large hand around her wrist and pulled her hand off his head, yanking her toward him in one smooth motion.

Kathy braced her knees against the side of the tub, struggling to keep her balance, struggling to catch her breath. "What. . . ?"

His eyes met hers and as suddenly as he'd grabbed her, he let loose. She staggered backwards. Her foot caught on the edge of the exercise mat, and she went down hard, landing on her backside on the mat.

He put his hands on the side of the whirlpool and raised up, peering over the side at her. "Are you okay?"

Still in shock at his almost violent response, she stared at him, rubbing her wrist where he'd touched her.

He let loose of the tub, looking dazed. "I. . .I'm sorry. Did I hurt you?"

She glared at him. "Good grief, did you think I was trying to drown you?"

He shook his head. "I guess my training kicked—" He stopped short. "Never mind. I'm sorry. Are you okay?"

She massaged her wrist. "I'm fine." But she felt responsible. She'd behaved in a stupid and unprofessional manner—not to mention she was flirting with a client—and now *he* was the one apologizing all over himself. She gave him a sideways glance. "Wheelchair or not, I wouldn't want to meet you in a dark alley."

He raked a wet hand through his hair, a sheepish expression painting his face. "Kathy. . .I'm really sorry. I'm not sure what happened. I. . .something about the way you—" He shook his head. "My instincts must have kicked in. . ." His voice trailed off and a faraway look came to his eyes.

She remembered a recent article in one of the news magazine that reported how many returning soldiers suffered debilitating flashbacks and recurrent nightmares that sometimes led to acute anxiety and depression. She wondered if Brian might have experienced something similar.

She tried for levity. "Well, remind me not to mess with you again anytime soon, will you?"

Her tack worked, and a smile lit his eyes. "Um. . ." He raised himself up in the tub, then slid down again, lifting one wrinkled hand out of the water. "I'm sort of turning into a prune in here. If I promise not to get you too wet, do you think you could help me out of here?"

Her hand went to her mouth. "Oh! I'm an idiot." Heat crept up her neck, and she could feel her cheeks turning ten shades of crimson. She was acting like a complete dork. He'd no doubt be calling his father in Cartagena and demanding her replacement.

She went for dry towels and came back to drape one over the back and seat of the wheelchair. Without speaking, she helped Brian over the side of the whirlpool and back into his chair. Her mind scrambled for a way to turn back the clock and don her professional persona again.

But it was too late. She'd been a fool. She'd let down her guard and sabotaged any respect he might have had for her. Not to mention she may well have compromised his emotional well-being in the process. He seemed fine now, but her horseplay had triggered that almost-violent outburst from him. She'd read many accounts about the deep psychological wounds many returning servicemen carried. She hadn't even considered Brian's mental state. But now she shot up a panicked prayer that her thoughtlessness hadn't inflicted any lasting damage.

Brian peeled off his wet T-shirt and dried off his face, chest, and arms. He patted the towel over his thighs and knees. Kathy took the damp towel and dried his lower legs and his feet. She worked a corner of the towel between his toes. He squirmed and grabbed the hand rims, threatening to roll away from her.

"Oops, sorry." She looked up at him. "Does that tickle?"

"I told you my feet were delicate."

She laughed, glad to be back on more lighthearted territory. "How do you dry your toes when you're here alone?"

He grinned. "Why do you think God created shag carpet?"

She threw back her head and laughed but stopped abruptly at his touch on her arm. She looked up into serious brown eyes.

"Hey. . .I hope I didn't hurt you. I honestly didn't mean to—"

"No. Please. . .don't think another thing about it. I shouldn't have been joking around. It. . .wasn't professional of me. I—"

"Hey, listen, I'm sick to death of 'professional.' I know you have a job to do here, and I'll try to cooperate, but it wouldn't bother me one bit if I never heard another 'professional' word out of you. Not to go over your head or anything, but I think the treatment plan I need most right now is a little bit of fun and a laugh now and then."

She finished drying his other foot and straightened. "Yeah, well, I'll see what I can do."

"You could even bring your bathing suit for the next session."

It was all she could do to resist snapping him with a corner of the damp towel. But she'd learned her lesson. She settled for a stern glower. "Don't push your luck, buddy."

His laughter was contagious.

Chapter 5

Brian placed his right foot on the floor and gripped the rails on the parallel bars tighter. He could easily propel himself the length of the bars using only the strength of his arms, but it was time to make his legs do the work.

The radio blared Simon and Garfunkel's "The Sound of Silence," and Kathy hummed along a half step off-key. Gingerly, he let his weight settle over his knees. It was an odd sensation, feeling the solid floor beneath his feet, letting his muscles remember what they were made for, what they'd done instinctively until a few months ago.

He took his eyes off the intricate tile pattern of the floor and looked up into Kathy's face. A renewed sense of resolve filled him, seeing the sheer determination in her eyes. Any casual observer would have thought *she* was the one trying to take these halting steps.

"You can do it, Brian. I know you can do it." She clenched and unclenched her fists at her side.

If he could harness sheer willpower, he would sprint across the room just for the reward of the smile of triumph he knew she held in reserve for him. But his muscles weren't so easily persuaded.

He planted his feet wide apart and balanced his body the way she'd taught him. His right leg could support his weight for several seconds, but to take a step, transferring all his weight to his left knee, was a challenge. He shuffled forward a few inches, and for a couple of heartbeats, his mangled knee held his weight. But too quickly, his leg wavered then buckled. He shifted his weight to his right leg and grabbed the bars before he could fall on his face.

His spirits sank, and he shook his head, hating that he'd disappointed her.

But her ever-present smile buoyed him. She stayed planted at the end of the bars and cheered him on. "You're so close, Brian. That knee is getting stronger every day. I can tell. Come on. You can do this."

Stabilizing himself with one hand, he pumped an imaginary—and unenthusiastic—pom-pom in the air with the other. "Rah-rah-rah."

Her face fell. "Hey. . ."

He was immediately remorseful. "I'm sorry, Kath." The nickname slipped out before he could catch himself. He hurried on hoping she wouldn't notice—or that if she did, she wouldn't care. "It's not that I don't appreciate your cheer-leading. I do. I just can't get quite as excited over one-tenth of a centimeter of progress the way you do."

She shook her head. "Those fractions add up, Brian. Every one of them is important. I don't think you realize how much progress you've made. You've come a long way. Not just in the four weeks I've been working with you, but. . .from the beginning. It's a miracle you're standing on that leg at all."

"It doesn't feel like a miracle." He glanced pointedly at the treadmill gathering dust in the opposite corner of the room. "In case you didn't notice, my dad's spent a fortune here. I'm pretty sure he expects to come home and have me jog out to greet him."

She studied him for a minute. "Oh, Brian, surely not. He'll just be glad you've made progress."

He shook his head. "You don't know my old man." Kathy had only dealt with the suave over-the-phone business side of Jerald Lowe. She hadn't met the man in the flesh.

"Do you want me to talk to him? Explain how—"

"Ha! I didn't come up against many army sergeants tougher than my dad. He'd chew you up and spit you out."

She looked doubtful.

He waved her off. "No, I'm a big boy. You don't need to talk to my daddy for me. Just forget it. . .I shouldn't have dumped that on you."

"You weren't dumping anything on me." She smiled. "Hey, as long as I'm here, I might as well play shrink, too."

"Now that *would* be a challenge."

He forced a grin, trying to reclaim the playfulness that usually marked their interactions. But Kathy frowned, her brow wrinkling. "You've never talked about. . .what happened.

In Nam. Can I ask?"

His pulse thrummed. He did an about-face and with all the grace of a toddler on a jungle gym, propelled himself along the parallel bars back to his wheelchair. He turned again and plopped into the chair, then sat there rocking the wheels to and fro, averting his eyes, wishing he could joke his way out of this conversation.

She pushed through the parallel bars toward him. "I'm sorry, Brian. It's none of my business. Never mind me. I can be a big snoop. Are you ready to work on the mat?"

"Sure." Taking hold of the hand rims, he wheeled his chair over to the exercise mat in the corner. "And no apology necessary. I. . .I'd just rather not talk about it. It was a bomb. A couple buddies and I were on patrol. . . . We walked into an ambush. Tim wasn't so lucky."

Kathy took in a sharp breath, and he quickly corrected her obvious assumption. "He's alive. But he won't ever be getting out of his chair. He lost his legs in the blast."

An image of his platoon buddy formed in his mind—the dull stare of a broken man hunched in a wheelchair, a heavy quilt where his legs should have been. Tim McKluskey's bitter words echoed in Brian's ears. "Take a good look at me, man. You look at these stumps and then try to tell me there's a God. No. . .you go peddle that rot somewhere else, my friend."

He never had gotten through to Tim. Last he'd heard, he was living in a V.A. hospital in Wichita, Kansas. It killed Brian to think of that.

"I'm so sorry, Brian." Kathy's soft voice broke through the painful memories.

"Hey, it's not your fault." A veil of melancholy settled between them. He didn't want the session to end this way. An idea came to him and he rolled toward the door, already set on her agreeing to it. "You want to take a tour of the house?"

Her eyes brightened. "Sure!"

He popped a wheelie and pivoted in his chair. "Follow me."

He led her out to the entry hall and into the dining room. The sun painted patches of divided light on the hardwood floor.

She stopped in front of the tall east window. "The first thing I'd do if I lived here is take these curtains down. These windows are too gorgeous to hide." She touched the heavy draperies that hung on either side below the fanlights then ran her hand along the polished wood of the window frame. She pushed back the drapes and leaned to look outside. Her breath caught. "Oh, man! What a view!"

He loved her enthusiasm for every little thing. "Wait till we get upstairs."

Their voices echoed in the cavernous room. She trailed behind him to the kitchen where she exclaimed over the granite countertops, the polished floors, and the pantry with its "secret" stairway.

"You can go up that way if you like."

"But what about you. . .you can't—"

He hooked a thumb over his shoulder. "Elevator."

"No kidding?" She clapped her hands. "Outta sight!"

He laughed at her childlike amazement. "Your choice. . ."

"I'll ride the elevator with you."

He pushed the button, and they rode up to the second floor. In the tiny space, her perfume—a soft baby powder scent—and her nearness made his pulse beat faster. He was grateful when the heavy doors slid open.

Kathy stepped into the upstairs hall and exclaimed over the grand double staircase.

"You're welcome to go up," he told her. "It's mostly just storage now, but if you want to look around, be my guest."

She put a hand on the dusty banister and winked. "I just want to sweep down the stairway once, like Scarlett O'Hara."

"Frankly, my dear"—he affected a deep Southern drawl—"I don't—mind if you do."

Giggling, she raced up the staircase, taking the steps two at a time. She crossed the landing and descended from the other side with a Scarlett-like flourish, nose in the air, and all the regality of a princess. That is, until her Dr. Scholl sandal caught in the belled hem of her jeans. Her shoe went one way and Kathy went the other. She caught herself and bounced down the last three steps on her rear end. She landed in a wide-eyed heap in front of Brian.

He bit his tongue, but the minute he saw she wasn't hurt, he let a snicker escape.

She giggled.

That was all it took. His laughter spilled out, doubling him over until he nearly fell out of his wheelchair.

Blushing like a tomato, she scrambled for the errant sandal. But it wasn't long before she was laughing, snorting along with him. Tears rolled down both their faces.

When they finally composed themselves, they wandered together through the second-floor rooms, with Kathy *oohing* and *aahing* like a little girl in a doll factory. It was fascinating to see his parents' home through objective eyes. Not that he cared that much about interior decorating, but he'd been a little disappointed to come home to his mother's update of the house. The orange shag carpeting and the color scheme Mom proudly called "harvest gold and avocado," along with the psychedelic wallpaper she'd hung in a few of the downstairs rooms, somehow seemed a betrayal of the mansion's heritage.

But Kathy declared the whole place "far out" and praised his mother's taste in décor.

When they'd made the rounds through the maze of bedrooms and the "servants' quarters," as his mom called the old sewing room and nanny's room, Brian led her to the guest room in the northeast corner of the house.

Below, to the east, the Mississippi sparkled in the afternoon sun. She crouched beside his chair, and together they gazed out on the summer afternoon. Neither of them spoke, and yet Brian had never felt more comfortable to sit in silence with another person.

Twenty minutes must have passed before Kathy looked at her watch. "Oh! We need to get busy. I've got another client in half an hour, and we still haven't done the mat."

He frowned. "The dreaded mat, you mean." He was teasing even more than she might guess. They had the exercises down to a science now. It was mostly resistance work, with her working the muscles he couldn't yet flex himself. It had become their time to talk. And the time he most looked forward to each day. She only came on weekdays, and now his weekends stretched into eternity. Monday had become his favorite day of the week.

Feeling an odd sense of envy at her mention of another client, he let her push his chair back into the elevator for the ride down. In the exercise room, she helped him transfer to the mat. He lay there on his back watching her. She knelt beside him and lifted his left foot, massaging the arch and ball of his foot, the muscles in his ankle, then working her way up his calf.

She had to remind him to work with her by pushing his leg against her hands. While they went through the routine, she hummed softly. She sang off-key, but he recognized the song. *Lean on me, when you're not strong. . .*

He smiled. How appropriate.

But a twinge of reality dimmed his smile. The forced intimacy of their workouts was becoming a distraction for him. Having her so close he could smell her shampoo, feel the warmth of her fingers as she worked his muscles, her curtain of silky hair shadowing her pretty face. . . . He shook off the dream. That was all it was. She no doubt had fifty clients who were equally enamored with her.

But sometimes he let himself fantasize that Kathy was more than a physical therapist to him. And sometimes, when she laughed at his jokes and smiled that sunny smile, it was all he could do not to grab the girl and kiss her.

Chapter 6

July 1972

Birds sang from every tree, and a warm summer breeze carried the fragrance of the old-fashioned roses that still bloomed thick along the mansion's stone foundation. Kathy jogged around the car and up to the entrance under the portico on the north side of the home where Brian had suggested she park.

She'd always enjoyed her work as a physical therapist, but these sessions with Brian Lowe had become the highlight of her days. In the five weeks she'd been coming here, she'd worked him hard. And he'd risen to every challenge she placed before him. It was easy to see now why he'd survived the war and the ugly aftermath it held for him. He was no coward; that was for sure. If only all her patients were like Brian.

She would have a good report to give his parents. After delay upon delay, Jerald and Madeleine Lowe were due home from Cartagena early next month. Brian had always seemed unconcerned by their absence, but she couldn't imagine having a son come back from the war, only to leave him, alone, mere days after he'd finally come home. Especially with the injuries Brian had suffered.

She suspected his parents' absence might bother him more than he let on. At any rate, she hoped she'd get to meet the Lowes and discuss Brian's progress with them.

And he'd made amazing progress. She rang the bell and waited for him to let her in. She had high hopes she would soon see Brian take his first solo steps. If only she could pretend he was still a new patient needing daily therapy. But she couldn't honestly tell his father that was true. She'd reluctantly cut back to three sessions last week; and in a normal course of therapy with any other client, taking into account the progress he'd made, she would probably be scaling back to twice-a-week sessions about now. But she couldn't bear the thought of cutting their time together even more. She already spent any day he wasn't on her schedule missing him.

The door opened and Brian sat there, grinning.

She wanted to hug the man but settled for a matching grin and a cheery "good morning." She'd seen him day before yesterday, but it felt like she'd just been reunited with a long-lost friend.

"Good morning back." His smile said he was just as happy to see her.

They had a routine down now, and they set to work right away. As always, they talked nonstop while she guided him through his core exercises. Later, while he soaked in the whirlpool, Brian mentioned that a friend and his wife were picking him up for church Sunday.

She jumped on the opportunity. "Have you always gone to church?"

He shook his head. "My folks never went—until recently. Dad was always working, and Mom never wanted to go alone. But Jeff and Patty—they were newlyweds—started having youth rallies at this coffeehouse downtown, and the girl I was dating then wanted to go, so I went with her." He shrugged. "She didn't last, but Jesus did."

She tipped her head. "Interesting. . .I didn't have you figured for a Jesus freak."

"Yeah, well. . .I'm just full of surprises. What about you?"

She laughed. "I was a Jesus freak before Jesus freaks were cool. We went to church every Sunday."

"With your parents?"

She shook her head. "My mom." Without warning, sadness clutched at her heart. "My dad died when I was a baby."

He hesitated. "What happened? . . .if you don't mind my asking."

She hadn't cried over her dad since the day she left for college, leaving her mother all alone. But the tears were thick in her throat now. "Korea," she whispered.

Brian lifted a hand out of the water and touched her arm. "I'm sorry, Kath. I didn't know."

"No. . .of course not. Why would you? I don't have any real memories of my dad. I was just a few months old when he died.

I have a picture of him holding me in the hospital." She tried to smile. "He looks pretty happy about it. Knowing that. . .carries me, if that makes any sense."

He nodded, and she knew he somehow understood.

She trailed a hand in the whirlpool. The water was growing cool, and she reached for a towel. "You're pruning. Better get out."

She helped him from the tub and dried his feet while he rubbed a towel over his hair and face. She risked a question while they were occupied. "You didn't. . .lose your faith over there?"

"No. Actually. . .it got me through. It was coming back here that really tried everything I thought I believed."

She looked at him. "What do you mean?"

"In case you hadn't noticed, people like me don't exactly get a hero's welcome when we come home."

His words pierced her like a knife. For a minute, she wondered if he somehow knew about her work at the Center for Peace. But one look at his eyes told her he didn't have a clue.

She was grateful when Brian glanced at the wall behind her and let out a low whistle. "Do you realize what time it is?"

She turned and followed his gaze. "Wow." The hour had dissolved like cotton candy, and her high spirits took a dip. The weekend stretched out in front of her—without Brian Lowe. It would be Monday before she'd see him again. "I guess we'd better wrap it up. But I've got a new set of stretches I want to show you before I go." It was the truth, but it felt like she was trying to extend their time artificially. "Do you have time?"

"No. I'm playing golf this afternoon." He bit out the sarcastic crack with a smile, but his frown told her it was said with anything but humor.

She winced. "Sorry. . .I didn't mean—"

Shaking his head, he held up a hand. "Don't mind me. You didn't say anything wrong. I'm just. . .feeling cranky all of a sudden."

She tilted her head and perched on the side of the tub. "Why are you cranky?"

His shoulders hunched. "I'm pondering the weekend. I'm bored out of my gourd just thinking about it."

"You need to get out of the house more. It's been gorgeous outside all week." She looked toward the tall windows that framed a sunny view of the grounds. "I know you can't drive yet, but do you try to get out some? Even just to ride around the grounds? Your mental health is important, too, you know. And trust me, the fresh air and sunshine will do wonders for your mood."

He rolled his eyes. "Yes, Mother."

She laughed. "Sorry. But I'm serious. When's the last time you got out of here?"

"I go out with Jeff and Patty every Sunday—except when they're out of town, like this week. And Mrs. Bennett drives me to my doctors' appointments."

"The housekeeper?"

He nodded. "We usually make it a lunch date."

"You take your housekeeper to lunch? That's sweet."

He grinned. "Yeah. I'm a sweet guy. Except when I'm cranky."

She checked her watch, an idea forming. She'd promised Charlie to go with him and the rest of the group from Hannibal to take part in a peace march in St. Louis tonight. They were organizing a caravan in about an hour. But Brian looked a little desperate and she hated to leave him. If she were in his shoes, she'd go nuts cooped up here all weekend—even though the mansion wasn't exactly a "coop."

It only took one more look at the pout he wore to make up her mind. She jumped up. "Get dressed."

"Huh?"

"Let's go for a drive. Get something to eat."

The grin that stretched his face convinced her she'd made the right decision.

Chapter 7

He truly hadn't been hinting, but as Brian locked up the house behind them and wheeled his chair out to Kathy's Volkswagen under the portico, he wouldn't have cared if he had. His spirits lifted at the sun on his shoulders. The breeze whipped his hair and carried the scent of sweet bay magnolia blossoms. "You really think you can get this big ol' chair in the trunk of that thing?" He indicated the front of the Beetle.

"We'll make it fit if I have to take it apart." She waited while he transferred into the front passenger seat, then folded his chair and wheeled it to the front of the car. She popped the trunk open. Through the crack under the hood, he watched her rearrange the contents and lift his chair. The little car rocked as she tried to wedge the chair in.

After trying for a minute, she hoisted the chair again and set it back on the drive. Brian held his breath, fearing the trip might be over before it ever started. But she started hauling things from the trunk, stowing them in the backseat.

He felt like a heel sitting there watching her while she wrestled to fit everything in. She lugged a toolbox and a lawn chair and made another trip with her duffel bag and some sort of homemade sign—heavy poster board nailed to a picket. He couldn't see what it said—until the wind caught it like a kite and it blew to the ground beside his car door.

He opened the door and leaned out to retrieve it for her. He stopped dead cold. For a moment he couldn't move, could only stare at the angry words, scrawled in bloodred letters, dripping with hate.

BABY KILLERS.

Realization knifed him when he looked up and met her eyes.

"I've got it, Brian." Her voice was cold, her lips pressed together in a tight line. She looked like he'd just caught her stealing the family silver.

He looked down at the poster again. "What is that?" He knew exactly what it was. He'd chosen not to revisit too often his memories of the reception he and four of his buddies had received when they'd come off the concourse at Dulles, coming home on leave after their first tour in Nam. They'd tried to joke about it in the cab on the way to the hotel, but the gags fell flat with the protesters' spittle still staining their uniforms.

Kathy snatched up the picket and turned the poster away from him. "It. . .it's nothing." She rammed the sign behind his seat, slammed the car door, and went to the front of the Beetle. After loading his wheelchair in the now-empty trunk, she came around and climbed behind the wheel. Her face was ashen.

His stomach churned and bile rose in his throat. "It's *not* nothing. Not to me." He nodded toward the backseat. "Why do you have that thing?"

Staring straight ahead, she turned the key in the ignition. "It was for a rally. . .a protest."

"A war protest?"

She nodded, still not looking at him.

"Baby killer?" Brian repeated the abhorrent phrase, aware of the incredulity stiffening his voice. Rather that than the disappointment tightening his chest. "Is that what you think I am?"

She turned to meet his gaze. "No, Brian. Of course not. Not you. . ."

"Who do you mean, then?"

"It's just. . .a slogan. I'm just trying to do something. . .to help end this war."

He jabbed a finger toward the backseat again. "And that's how you're doing it?"

"It's just a sign, Brian. I'm trying to get guys like you home. Guys like John." She held out the wrist that sported the POW bracelet.

He'd noticed it before, of course. Admired her for being involved as a civilian, supporting the troops—he'd thought.

She shifted the car into gear and started down the long drive.

Brian clutched at his door handle. "Stop the car."

"What?"

"Stop this car." He fought to keep his voice steady.

Kathy stopped the car at the end of the lane and turned to face him. "Brian, come on. You're overreacting. It's not person—"

"I'm overreacting? You call me. . .and my buddies who died in that hellhole. . .baby killers, and I'm supposed to just brush it off?"

Her face reddened. "Are you going to sit there and tell me there's no truth to it?" Pain filled her eyes. "What about My Lai? Babies and children were killed in some of those villages. I saw the photographs, Brian." Her voice dropped to a whisper. "You can't deny it happened."

Everything started to spin around him. His ears buzzed, and Kathy's voice receded while the *rat-a-tat-tat* of machine-gun fire spit around him and the heavy jungle air filled his lungs. He knew it wasn't real, but he couldn't seem to turn it off, either.

"Brian? Are you okay?"

He pressed his hands against the dashboard and forced himself to take deep breaths. He had to get out of this car. He wanted to run as far as his legs would carry him. But of course that wasn't an option.

He pushed open his door and let the night air lave over him. But the giant lump in his throat wouldn't seem to go down. "You remember me telling you about my buddy? Tim?"

She nodded, and he thought he saw fear in her eyes.

"Tim woke me up one night about a week after we were deployed. He was crying like a baby. . .told me his patrol had come across a little kid in a rice paddy that morning. Said the boy couldn't have been more than five or six. The kid yelled at the GIs, and when they came toward him, he pulled the pin from a grenade and lobbed it at them."

Kathy didn't move, and Brian held her gaze. "The bomb went off, and one of Tim's guys fired back. They got out of there. Tim never knew if they hit the kid or not, but it haunted him. It'll haunt him the rest of his life, Kathy. So yes. It happens."

Her chin quivered and she shook her head.

"War is ugly." He tried to soften his voice, but his words shot out like bullets. And he suddenly didn't care anymore how they sounded to her. "Nobody knows more than I do that war is a hateful, evil thing. I thank God every day that I was never put in the position Tim was. I don't know what I would have done. Nobody can know until they're in the thick of it. But if my men were in danger. . ." He shook his head, unwilling to go on.

She held the steering wheel at ten and two, her knuckles turning white. "Brian. . .I'm sorry—"

He softened a little at the contrition in her voice. "No. Don't be sorry. If you believe in what you're doing, I can't expect you to do anything else."

"Somebody has to make people understand. This war is destroying us and nobody seems to care! People have to know the truth."

"Then make sure *you* know the truth," he spat. "You seem to think anybody in uniform is laughing it up, having the time of their lives over there."

"No, of course not! It's—"

He didn't let her finish. "Well, they're *not*, Kathy. They're fighting because—right or wrong—they believe they're making this world a safer place. They believe they're preserving the right for people like you to carry signs like that one you carry. And so your kids and grandkids can carry them, too."

"I don't know what to say. . ."

He dropped his head, composing himself, before he dared meet her gaze again. "And I don't know how to make you understand."

She shook her head, tears brimming in her eyes. "I don't know if we can ever agree on this, Brian."

In spite of the ire she'd roused in him, he longed to soothe the grief that threaded her voice now. "I think. . ." He forced his voice lower. "I think we both want the same thing, Kathy. We're both fighting for peace." He shrugged, attempting a smile and failing. "That probably sounds like an oxymoron to you."

She nodded. "Yes, but. . .maybe you're right. Maybe we just have different ways of going after it."

His smile came easy now. "I'm willing to. . .to try to understand where you're coming from if—"

She finished his sentence for him. "I'll do my best to hear you out, too."

Chapter 8

September 1972

Kathy paused in the doorway under the portico, waiting for Brian to lead the way to the exercise room.

But he headed toward the kitchen instead. "I made you some coffee."

This was something new. "Well. . .that was nice of you." She slipped off her shoes by the door and followed him. The gesture touched her, even if it did add another wrinkle to the guilt that garbed her. Too much of their time together these last weeks was stolen in conversation and laughter—and flirting. She always subtracted their "social" time from her billable hours, but still. . .

Since that day Brian had discovered her involvement with the Center for Peace, they'd spent the hours of his therapy sessions in their own sort of therapy—talking, often arguing passionately, but trying to work through their differences. As she learned to know Brian better, she saw a whole different side to the struggle for peace. She still didn't necessarily agree with him on every point about the price of war and the best way to advance the cause of peace.

They would probably always attack the issues of war and peace from different perspectives—but maybe that was okay. As Brian had told her more than once, "God gave us different gifts for a reason."

They'd discovered some common ground, too. And each of them had softened a little. Because of Brian's perspective, she'd convinced Charlie Morgan to tone down some of the approaches the center used in their rallies.

Her picket sign with the slogan that had hurt Brian so deeply had been relegated to the incinerator. Brian had painted her a new one that said, GIVE PEACE A CHANCE. He offered to make another one that read, SUPPORT THE TROOPS, but she thought that might be pushing it for Charlie.

The director was already a little put out with her. On account of Brian, she'd missed the St. Louis peace march last month, and she'd shown up two hours late for a sit-in Charlie organized over at the VFW post last Thursday—also on account of Brian. Charlie was starting to figure out that something was going on with her and "that Brian dude," and she didn't look forward to explaining it. Not that she owed Charlie anything.

And not that she knew how to explain her relationship with Brian, even to herself. They were friends. . .but they'd become so much more. It frightened her to think too far into the future.

"I already lifted weights so we can skip that today." Brian's voice was a welcome intrusion on her thoughts. He wheeled toward the kitchen, calling over his shoulder, "You take sugar? Or cream?"

"No, thanks. Black is fine." She started after him. "You need some help?"

"Sure. You want something to eat? Eggs or something?"

She shook her head. "I stopped for a bagel on the way over."

"Oh. . .and coffee, I bet. . ." Disappointment tinged his words.

"I only had one cup." She took a whiff of the rich aroma coming from the kitchen. "And this smells good."

"It should. It's fresh from Colombia."

"Oh? Did your parents send it?"

"Better than that. They delivered it in person." His smile didn't quite reach his eyes.

"They're home? I thought they weren't due until next week."

He nodded and glanced at his watch. "They had a breakfast fundraiser this morning, but they should be back before you leave. They're looking forward to meeting you."

She glanced down at her blue jeans and sleeveless peasant blouse, wishing she'd dressed a little more professionally. Oh well, the Lowes would just have to take her as she was. "So what did they think? About your progress?" Brian was now able to bear his weight for five or six seconds at a time recently. He was a long way from walking, but it was progress.

He puffed out one cheek. "Mom seemed pretty happy

about it. My old man reacted about like I expected." He tapped a rhythm-less staccato on the side of his wheelchair. "He tried not to let on, but it's obvious he's disappointed I'm still dependent. . .on the chair." He shrugged and looked away.

She put a hand on his arm. "I'm sorry, Brian. I'm. . .anxious to talk to him. Help him understand the progress you've made. He should be—"

"Don't waste your time."

She took a step backwards, the bitter tone in Brian's voice catching her off guard. "I don't get it. . . Is everything okay?"

He blew out a breath. "Never mind. It's. . .not like I was expecting anything else."

"But he hasn't been here to see how hard you've worked. How much progress you *have* made."

He shrugged again. "Forget it. It's no big deal."

"I think it is," she said softly. Brian had never failed to do her prescribed workouts, never failed to give her one-hundred-and-ten percent. She would make it a point to tell Jerald Lowe just that. Her jaw clenched, thinking about what a jerk the man must be to express anything but admiration and pride in his son.

The truth was, Brian's work ethic threatened to render her unnecessary. Of course, she wouldn't tell *that* to the man who wrote the checks. Still, if not for the fact that Brian needed someone to help with the resistance exercises and parallel bars, and to assist with the hydrotherapy, she'd be out of a job here.

She was more than a little curious about Jerald and Madeleine Lowe. How they could remain so uninvolved in their son's life was beyond her. Right now she just hoped she could refrain from giving the man a piece of her mind. Brian was so different than she'd expected the boy who grew up in the mansion on the hill to be.

How had Brian remained unaffected by his wealth? There was something about his strength that drew her. Confined to his wheelchair, unable to do physically what most men did without a thought, he was still somehow stronger than any man she knew. And the closer they'd become, the more it became clear that he drew his strength from his trust in God—a faith that had somehow survived horrors she could scarcely imagine.

Knowing that, she didn't like the bitterness she saw in his eyes now. It didn't fit with what she knew of him. She didn't blame Brian, though. Instead, she despised his father for inducing that kind of resentment.

She feared under the same testing, she might find her love for God, her trust in His goodness, wavering. Did she dare examine her own faith under a microscope?

"Hey you. . ." Brian's low voice tugged her from her reverie. "Are you just going to stand there all day?" He wore a thin smile, a brave face for her sake, no doubt. "I could use a little help with the coffee."

She smiled and followed him back to the kitchen. He poured coffee, and she carried the two steaming mugs into the exercise room.

They joked around, chatting while they finished their coffee, then worked on the mats for twenty minutes, before moving to the parallel bars.

In spite of his steady progress, Brian had grown frustrated with how slowly things were moving. He still couldn't bear enough weight on his left knee and foot to take anything that he'd allow himself to count as a step. Lately, they'd concentrated on getting his other leg strong enough that he could maneuver on crutches for a few minutes at a time. She held out hope that one day the muscles and tendons in his left leg would become strong enough to bear his full weight.

She didn't push him on the bars today. In silence, they went through the routines they both knew by heart. Several times she caught him watching her, an expression on his face she couldn't quite decipher. She wished there was something she could say to get him out of this funk he was in. She wanted to get back the smiling, joking Brian she loved.

Loved? Where had that come from? That was a strong word. But it had come to her mind as clearly as if she'd spoken it aloud. She stole a glance at him, almost afraid he'd read her thoughts. But he was still in a mood, his shoulders hunched, just putting in his time, his heart obviously not in what he was doing.

After ten minutes she walked over to the whirlpool and started the water running. "Why don't we finish up here?" She glanced at her watch. "You said your parents will be home before I have to leave?"

He lifted one shoulder. "They said they would."

"Okay." She filled the tub while he stripped down to his swimming trunks and T-shirt. Here, too, they had a routine they both knew by heart, and she helped him into the tub with minimal effort.

While he soaked his legs, she massaged his shoulders, wishing she had some magical bag of tricks that could have him walking by the time he got out of the tub and dried off. Before she had to face his father.

She hoped she'd have an opportunity to talk to Brian's dad alone. To impress on the man how important it was to encourage Brian, not to expect too much too soon. Even to prepare him for the possibility that Brian may never completely regain the use of his left leg.

She would never take that hope away from Brian, of course. And she knew him well enough by now to know that he wouldn't appreciate most of what she planned to say to his father.

She rubbed the taut muscles in the back of his neck, brushing his damp hair out of the way, struggling to remain clinical. It was a struggle that had become more difficult as the weeks went by. Working her fingers in circles on the warmth of his skin, she pushed that word—*love*—to the back of her consciousness. She didn't dare examine her feelings for this man—for her *client*—too closely.

Chapter 9

Brian leaned forward in the whirlpool, forcing himself away from the gentle touch of her fingers. "That feels. . .incredible," he said, not daring to look at her. "But you're going to put me to sleep if you don't quit it now." It felt incredible all right, but drowsiness wasn't exactly his real reason for asking her to stop.

She slid off the stool at the side of the tub and reached for the towel hanging on the back of his wheelchair. He boosted himself out of the water and allowed her to help him lift one leg over the edge of the steel tub. But somewhere in the process of the transfer, she lost her balance. Rather than risk him falling, she leaned into the tub and guided his leg back into the water.

But instead of letting loose, he clung to her. Feeling unaccountably brave, he pulled her toward him.

"Brian!" She braced one knee against the side of the stainless steel tub and battled to stay on her feet.

He saw to it that it was a losing battle.

Giggling, she listed dangerously toward the tub. "You crazy man! Stop it! You're going to make me fall in!" Her laughter started as the familiar teasing kind they'd shared almost from the beginning. But then her eyes met his and a nervous tremor crept into her voice.

His teasing had turned to something more. Something serious and bold. He knew it, and he didn't care. He'd held back as long as he could, keeping his true feelings for her hidden behind their playful banter. He was tired of pretending he didn't have feelings for her. With one arm around her waist, he pulled her closer still.

"Brian! Cut it out." She tugged against him, but he was sweetly familiar with her physical strength, and she wasn't trying very hard to get away.

But when he reached for her with his other arm, the water buoyed him and he lost his balance. Flopping back into the tepid water like a marooned mackerel, he clutched for the side of the tub. He snagged her long hair and his fingers got tangled in its silky threads.

"Ow! Ouch!" She bent at the waist and, hopping on one foot, dipped her head toward him, trying to disentangle herself.

She finally managed to yank her hair loose, but apparently the floor was wet from all their splashing. She slipped, letting out a piercing squeal on her way down.

Somehow, she ended up on his lap in the water, her feet and legs hanging out of the tub, lopped over the side like a limp beach towel.

She floundered, trying to get out, and he tried to assist her. But the harder they tried to right each other, the more water sloshed out of the tub and the harder they laughed.

All at once—and he honestly wasn't sure exactly how it happened—Kathy had her arms around his neck and he had his arms around her waist. They were so close he could smell the peppermint gum on her breath, and it seemed like the most natural thing in the world to just kiss her and get it over with.

Looking her in the eye, he leaned forward. She met him halfway and kissed him back exactly the way he'd imagined in his dreams. For one minute he hoped the doctors would prescribe years and years of this particular brand of physical therapy.

"What in the world is going on?"

At the bark of his father's voice, Brian let go of her, put his hands on the sides of the tub, and heaved himself up in the water. His effort pushed Kathy high enough to slide over the edge and land feetfirst on the floor. She stood there sputtering and stammering, dripping water all over the expensive tile floor.

Brian put both arms over the back of the tub and straightened to the closest thing he could call standing at attention. "Dad. Hi. Um. . .this is Kathy—Kathryn Nowlin."

His father looked from Kathy to him and back again. "This is. . .?" He shook his head, a look of derision defining his sharp features. "Well, that explains a lot. Your. . .services will not be required any longer, Miss Nowlin. You can gather your things and—"

"No, Dad. Wait. . .I can explain."

"That I'll be interested to hear."

A door slammed out in the entrance hall, followed by his mother's cheery voice. "Jerry? Brian? Where is everybody?"

Great. He might have a prayer of explaining the whole fiasco to his father, but Mom was another matter altogether.

Apparently his father had the same thoughts. "Get this mess cleaned up," he snapped at Brian. He didn't even give Kathy the benefit of a glance.

"Yes, sir." Yeah, right. As if he could just hop out of the tub and start mopping things up.

"I'll try to head off your mother, but you better come up with something."

Kathy yanked the soggy towel from the back of his chair and came at him with towel outspread and a panic-stricken expression.

"Hey," he whispered. "It's okay. His bark is worse than his bite."

"That's not what you were saying half an hour ago."

She had him there. "It'll be okay." He put his hands under his right thigh, trying to lift his leg over the side. "Here. . .give me a hand, will you?"

She jumped to help him. But a minute later, when he was safely in his chair drying off, he was surprised to see tears spring to her eyes. "I don't know what I was thinking. I'm so sorry, Brian." The furrows in her forehead deepened.

He touched her arm. "Cut it out! It wasn't you, Kath. I take full responsibility."

She hung her head, shaking it slowly like someone coming

out of shock. "I. . .I don't even know how we. . .how that happened." She looked back toward the tub as if it was the scene of an accident.

He smiled. "Um. . .I'll explain it to you later. Right now I think the best thing would be to mop up this floor. If you think my dad is a dragon, you haven't seen my mother in the face of buckling tile."

Kathy grabbed another towel from the pile on the stool in the corner and sopped up the water puddling on the tiles as if her life depended on it.

He laughed. "I'm kidding. Well, exaggerating anyway. . ."

That coaxed a little smile out of her. "Maybe," she said. "But I'm not taking any chances."

Chapter 10

Kathy was on her hands and knees blotting up water from around the base of the whirlpool tub when Brian's parents came through the door. She scrambled to her feet and tried in vain to keep her soaking wet jeans from dripping on the floor under her bare feet.

Brian gave her a conspiratorial wink before making formal introductions. "Dad, you've met Kathy. Mom, this is Kathryn Nowlin, my physical therapist."

Kathy could almost hear him thinking, *emphasis on the physical.* She curbed a nervous smile, not daring to meet Brian's eyes, and reached a hand out to Madeleine Lowe.

Brian obviously got his good looks from his mother, but it was a bit disconcerting that Madeleine Lowe didn't look a day over thirty-five. Her black hair was teased into a bouffant, her makeup was flawless, and she wore a sleek pantsuit that hugged a trim figure. No matter how she tried, Kathy had a hard time envisioning this woman wearing a carpenter's apron and wielding a hammer in the Colombian rain forest. Or Brian's father for that matter.

Mrs. Lowe took her hand, but her smile faded when her gaze landed on Kathy's soggy clothes. She extricated her hand from Kathy's and took a step backward, putting a hand to her throat. "What on earth happened?"

Brian wheeled his chair closer. "Mom. . .we sort of. . .um. . . had a water fight. Everything's fine now."

Jerald Lowe put a hand on his wife's back. "I think you can go now, Miss Nowlin. Have your bill sent to me here at the house."

"Mr. Lowe, I—"

"*That* will be all."

"Dad. Stop it."

Mrs. Lowe looked from her son to her husband. "What is going on? Jerry?"

"I'll explain later." He turned back to Kathy, crossing his arms over his chest. "Miss Nowlin?"

Her spirits plummeted. He was serious. He was firing her.

Brian grabbed the hand rims and wheeled his chair forward, positioning himself between her and the Lowes. He set the brake and looked up at his father. "This is my fault. Don't blame Kathy. She's done an incredible job. You may not realize it, Dad, but I've made a lot of progress and—"

"He has," Kathy said. "He's getting stronger every day. His knees are healing, and he's learning to use other muscles to compensate for—"

"I *said* that will be all." Jerald Lowe leveled a callous gaze at her.

Brian flipped the brake off and popped the front wheels of his chair an inch off the floor. "Dad. You're not being fair."

Lowe ignored him.

Kathy felt like a rope in a tug-of-war. If she stayed, she forced Brian to fight for her. A fight it didn't look like he had a prayer of winning. But if she walked away, she might never see him again.

She'd been such a fool! Why had she let this happen? Her training had drilled into her how important it was not to allow exactly this kind of emotional attachment. And she'd seen it coming from the moment she met Brian. They'd clicked. She should have gotten out before her feelings for him overwhelmed her.

Yes, Brian had initiated what happened today. But she'd been acutely aware of his intentions the minute he grabbed her arm. She'd *wanted* him to kiss her. Had been wanting that for a long time. She saw that all too clearly now. And it had affected the quality of her work with Brian. She'd wasted far too much time flirting and "playing" with him. Maybe Jerald Lowe had a point. Maybe Brian would be on his feet by now if he'd had a therapist who wasn't preoccupied falling in love with him.

She groaned. She had no choice but to leave. Brian would have to work things out with his father, but she wasn't going to stand between them. It was bad enough she'd violated that sacrosanct space between client and therapist.

She touched Brian's shoulder. His T-shirt was still damp and clung to his chest. The warmth of his skin soaked through the thin cloth. "I'm sorry, Brian. I. . .need to go."

She went to the corner by the door, slipped into her sandals, and started gathering her things.

"Wait, Kathy." Pumping his arms, he wheeled toward her. "You don't have to leave."

She slung her purse over one shoulder and straightened, facing Brian. "I think I do."

"Kath—"

With his voice echoing in her ears, and feeling as if she were carrying a concrete block on her shoulders, she went through the door and crossed the hallway. The familiar whisper of his wheels on the tile behind her was conspicuously absent, and a feeling of emptiness rocketed through her.

She let herself out the side door and ran to the VW. Her mind began to process all the ramifications of today's firing. Her monthly check from Jerald Lowe represented a hefty portion of her income. She would need to fill those hours. She hoped Brian's father wasn't vengeful. He was well connected in Hannibal, and he certainly had the power to blackball her all over town if he so desired.

As she wound her way down the hill, she didn't allow herself so much as a glance in the rearview mirror. Her hands started to tremble and the tears came. She prayed aloud over the whine of the Bug's engine. "Oh, Lord. What have I done? I really blew it this time."

She turned onto the highway and punched the accelerator. Keeping her eyes trained on the road in front of her, she flipped on the radio. Carole King's mellow voice filled the car. *It's too late, baby. . .*

She'd made a mistake that might change the course of her life. And yet, one thing kept intruding on her common sense: how it had felt to be in Brian's arms, to finally know what it was like to have him kiss her. But what if that first kiss had been their last?

Brian pushed open the door and jammed his wheelchair through it, not caring if he scraped the fine wood. He propelled the chair the length of the wraparound porch and rolled down the ramp and into the driveway. Every muscle burned from the effort.

Kathy's Volkswagen rounded a curve in the drive and picked up speed. "Kathy!" His mind registered how foolish it was to yell at her. There was no way she could hear him. But he had to stop her somehow.

Her car slowed at the bottom of the hill, and Brian raced after her, his chair picking up speed with the momentum the steep grade offered. His wheels wobbled on the uneven pavement, and he struggled to keep his balance. Behind him, his mother's shrill voice begged him to stop. He took his hands off the wheels and let the chair fly of its own accord.

At the bottom of the hill, the driveway inclined slightly before it fed onto the highway. When the incline slowed him enough to make it safe, he captured the hand rims again and powered himself up the slope until he could see the highway. The VW was still in sight, but it grew smaller and smaller as it picked up speed and finally disappeared over the hill.

Sweating and out of breath, he turned the chair around

and started back up the hill. It was odd to see the house from this perspective. Except for Sunday mornings and his doctor's appointments, and an occasional jaunt beyond the porch when the paperboy's throw was off, he rarely went beyond the porch rails of this house.

Even though his hands were blistering and his muscles burned, he relished the feel of the wind in his hair. It felt good to be in the sunshine. Good to be breathing fresh air.

He saw his parents up on the porch, waiting for him, and slowed his pace. He had no idea how he would explain Kathy to them. He couldn't very well tell them the truth.

He stopped his chair in the middle of the driveway and turned to look back down at the highway. The silver ribbon of road was empty except for a semitrailer belching black exhaust. What was the truth?

He loved her.

The thought took his breath away. But then the arguments started in his brain. *You don't know what love is. You've barely known the woman for three months. Besides, now you'll never see her again.*

He broke into a cold sweat. What if that were true?

"Brian?" His father's voice ricocheted through the red cedars that dotted the hillside.

"I'm coming." Defeated, he turned around and started back up the hill.

The driveway inclined sharply to the house, and by the time he was within earshot of the house, he was utterly exhausted and drenched in sweat.

His mother had disappeared, but his father hung over the porch railing, his mouth set in a hard line. "Hurry up. Your mother is worried about you."

"I'm fine." He slowed to a snail's pace, keeping his head down. He didn't have the energy for an argument with his father.

But Dad met him at the top of the ramp and put a tender hand on his shoulder. "We'll find someone else to do your therapy. Your mother is on the phone right now. We'll get something arranged before we have to leave next week." He sighed. "I'm sorry I can't just stay and supervise all this myself, but I'm sure there are any number of competent—"

Brian wriggled out from under his father's touch. "I don't want anyone else, Dad."

"I'm not going to let you give up. You are going to walk again, son. I know you are."

Brian lifted his head, jaw clenched, suddenly empowered by the ire flowing through his veins. "You just don't get it, do you?"

"I. . .what. . . ?" For once his father seemed at a loss for words.

"Kathy was the best thing that ever happened to me. You had no right to send her away." If the fury he felt could have been harnessed, he would have risen from this blasted chair and marched into the house.

But his words apparently zapped the tenderness right out of Jerry Lowe because he responded with equal fury, his face turning from pink to crimson. "I had *every* right! I have not been paying these exorbitant fees so you can have some floozy at your beck and call. It's no wonder you're still in that chair if that's the kind of *therapy* she's been offering. She ought to have her license revoked."

"What?" Brian sputtered, groping for the right words. "You've totally misjudged this whole thing, Dad. It's not like you think. It is not like. . .it looked." He took a shallow breath. He could hardly fault his father for assuming the worst. He *could* imagine how things must have appeared.

His father paced the length of the porch and back. "If you think there's any way you can explain away what I saw when I walked into this room. . ." He shook his head and paced some more.

Brian tried to put himself in Dad's place. *God, please give me the words to soften his heart, to help him understand.* "Dad. . . please let me explain."

He paced some more and came to stand in front of Brian's chair, leaning against one of the porch's concrete balusters. "I'm listening."

"What. . .what you saw today just—happened. Kathy and I have become friends. She's good at what she does. Maybe you don't see it, but I've improved a lot since she started helping me with the PT."

"I. . .I thought—" His father's voice broke and he bowed his head, obviously struggling for control. Finally he looked up, his eyes red. "I thought you'd be walking by the time we got back. I prayed so hard, Brian. Your mom and I both did. I was so sure God would answer. After the sacrifice you made. . .how could He not?"

"Dad. . ." Deep inside him, a hard place began to soften, and an old wound began to heal. "I'm going to be okay, Dad."

His father regarded him, his face a mask of grief.

Brian tried to muster a smile. "I may not win any marathons, but I get around all right. I think I'll walk again someday. These things—they take time. But even if I don't, I—" His voice fractured. "I came home with so much more than some of the guys."

His father nodded, his Adam's apple working in his throat, his eyes still wet. Brian couldn't quite decipher his expression.

But he didn't need to when Dad came to put a hand on his shoulder. "I wish I had your faith, son. I wish I did."

Not knowing how to respond, Brian placed his hand over his father's. He was startled to realize that his was the larger. The symbolism did not escape him. In spite of their differences, he loved his father. But he had to start making some decisions for himself.

It was time for him to finally grow up and act like the man he was. Odd that he'd fought a war—almost lost his life—before learning that lesson.

Chapter 11

Wᵢth the windows open to the *chirrup* of cicadas and the distant noises of the city below, Brian plumped his pillow and positioned it back under his neck. He could hear the faint murmur of the television upstairs in his parents' room. It was odd having someone else in the house. He'd grown accustomed to the silence.

He sighed and closed his eyes, then opened them again. As exhausted as he was from the stress of the morning, sleep wouldn't come. The events of the day played through his mind as if they were burned on a sixteen-millimeter reel. He kept rewinding to the part where Kathy's lips touched his.

Thanks to his father's tirade, he hadn't really had time to explore his feelings about that kiss. The radio on his nightstand was turned low, and the lilting harmonies of the Temptations played a wistful soundtrack for his memories. *Just my imagination. . .running away with me. . .*

He closed his eyes again, reliving the moment. He and

Kathy wrapped in each other's arms, the lukewarm water buoying them, lapping over them. . .kissing her. . .*her kissing him back.*

The thought jolted him. And it *wasn't* just his imagination running away with him. His memory was keen on that point. Kathy Nowlin had kissed him back—and good. What was he supposed to make of that?

Mind racing, he threw off the covers. He had to talk to her. Should have called her long before now. He scooted up in the bed and flipped on the bedside lamp. She'd given him her phone number when he first started working with her, but he'd never used it. He wasn't even sure where he'd put it now. The telephone book in his nightstand drawer was two years old, but maybe she was listed in there.

He plunked the bulky book on his lap and riffled through the pages. *Nowlin. K.* on Broadway. That had to be her. He remembered her talking about her loft apartment on Hannibal's main thoroughfare. He dialed the number. His hands grew clammier with each ring she didn't answer.

Finally on the sixth ring, her voice came softly. "Hello?"

"Kathy, it's Brian."

"Brian—"

"Listen, I'm sorry about today. About my dad. I don't know why—" He blew out a heavy breath. He was doing this all wrong. It wasn't his father's fault. It was no one's fault but his own. He should have stood up to Jerry Lowe long ago. And he should have stood up for Kathy before his father sent her away.

He started over. "Kathy, I'm sorry. I shouldn't have let Dad send you away like that."

"Why did you?"

That threw him for a loop. "I guess. . .I'm a coward."

"Stop. I know better than that."

"Well, when it comes to my father, apparently I am."

"You're sure. . .it wasn't because *you* wanted me to leave?"

"What do you mean?" For some odd reason, his heart started to pump the way it had wheeling down the driveway after her this morning.

"What happened this morning, Brian?" Her voice grew softer. "Between us. . ."

He took a wavering breath. "I was hoping you could tell me."

"I asked you first."

The grin he heard in her voice made him smile. "Okay. But. . . I don't really think this is a conversation for the telephone."

"You want me to come over?"

"Would you?"

"Give me ten minutes."

❖

How can you mend a broken heart? The Bee Gees ballad came on the car radio as Kathy merged onto the highway and headed out to the House on Cranberry Hill. She hoped she wouldn't be asking that same question by the time this night was over. Her nerves skittered as she tried to analyze her own emotions, let alone think of how she could explain them to Brian.

When she reached the top of the hill she saw him sitting on

the porch, waiting for her. Even under the taut circumstances that had brought her here tonight, seeing Brian sparked something inside of her—a feeling of anticipation and connection she'd never felt with anyone else.

His face gave away nothing as he lifted a hand in greeting. She turned off the car and got out. Walking slowly up to the porch, she never let her gaze leave his.

"Hi." He rolled his chair to the edge of the porch and held out his hand, palm out. She put her hand in his, her heart soaring, a sure knowledge building inside her as he knit his fingers with hers. *Oh, please, Father. . .let this night end the way I hope it will.*

"Do you want to go inside?"

She looked toward the house. The windows were lit upstairs and down. "Your parents are here?"

He nodded. "It's okay. They're not going to kick you out."

She gave a tentative smile. "You're sure."

"Positive." He squeezed her hand. "I talked to my dad."

"About?"

"About your job."

Her hopes mounted. "Is. . .is he reconsidering?"

Brian chewed the corner of his lower lip. "No. *I* reconsidered. I asked Dad not to hire you back, Kathy."

As quickly as they'd soared, her spirits plummeted. "But. . ." She took a step backwards, tugged her hand away from him. "I. . .I don't understand."

"It's not right. What happened today. What we've been feeling for each other."

No! He was wrong. She loved him. Couldn't he see that? Hadn't he made her believe that he had the same feelings for her? How could she have misread things so badly?

She felt numb. "Then. . .what *was* that today? What happened? You. . .you kissed me, Brian. I thought—" Her voice broke.

He gripped the hand rims and with one stroke wheeled himself in front of her. He reached for her hand again. "Kathy. No. Don't cry. Let me explain."

"Come here." He put his free hand around her waist, and with one fluid, graceful motion, pulled her onto his lap.

Her arms had nowhere to go but around his neck.

"I asked my father to find someone else for my therapy because. . .I know it violates your professional code to be kissing your patients. I don't think I can be responsible for holding you to that."

His meaning registered, and joy coursed through her veins.

But he turned serious again. "I think what happened today, Kath, is that we both finally admitted—maybe to ourselves as much as to each other—what we've been feeling for a long time."

She smiled. "You, too? Really? You've. . .felt it, too?"

He nodded, running a finger whisper-soft along her cheek. "Really. A lot. For a long time."

She pulled back just far enough to study his face. The smile he gave melted her. "Oh, Brian." She rested her palm on his cheek, enjoying the prickle of his day-old beard beneath her touch.

He closed his eyes. "I didn't dare think you might return my feelings. I'm not exactly gainfully employed, Kath. Even though Dad has a job waiting for me when I'm done with therapy," he added quickly.

She stroked his cheek and smiled up at him. "I don't care about that."

"And I"—he looked over her, at his feet on the chair's footrests—"I don't know how this will end up. . .whether I'll ever be able to walk."

She started shaking her head. "I don't care. . . . I don't care, Brian. That's not important. It's who you *are* that matters to me. And. . .I *love* who you are."

"You're sure?"

"I've never been more sure about anything in my life."

Behind him, the House on Cranberry Hill towered over them, and for a fleeting moment, she let herself imagine what it might be like to share this house with Brian Lowe.

He tipped her chin, coaxing her gaze back to him. He threaded his fingers through her hair, then traced her lips with a feather touch. "It's been three months since I rolled this chair through those doors after. . .a very long two years in Nam." He nodded behind him toward the wide front entry. "But tonight, Kathy, for the first time in my life, I feel as if I've finally come home."

DEBORAH RANEY

Deborah dreamed of writing a book since the summer she read all of Laura Ingalls Wilder's *Little House* books and discovered that a little Kansas farm girl could indeed grow up to be a writer. After a happy twenty-year detour as a stay-at-home mom, Deb began her writing career. Her books have won the RITA Award, the HOLT Medallion, the National Readers' Choice Award, and the Silver Angel from Excellence in Media. Deborah's first novel, *A Vow to Cherish*, inspired the World Wide Pictures film of the same title. Deb also serves on the advisory board of American Christian Fiction Writers. She and her husband, Ken Raney, have four children and enjoy the small-town life in Kansas that is the setting for many of Deb's novels. Visit her Web site at www.deborahraney.com.

THE PRETEND
FAMILY

by Joyce Livingston

Dedication

Since Missouri is where I began, having been born in St. Joseph, I feel it most fitting to dedicate this book to my parents: Dorothy and Louis Sampson, who divorced when I was twenty-three and passed away a number of years later. I wish I could say they knew the Lord, but I am sad to say of that I can't be sure, even though I witnessed to them many times.

If you are reading this book and you do not know for sure where you will spend eternity, please—like my hero, Tadd Winsted, does in this story—make your peace with God before it is everlastingly too late. God created you, He loves you, and He has a plan for your life. Be open to His will. It is the only way you will find true happiness and contentment. I love each reader and although I don't know all your names, I pray for you often.

Chapter 1

Present Day

Tadd Winsted picked up the phone and dialed his parents' number in Germany. Though he loved his visits with his mom and dad, he hated the way their conversations always ended up with the same question. "When are you going to get married and have children?" The way they badgered him about it drove him crazy. You'd think they'd get used to the idea after a while, he told himself as he waited for the first ring. Just because his younger brother, Charles, had opted to remain in Heidelberg and join the family business didn't mean he had to, too. Good old Charles, definitely a chip off the old block. He looked like their father, talked like him, and was even left-handed. And to both his mother and father's delight, Charles had married the socialite daughter of their closest friends, and the two had presented Mr. and Mrs. Winsted with a pair of perfect little grandchildren, one of them left-handed, the other the spittin' image of both father and grandfather.

A heavily accented voice answered almost immediately. "Good morning. Winsted House."

Tadd couldn't help but smile. It was Olga, his parents' housekeeper. "Hi, good-lookin', this is the rebel son. Mom or Dad around?" He could almost see the smile on Olga's face. She had been the only one in his parents' home who seemed to appreciate his boyhood antics.

"How do you know I'm good-looking? You haven't been home for nearly two years."

"Hey, Heidelberg is a long way from Hannibal. I'd like to come, but running my restaurant takes all my time—and then some."

"Your mother and father would like to see you, Tadd. They're concerned about you."

He harrumphed. "They could come and see me. Planes fly from Heidelberg to the good ol' USA every day."

"And they fly from Hannibal to Heidelberg every day, as well," she countered, a slight snap in her answer. "Your parents miss you."

Tadd glanced at the photograph on his office bookshelf. "Probably not very much. They have Charles."

"But Charles isn't you. Hold on," she spoke quickly. "Here's your father."

"Tadd, boy, it's good to hear your voice. How are things in America? The House on Cranberry Hill restaurant doing well?"

"Everything's great, Dad. Sorry I didn't call you last week. How are you and Mom doing?"

"We're both fine. I'm as busy as ever, although Charles is beginning to take over more of my responsibilities."

Tadd grimaced. He knew what was coming next.

"I wish you were more like Charles. That boy has a good head on his shoulders. You should see the way he handles our clients."

I must have a good head, too, Dad, he wanted to say but didn't. *Otherwise this old mansion I've turned into the area's finest restaurant wouldn't be functioning half as well as it is.*

"And you should see his children," his father continued. "Young Charles is already taking an interest in our business, and little Sarah has learned how to curtsy and serve tea."

Tadd rolled his eyes. "Serve tea, huh? That's quite an accomplishment. Before long, that little girl will be writing her own book on etiquette. And Charles, at only eight, is taking an interest in the business? I can see why you're so proud of them. They sound like child protégés."

"Don't make fun of your brother's children, Tadd. Someone in this family had to stay in Heidelberg and follow my example. I've worked hard to build our business to what it is today. If it weren't for Charles—"

Though Tadd flinched at his father's words, they didn't surprise him. The same conversation occurred nearly every time he phoned home. "I know," he said, interrupting. "If it weren't for Charles, you wouldn't have a son to keep it going when you finally decide to retire."

"Tadd, aren't you ever going to settle down and find yourself a wife? You're not getting any younger, you know."

Tadd had answered that same question, too, so many times he couldn't count them. A sudden thought occurred to him. What if he didn't answer the same way? Maybe said something different? Something that would, at least temporarily, get them off his back?

"Tadd? Are you still there? Did you hear me?"

"Yeah, Dad, I hear you." He paused a moment; then, without taking time to think through the consequences his answer might bring, he blurted out, "Actually, I got married last week."

His father's voice boomed a loud "What?" into the phone. "What did you say? We must have a bad connection. It sounded like you said you got married."

"I did, Dad. I married a lovely woman from right here in Hannibal."

"Tadd, we had no idea you were even dating! Why didn't you tell us you were getting serious with someone? We haven't even met this woman."

He frowned. Maybe he should have given his statement more thought before springing something like that on his parents. "Yeah, I know. But I'm sure you'll like her," he hastened to add.

"I've heard many American women prefer a career to having a family. How does she feel about having children?"

Uh-oh. How was he going to answer that one? "She—ah—she loves kids. In fact, she—she already has a daughter."

"Oh, son, I hope there isn't an ex-husband in the picture. Situations like that can be quite sticky."

"Ah, no—no ex-husband. Her husband—died—several years ago."

"Why didn't you tell us you were getting married? We should have been there."

"It was a small wedding. I figured, with you being so busy and Mom's brother as ill as he is, you wouldn't be able to come."

"We would have tried. We were both beginning to wonder if you were ever going to have a family." His father's voice actually carried a bit of excitement. "When are we going to meet your lovely bride and her child?"

"In time, Dad. It's hard for me to get away, too, but maybe we can plan a trip to Germany in a few months." He hated to deceive his father, but the constant questioning and the inferences that they thought he was less than complete because he had chosen to remain unmarried and childless were getting on his nerves. Maybe telling them he had a new wife would work out well after all. For a few months, he'd let them enjoy the idea that he had married and was now a stepfather, then he'd simply tell them it hadn't worked out and he and his new wife had decided to call it quits, like his sister and her husband had. His parents had been unhappy about their breakup, but they had adjusted to it more quickly than he'd thought they would. In the meantime, on his weekly calls he could toss in a few facts about his made-up wife and child, enough to keep them appeased. Living in Germany, it was unlikely they'd ever know the difference. How many times had he asked them—no, begged them—to come to America to see his restaurant, and they'd been too busy and too tied up to leave? Maybe now that they thought he was interested enough in women to have actually caught one, they'd leave him alone.

"Good. We'll count on seeing you in a few months. Your mother isn't here right now or I'd put her on the phone. Why don't you send us each a copy of your wedding picture? I'd like a set one on my desk at the factory, and I know your mother will want one, too. Maybe you can even send one for Charles."

Pictures? How could he produce pictures of people who didn't exist? "I'll—I'll call and see if the photographer can make some for you."

"Splendid. I can hardly wait to see them. Maybe we can all get on a conference call soon and you can introduce us to your new family."

Tadd swallowed hard. Conference call? When he had the sudden inspiration to create this farce, he hadn't realized how rapidly it could snowball on him. "Maybe. We'll work on it. Right now the three of us are concentrating on getting settled." He had to change the subject. "Tell me about Charles. What's going on in his life besides work?"

They visited a few more minutes then Tadd hung up the phone. How was he ever going to be able to produce wedding pictures? Maybe he could find a woman and child who would be willing to pose with him. But how? Where would he look? He couldn't just walk up to someone on the street and make such a request. What had he gotten himself into? Maybe he should call his father back and explain it had all been a joke.

No, that would never work. They would be furious with him for making light of something as serious as marriage.

He snapped his fingers as an idea hit him. He would *hire* a woman and a child. The Molly Brown Theater, right here in

Hannibal, had a long list of actors. Surely some of them would be interested in earning a little extra money by having their pictures taken. He'd simply hire a woman and her child, rent a tux, a bridal gown, and a dress for his make-believe daughter, have a photograph taken, and his problem would be solved.

❀

"I have just the woman for you." Doug Barkley, the manager, told him when he dialed the theater a few minutes later. "She's a single mom with an eight-year-old daughter, and she can really use the extra money. They're both in our latest production. If you like, you can come tonight and take a look at them, make sure they're right. You gonna tell me what this is for?"

Tadd smiled into the phone. "Just a little project I have going. Thanks, Doug. I'll see you tonight."

❀

Tadd arrived at the theater just as the play was ending. Hurrying inside, he made his way backstage in search of Doug.

"Sabrina and Megan will be here in a minute," Doug told him, reaching out to shake his hand. "They're changing into their street clothes." He had no more than said the words when a beautiful flame-haired young woman with an equally beautiful flame-haired girl at her side appeared from a nearby dressing room. *Wow* was the only word Tadd could think of to describe the woman. He nearly wilted when her green eyes zeroed in on him.

"Sabrina," Doug said, apparently noticing Tadd's reaction to her appearance. "This is Tadd Winsted, the man I told you about. Tadd, this is Sabrina Stewart and her daughter, Megan."

The woman reached out her hand. "Nice to meet you, Mr. Winsted. What exactly is it you want us to do? Something about having a picture taken with you?"

Still in awe of her beauty, Tadd gave her hand a shake. "Yes, in wedding clothes."

She eyed him suspiciously. "That seems like a strange request. May I ask what the picture is for?"

He searched for the right answer, one that wouldn't require going into detail. "Actually, I'm playing a joke on someone."

Her gaze narrowed. "I'm not getting my daughter and myself into something illegal, am I?"

Doug came to his rescue. "Mr. Winsted owns the House on Cranberry Hill restaurant and is one of Hannibal's most highly respected businessmen. He'd never be involved in something illegal."

Tadd gave him a nod of appreciation. "Like I said, I'm playing a joke on someone and need your help to do it."

She frowned as if giving her answer some thought. "And all we have to do is have our picture taken with you? It would have to be done some morning between eight and ten. I'm due at work by eleven."

He nodded. "That's fine. It shouldn't take more than an hour of your time. Give me yours and your daughter's sizes, and I'll have the wedding clothes delivered to your home."

A slight frown creased her forehead. "I'd prefer that you have them delivered to the theater. I'll pick them up here."

"Wherever you wish. Write your phone number down, then. I'll set the time up with the photographer and give you a call." He waited until she wrote down her number and said good-bye; then he watched as she exited through a side door. "Is her daughter always that quiet?" he asked as the door closed behind them.

Doug nodded. "Yeah, she's pretty quiet, but I'll tell you one thing. She's one of the best little actresses I've ever hired."

In that case, she should work out just fine.

"But why, Mama, why does he want his picture taken with us?"

Sabrina opened the car door then motioned her daughter inside. "I have no idea, sweetie, but the money he's paying us will really come in handy."

Though she tried to appear unconcerned, she wasn't. Something about the whole situation seemed weird. What grown man, especially one as handsome and successful as Tadd Winsted, would hire a woman and child for a wedding picture? And why? What kind of joke could he possibly play on a person with a wedding picture? She shrugged as she inserted the key in the ignition and gave it a twist. *Doug did speak well of the man. I guess we'll just go through with it and hope for the best.*

Bo Dawson made one final lighting check then moved behind his camera. "Could you two stand a bit closer together? Now, Mr. Winsted, tilt your head slightly toward Ms. Stewart. That's it. All right, everyone. Look happy. I need big smiles."

Sabrina was smiling on the outside, but inwardly she was fighting off tears. After losing her beloved Mike, she'd never expected to wear a wedding gown again. Yet here she was, standing by a stranger, having a wedding photo taken.

"Can we have a picture, Mama? Can we?" Megan asked when they'd finished.

She scowled at her daughter. "No, Megan. The pictures belong to Mr. Winsted."

Mr. Winsted turned toward Megan with a smile. "Of course you can have a picture. I'll mail it to the theater. But I do want to thank you both for doing this for me." He reached in his tuxedo pocket and pulled out an envelope. "Here's the money I owe you. I think you'll find it more than adequate."

"Thank you. I just hope your joke works out as you planned." Sabrina took the envelope then reached for her daughter's hand. "We'll leave these clothes in the dressing room. I'm sure you'll want to return them as soon as possible."

He nodded. "Good idea. By the way, why don't you and your daughter come by the restaurant some night and be my guests for dinner?"

Megan's eyes lit up at his invitation. "Can we, Mama? I've never been to Mr. Winsted's restaurant before. Can we?"

"We'll see. But with our schedule at the theater as it is, it might be difficult."

"Please, Mama, I'd really, really like to go."

"I'd love to show you around the place," Mr. Winsted inserted, making it doubly hard for her to refuse her daughter.

"We'll try. I'm just not sure when we can make it."

"Anytime is fine. I'm there day and night—" He paused long enough to give her a shy grin. "Unless I'm off somewhere having my picture taken."

Tadd let out an exaggerated sigh. Even though he felt like a heel for deceiving his parents, he had pulled off his charade without a hitch. Within days, he'd have the photographs to send to Germany. During his weekly calls to his parents, he would mention a few details about his new wife, sprinkle in a few complimentary words about his new daughter, then, in a few months, he'd explain things weren't working out and the two had decided to separate for a while. A couple of months after that, he'd drop the divorce announcement on them. They'd give him all the reasons he shouldn't divorce his new wife. He'd counter by telling them how hard he'd tried but she had insisted they simply weren't compatible and wanted a divorce. There had been nothing he could do to stop it. That should put an end to all the talk about him and his bachelorhood. But would it put an end to his feelings of guilt?

A week later, Tadd slipped three photographs, bearing the inscription *With love, Tadd, Sabrina, and Megan*, into a box along with the lovely gold Byzantine bracelet he'd selected for his mother and a new leather wallet he hoped his father would like, addressed, and sealed it, then personally hand delivered it to the Hannibal post office.

"Your mother is on line one," the cashier told Tadd a few days later as he hurried into the restaurant's foyer.

He nodded a thank-you then scurried into his office and punched the speaker button on his phone. "Hi, Mom. Did you get my package?"

"Oh, yes, dear. It arrived this morning. Your new bride is lovely, and that precious child, Megan, is adorable. Oh, and I love the Byzantine bracelet. I'll think of you every time I wear it."

"Glad you liked it." Tadd grinned with satisfaction. "Did Dad like the wallet?"

"I sure did," his father's voice boomed with exuberance as he got on the line. "Good timing, too. My old one needed replacing. By the way, it looks as though you've done yourself proud. Sabrina is beautiful and so is Megan. I can't believe you've finally married. But, from the looks of things, I'd say those two were worth the wait. "

"I'm so anxious to meet them, Tadd."

He could tell by the lilt in his mother's voice that she was as happy about his so-called marriage as his father was. "We're pretty busy right now. You know, getting settled as a family, setting up housekeeping, working at the restaurant, but we'll come and visit you as soon as we can."

"That's why we've called you, dear. We have a surprise."

Tadd chuckled. "Don't tell me. I know what it is. You're getting us one of those fancy-carved, German Black Forest clocks as a wedding gift, like the one you got Charles. I've always wanted—"

His serious-minded, sophisticated mother let out an uncharacteristic giggle. "No, not a clock. Something much better."

"You don't have time to come and see us so...we're coming to see you!"

His father's announcement threw Tadd in a sudden state of shock. "You can't!" *No, this can't be happening.* "You can't come!"

"Can't come? Of course we can come. Your mother and I have it all planned out. She's even hired a nurse to stay with her brother."

"Your father has already called the travel agency and worked out the schedule," his mother added.

Tadd's mind raced. *Think! Think!* "But, Dad, what about the stockholders' meeting? It's always this time of year. You can't miss that. You're the president and CEO!"

"That meeting was last week. Everything is under control. Charles has agreed to take over my duties in my absence. We'll be arriving in St. Louis one week from today. You will pick us up at the airport, won't you?"

Desperate to come up with a valid reason why they shouldn't come, Tadd dropped into his desk chair and cradled his head in his hands. What a mess he'd gotten himself into, all because of a stupid lie. "It's a long flight from Germany to Missouri. Are you sure you two are up to it?"

"Of course we are. Nothing is as important as getting to meet our son's new wife and daughter. Charles and his family wanted to come, too, but your father needs him here. They said they'd try to come later."

"Going through airport security can be a real hassle," Tadd countered, hoping that would be enough to discourage them and make them rethink their plans. "Sometimes it can take hours."

His father let out a snort. "Are you forgetting I fly all over Europe on business? Security here hasn't gotten any easier, either. I'm sure we can handle it."

"But, Mother, what about your arthritis?"

"The doctor gave me a new prescription. It is working wonders on my hands. Besides, the change of scenery will be good for us. We've missed you, Tadd."

"I've missed you, too, Mom." Tadd was out of ideas. He needed more time to think. Surely, other than telling them the truth, he could come up with a way to keep them from traveling to Missouri.

"You do want us to come, don't you, son?"

His father's question ripped at his heart. He'd had no idea the farce he'd created on impulse would come back to haunt him this quickly. "Of course I want you to come. I've been trying to get you to come ever since I moved here. It's just—"

"Just that you're overly concerned about your mother and me? Well, you needn't be. There's nothing that would make us any happier than to come to Hannibal, see our son, and meet his new wife and child."

For once, Tadd found himself speechless. What other excuses could he offer? He couldn't tell them he'd hired the woman and child in the picture to get them off his back. It would break their hearts to know he had deliberately deceived them.

"Then it's settled." The words came out in his father's customary take-charge manner. "I'll e-mail you with our flight plans so you'll know what time we'll arrive and at which gate."

"Tell Sabrina and Megan we can hardly wait to meet them,"

his mother added. Tadd could almost see the smile on her face. "I am really proud of you, dear. It looks as though you've made a wonderful choice for a wife. The two of you look so content with each other in that picture, it makes me want to cry with happiness."

Makes me want to cry, too, but not with happiness. My idiotic plan to deceive you was the dumbest idea I have ever had. Trying to, momentarily, put aside his quandary, Tadd told them how much he loved them and looked forward to seeing them then hit the OFF button on his phone. *I can't hurt their feelings by admitting that I lied to them. Where do I go from here?*

He spent a sleepless night turning over various options in his head—none of which had any value. But by dawn, he'd come up with an idea, one even more bizarre than his original one about the photograph. He waited until nine then dialed Sabrina's number. Megan answered on the first ring.

Not used to carrying on a conversation with an eight-year-old, he got right to the point. "I need to speak with your mother."

"Is that you, Mr. Winsted? It sounds like you."

Considering their brief time together, he found himself both surprised and pleased she'd recognized his voice. "Yes, Megan, it's me. Did your mother get the photograph I sent?"

Megan let out a childish giggle. "I think my hair looked funny."

He pulled his copy from atop his desk and gazed at it. Her hair looked fine to him, but what did he know about children's hairstyles? "You don't look funny. You look—cute."

"I was having a bad hair day. My hair was all frizzy."

Tadd gave his head a slight shake. Did she say bad hair day? He thought only grown-up ladies made statements like that. "Believe me, your hair looked fine. Would you please call your mother to the phone?"

"She's working some extra time at the grocery store, but she'll be home for lunch. She can call you back."

"You're home alone?"

Another giggle sounded. "No, silly, I'm only eight years old. My babysitter is with me."

He should have realized Sabrina would never leave her child alone. "Have her give me a call. It's important." He thanked Megan then said good-bye.

When she hadn't returned his call by one o'clock, Tadd began to wonder if Megan had even remembered to give her mother his message. Maybe he should call again. But, as he headed for his office, the cashier waved at him to get his attention then held the phone up in one hand. Tadd nodded then hurried into his office. "Tadd Winsted. How may I help you?"

"Mr. Winsted, this is Sabrina Stewart. Megan said you needed to speak with me?"

"Yes, Ms. Stewart, but I'd prefer not to do it over the phone. I was wondering if you and Megan could come and have dinner with me tonight, here at my restaurant."

"Your offer is very kind, Mr. Winsted, but I'm afraid I'll have to refuse. Surely we can discuss whatever is on your mind over the phone."

No, I need to do this in person. "Are you sure you can't make it? I guarantee you'll have a good meal, and I'd love to show you and Megan around the place. Please say you'll come."

"Well, we don't have a performance tonight, so I guess we could, but we'll have to make it early."

Tadd breathed a sigh of relief. "Early is fine. Come anytime you like. I'll be watching for you."

"Megan, I know you're excited about coming here tonight, but we're not going to stay very long. We'll have a nice dinner, hear what Mr. Winsted has to say, take a quick look around his restaurant, then get out of here. I have no idea what he has on his mind, but we're certainly not going to get ourselves caught up in another of his crazy ideas. Do you hear me?"

Megan nodded as she crawled out of their small car. "Maybe he wants us to have another picture taken."

"Nothing would surprise me."

Tadd greeted the pair at the door then ushered them to a table in front of a large window along the far wall. It afforded a magnificent view of the river and of the huge stained-glass window that was the restaurant's main focal point. "I'm so glad you could make it." He pulled out a chair for Sabrina then seated Megan before sliding into his own chair.

"Your restaurant is beautiful," she said, glancing from the magnificent staircase to the enormous stained-glass window that nearly filled one whole wall. "I had no idea it was so— grand."

"I fell in love with this place the minute I saw it, and I knew the main floor would make an incredible restaurant—and, with all the bedrooms on the second floor, it is a perfect home for me, as well." He smiled, pride evident on his face. "The House on Cranberry Hill was originally built by a sea captain for his family. The place even has a widow's walk. The staircase and the stained-glass window were in good condition when I bought the place, but I can't say as much for the rest of the house. It took months to remodel and update it, but I knew it would be worth it. It has become quite a showplace. Because of its history and uniqueness, it's been featured in a number of gourmet and fine foods magazines, which has really helped my business."

"I can see why. It's truly lovely."

After their waiter had filled their water glasses he asked Megan, "Do you like shrimp, Megan? We're famous for our deep-fried shrimp."

Sabrina gave her head a slight shake as she lifted her menu. "Megan and I rarely eat fried foods."

Tadd's brow rose. "Does that rule out hamburgers? We make great burgers, all from extra-lean, top-quality sirloin. Terrific fries, too."

"Please, Mama, just this one time? I love hamburgers."

Sabrina rolled her eyes. "Okay, just this once, but no french fries."

"What'll you have, Ms. Stewart? I recommend the filet mignon. Our patrons love it."

"I'm not much of a meat eater. I prefer chicken or turkey."

"Okay, then may I suggest our chicken Alfredo? Surely you like pasta."

Realizing how unreasonable she must seem, Sabrina smiled.

"I love pasta, Mr. Winsted. The Alfredo sounds wonderful."

"My mom is kinda picky about our food," Megan volunteered as she unfolded her napkin and spread it in her lap. "She says animal fat will kill you."

Sabrina's jaw dropped. "Megan! I am not picky. I'm merely concerned about our health."

"Your mother is right, Megan. We try to keep the fat content as low as possible in all our entrées. After we finish dinner, I'll take you into our kitchen and have one of the chefs show you around."

Megan leaned back in her chair and crossed her arms. "We won't be here very long. My mom said we're going to have a nice dinner, take a quick look around, then get out of here."

"Megan!" Sabrina couldn't believe the words that had come from her daughter's mouth—twice. "I—I simply meant we didn't want to take up Mr. Winsted's time. He—he has a restaurant to run." She wondered if her face was as red as it felt. What must he think of her as a mother, to have not trained her child to have better manners?

As if aware of her discomfort, Mr. Winsted gave her a consoling smile. "Even the boss needs a little time off now and then. Tonight's my night."

When their food arrived, Sabrina reached for her daughter's hand. "Megan and I always thank the Lord for our food. Do you mind if I pray?"

"Ah, sure. Go ahead. It's fine with me." He gestured toward the many people seated around them enjoying their dinners. "A lot of my customers pray before their meals. I think it's—nice.

My grandmother used to pray with me."

She nodded then bowed her head and said a simple prayer. When she opened her eyes and found him staring at her, she simply smiled and unfolded her napkin.

After they'd finished their meal, Megan wiped at her chin with her napkin. "That was a good hamburger."

Tadd gave her a satisfied smile. "I'm glad you enjoyed it. Now, how about dessert?"

Megan lifted her hand. "I'll have chocolate cake and ice cream."

Sabrina gave her head a quick shake. "No, Megan, no dessert for either of us. We've already eaten far too much. I don't want you waking up in the middle of the night with a tummy ache."

Megan rolled her lower lip. "Please, Mama."

"Sorry, honey, but the answer is no."

❋

Tadd decided it was as good a time as any to change the subject and bring up the reason he had invited them there. He waited until the busboy had cleared their dishes, then he turned to Sabrina and gazed at her for a moment before speaking. Had her eyes been that green when they had posed for their picture? "I know you're wondering why I invited you here tonight." He cleared his throat nervously. "It—ah—seems I've gotten myself into a bit of a bind, and you and Megan are the only ones who can get me out."

Sabrina bristled at his statement. "I knew it. Your joke backfired, didn't it?"

Megan tugged on her mother's arm. "What does 'bit of a bind' mean?"

Without taking her eyes off Tadd, she answered in a slightly irritated voice. "It means he's gotten himself into some sort of trouble."

"Not trouble exactly. A predicament that I can't solve by myself would be a better description." Admitting to what he had done was even harder than he had imagined.

Sabrina leaned back in her chair and crossed her arms, then glared at him. "Would you care to explain exactly what you do mean?"

"Yes, but let me start at the beginning. All my life I have been overshadowed by my younger brother. Charles just happens to be perfect and also has a perfect family, plus he is the image of my highly successful father. I, on the other hand, have been the rabble-rouser of the family. Not that I've done terrible things, but I've always walked to the beat of my own drum. Even though I am the eldest son and first in line to eventually take over the reins when my father retires, the family business has never had any appeal to me. But to Charles it means everything. He's more than content to stay in Germany, working alongside our father and learning the business. Eventually, he'll move into the CEO position my father had intended for me. Not me. I wanted to come to America and live the American dream. For years, my goal has been to start my own business. That goal eventually turned out to be this restaurant."

"Much to your parents' disappointment?"

He nodded. "Yes."

Sabrina's expression softened. "But you've fulfilled your dream. Surely they are as proud of you as they are of your brother."

"I think your restaurant is nice," Megan chimed in.

Tadd couldn't help but smile. "Thank you, Megan."

Sabrina sighed. "So far I can't see what any of this has to do with us."

"Let me finish, then you'll see." He took a slow sip of water. Why did his throat suddenly seem parched? "Although my parents would have much preferred I stay in Germany and become a part of the family business, I think they've finally come to grips with the fact that staying there wasn't what I wanted to do. But I've disappointed them in another way, as well—one extremely important to them."

Sabrina started to rise. "I'm quite uncomfortable with this, Mr. Winsted. Your personal family history is none of my concern. Perhaps—"

He cupped his hand over her wrist. "Please. Stay. Let me assure you this does concern you."

With her gaze still fixed on him, she slowly sank back into her chair.

"I—I've never married, Ms. Stewart, and Mom and Dad have been on my back for years about it. Sometimes I think they wonder if I'm—you know."

She gasped. "Surely not."

"I hope that's not what they think, but they are extremely disappointed I haven't provided them with daughter-in-law and grandchildren. Like my brother."

Sabrina's eyes widened as her jaw dropped. "Oh, no! Don't

tell me that picture was meant for them!"

"Yes, I'm afraid it was," Tadd forced himself to admit.

She glared at him. "You should have told me. If I'd known that photograph was for your parents I would never have agreed to it!"

"I'm sorry, Ms. Stewart. I had no idea this thing would snowball as it has. I thought if I sent them a picture of my new wife, one who already had a daughter, they would be satisfied for now and quit bugging me."

She let out a huff as her hands anchored on her hips. "Surely you didn't think you could get away with such a farce. They were bound to find out eventually. Didn't you think of that? Just what kind of a man are you?"

"I guess I'd convinced myself that my plan was in everyone's best interest."

"Your best interest, not theirs! You lied to them! And you made my daughter and me a part of that lie. The Bible says lying is a sin."

He sighed. "You're right, I know it does. I remember my grandmother telling me that when I was a teenager and lied to her, but at the time, it didn't seem like such a big thing. I've always tried to live a good life. But sometimes circumstances require a little white lie. This was one of those times."

"I doubt your parents would feel that way if they knew you had lied to them. A lie is a lie, no matter what color it is."

"That's exactly the reason I don't want them to find out. In a few months I was going to explain my wife and I were having marital difficulties and some irresolvable issues, so we'd decided to separate for a while to try to work things out. Then, a few weeks after that, I planned to tell them things hadn't worked out and we'd decided to divorce. I knew they'd be upset about it, but at least they would have thought I had given marriage a try."

Her troubled expression turned to one of anger. "Marriage should be sacred. Are you so opposed to marriage that you weren't even interested in finding yourself a nice girl and settling down?"

Tadd glanced around and found a number of his patrons staring at them. He leaned toward her and answered in a soft voice. "I am not opposed to marriage, Sabrina. In fact, someday, when the timing is right, I'd love to have a family, just not yet. Is that such a bad thing?"

"Not a bad thing, but not a good thing, either. Many men pursue careers *and* have a family at the same time," she countered, her voice tinged with agitation.

He had to make her understand. "I'm sure they do, but a good many of those who do short-change their families by being so busy they don't have time for them. Like my father. He was totally dedicated to his business and rarely at home when I was a kid. Not once did he play ball with me, go to any of my school programs, help with my homework, any of the things that were important to me. When I have a family, I'm going to spend every possible minute with them—be the father my own father didn't take time to be. Can't you understand that?"

Sabrina's gaze narrowed. "If every man waited until he was successful, most would never get married and have a family. Are you sure there's not some other underlying reason?"

"Look, Ms. Stewart. You're talking about *most* men. I'm not like *most* men. And, contrary to what you may be thinking, I'm not delaying marriage because I'm in debt after all the extravagant remodeling and refurbishing of the House on Cranberry Hill to its previous glory. Honest I'm not. My grandfather left my brother and me each a substantial inheritance—an inheritance that has allowed me to enter into this entrepreneurship nearly debt-free. But the one thing he couldn't leave me was the time and hard work necessary to build the business. I owe it to him, as well as to myself, to make it a success, which leaves no time for a wife, and certainly not children. If the restaurant continues its growth, within a very few years I'll be ready for a family."

"Have you explained it that way to your parents?"

"Yes. They listen but they don't understand. The family business was already established and doing well before my father was out of diapers, thanks to my grandfather who laid the groundwork and shed the blood and tears to get it on its feet. My father and mother have had everything they could possibly want all their lives."

"But from the sounds of it, so have you."

"Yes, I have, materially. But as I told you, those things weren't nearly as important to me as my father's time and attention. And I know, if my mother were honest, she'd admit she hated all the time my father spent away from home. As a result, over the years those two grew apart with each doing their own thing. Now that my father is partially retired, they're more like friends and lovers, which delights me. I wish it could have been that way back then. I have no intention of doing that same thing to my family."

"I'm sorry, Mr. Winsted. I can see why you feel a certain amount of resentment, but it sounds to me like your parents love you and want the very best for you."

"I'm sure they do, but what *they* think is best for me is a wife and children—now. I'm not ready. Despite what I may have led you to believe, I love my parents and would never deliberately hurt them."

"But you lied to them." She gave her head a sad shake. "How could you do such a thing?"

"You really want to know? I figured it was better to lie to them than tell them the truth—that my dad had been a lousy father and I never wanted to be like him."

"I think you'd make a good daddy," Megan, who had been surprisingly quiet, offered. "I think you're nice."

Sabrina gave her daughter a slight frown. "Just sit quietly, Megan. This is grown-up talk." Then, turning to Tadd, she let out a slow sigh. "Didn't it occur to you that your parents would insist on meeting your new family?"

"I doubted there was a chance that would happen. My mother hates traveling and my father gets his fill of it crisscrossing Europe on business. I've invited them to come here many times, but they always say no. Instead, they expect me to go over there, but I've explained I'm too busy here with the restaurant to even consider it."

"Sounds like you did, indeed, think you had all your bases

covered, but I still don't understand why you're telling me all of this."

"I did think my bases were covered until I got a call from my parents yesterday. They'll be here in a week."

Sabrina let out a squeal. "One week? What are you going to do?"

"That's where you come in. I want to hire you and Megan to be my family."

Chapter 2

"You what?"

"You heard me. I want to hire you to be my family. Just for the few days my parents will be in town, that's all, and I'll pay you handsomely for it."

Her jaw dropped as her flattened palm went to her chest. "You want *my* daughter and me to pose as *your* family? You have to be out of your mind. The answer is no, Mr. Winsted. No!"

Tadd found himself ready to plead with her. Beg, if necessary. Even on his knees. "You're already a part of it, Ms. Stewart. They've seen your picture. I can't hire anyone else. Please, I need you."

She stood quickly and grabbed onto Megan's hand, nearly jerking the child out of her chair. "Come on, Megan. We're finished here. Let's go."

Swirling around, she glared at Tadd. "I *could* thank you for the nice dinner, but I won't. Megan and I will be paying for our own dinner."

Tadd hurried after the pair but before he could catch them, Sabrina had opened her purse, pulled out a few bills, and tossed them onto cashier's counter, then rushed her way out the door toward the parking lot. He hurried out onto the porch and watched with disappointment until their car disappeared down the hill. "There goes my only solution."

Sabrina's keys hit the table with a thud as the two entered their apartment. "The nerve of that man. I'm still in shock that he would even consider us being a part of his deception," she said, more to herself than to her daughter.

Megan pulled off her sweater then sat down on the faded loveseat. "You're too mad, Mama. It's not good for you. Remember Jesus said you shouldn't be angry when the sun goes down."

"You're right, sweetie." Sabrina tried to regain her composure, but it was hard. "I shouldn't be so angry, but I can't believe Mr. Winsted could lie to his parents like that." For her daughter's sake, she forced a smile. "Let's forget about it. It's his problem, not ours. Maybe we should go over your lines for the new play."

"Do we have to?" Megan asked in a near groan. "I already know them."

"I just want us to be ready when rehearsals start, that's all."

"I wish I had a daddy."

An ache pierced Sabrina's heart. "I know, honey, I wish your father was here with us, too. He was a wonderful man. You would have loved him."

Megan lifted her beautiful green eyes to her mother. "Would he have spent time with me like Mr. Winsted wanted his daddy to do?"

Sabrina gazed at the face she loved more than anything on earth. Then she sat down beside her daughter and pulled her into her arms. "Oh, yes, I'm sure he would have."

"But wouldn't he have had to go to work every day?"

"Yes, but he would have managed to have plenty of time for the two of us. He loved us."

"Mr. Winsted said his daddy loved him. Why did he go to work so much?"

"I guess he thought making money was more important than his family."

Megan frowned. "Then I think he should be mad at his daddy. His daddy should have spent time with him."

"I'm not sure he's exactly mad at his father, I think he's disappointed in him."

"I'd be mad at him. Daddies need to be with their children. That's why God made daddies."

Sabrina couldn't argue that point. She felt as strongly as Mr. Winsted that people shouldn't have children if they didn't intend to spend time with them, teach them, play with them, and set a good example. "The relationship between Mr. Winsted and his parents is none of our business, but we do need to pray for them. Okay?"

Megan nodded. "Can I watch one of my videos before I go to bed?"

"Just one, honey, but get your jammies on first. When your video finishes, I'll come in and read to you from your Bible storybook." She watched as Megan dutifully went off into the small bedroom the two of them shared. Would she ever be able to provide a decent place for them to live? It wasn't that she wasn't thankful for their small apartment, her near minimum-wage job at the grocery store, and the extra money their bit part, occasional acting jobs provided, but it was never enough. Each month, instead of being able to save a few dollars, she was getting further and further behind. She had no idea what she was going to do to subsidize her income when the theater season ended and tourists no longer flocked to Hannibal on vacation. But, even though her faith seemed to constantly waver, the Lord always came through and provided for them in one way or another. Surely He'd see them through this time.

After she had read to her daughter and tucked her into bed then prayed with her, Sabrina picked up the day's mail from the coffee table. She began to shift through the assortment of bills, with the contents of each envelope sending her deeper into the depths of financial despair. But it was the last envelope she opened that pushed her over the edge. One from her landlord, and it simply said *The City of Hannibal has purchased your building for a parking lot. You have until the thirtieth of next month to vacate.*

"Vacate?" she screamed aloud, tears bursting forth and tunneling down her cheeks. "Vacate to where? These are the lowest price apartments in town! How am I going to pay for a more expensive one?"

"What's wrong, Mama?"

Sabrina turned, realizing her scream must have awakened her daughter. She grabbed onto Megan and held her tight. "I'm sorry, honey. I didn't mean to scare you. I just found out we're going to have to move and find another apartment. I guess the news upset me more than I realized." Then burying her face in her daughter's red curls, she whispered, "Go back to bed. This is nothing for you to worry about. Mama will work things out."

Megan lifted her face and gazed into her mother's eyes. "Don't worry, Mama. Jesus knows where we should live."

Her child's words went straight to her heart. If only trusting in God to provide for them was that simple, considering the fact that, lately, most of their prayers for help seemed to go unanswered.

Though her night was mostly sleepless, Sabrina forced herself to get out of bed the next morning and don a happy face. "I have a surprise for you," she told Megan brightly as she bent and kissed her sleeping child. "We're having bacon and eggs for breakfast." It was something she did rarely, considering bacon's fat content, but Megan loved bacon and eggs. By the time she was ready to leave for her job at the grocery store, she had convinced herself that, somehow, this setback was going to turn out for the best.

That is, until she crawled into her sixteen-year-old car and turned the key in the ignition.

Nothing. Not even a grind or a groan sounded from the car that had recently begun behaving as cantankerously as a crotchety old man. "Come on, come on, don't fail me," she told the car while patting its steering wheel. "I can't miss work. Please start." Although she did everything she could to get it started—checking the battery terminals, the water, and the gas gauge—the car wouldn't respond. Swallowing at the lump in her throat and fighting back tears, she grabbed her purse from the seat, crawled out the door, and walked the ten blocks to the store, arriving nearly twenty minutes late.

Her boss, well known for his undeserved tirades, was livid. "How could you be late today of all days?" he railed at her, waving his arms in the air. "You know Saturdays are our busiest days. Thanks to you and your tardiness, I've had to close one of the checkout lanes."

"I'm so sorry. My car wouldn't start and I had to walk. It won't happen again, I promise."

"Look, Sabrina, this is the third time, maybe the fourth, that thing wouldn't start and you've been late to work. You should've gotten rid of that heap long ago. That old battlewagon is nothing but a piece of trash. I doubt even the junkyard would take it." He pointed to the closed lane. "Get your apron on and get busy. We'll talk about this later."

For the sake of her customers, she made herself smile and act like her normally courteous self, but inside she was miserable. What if he wanted to talk to her later so he could fire her? With the Hannibal tourist season nearly over, his business would drop, too. He could easily get by with one less cashier and not even miss her. Sabrina had never felt such hopelessness. When five o'clock finally came around and her shift ended, she walked the ten blocks to her house then knocked on her neighbor's door, hoping to beg a ride to the theater for that night's performance.

"No, I won't drive you," the woman told her, "but I'll loan you my car and you can drive yourself."

Overwhelmed by the woman's generosity, especially since she wasn't much better off than they were, Sabrina thanked her and took the keys from her hand, promising to be careful.

The evening went well. The house was packed, and no one forgot his or her lines. As usual, when the play ended, the cast moved into the lobby to meet the audience. Everyone raved over Megan's and her performance. While she appreciated their kind words, she couldn't get her apartment and car situation out of her mind. The two changed into their street clothes and were just about to leave the theater when someone approached her. It was Mr. Winsted, the last person in the world she wanted to talk to at that minute.

"Please," he said in a kind voice, hurrying toward them. "Wait. I need to talk to you."

"Look, I've had a rough day. I received notice that I have exactly thirty-three days to find an apartment I can't afford, my sixteen-year-old car quit on me. I still owe money to the repair shop from the last time it broke down. I don't have money to fix it up again or buy a new one, and I'm close to losing my job. Plus, the dentist says my daughter needs braces." Sabrina turned her back on him and reached for the doorknob. "You have your problems, and I have mine. Believe me, there is nothing you can say that I need to hear."

Stepping between her and the door, he blocked her way. "I may have the answer to your problems."

Pushing his arm to one side, she scowled at him. "You mean by helping you lie to your parents?"

"What I mean is—I'm offering you more money than you can make in two months or more at that grocery store if you'll do this acting job for me."

She huffed. "You call that an acting job?"

"A five-thousand-dollar acting job. If things are as bad as you say they are, it might be wise to carefully consider my offer before you refuse."

Five thousand dollars? In her lifetime, she'd never had five thousand dollars all at once.

"Think of Megan. If you won't do this for yourself, do it for her."

Five thousand dollars. With that kind of money she could buy another cheap car and have enough left over to pay a higher rent until the next tourist season started, then she'd be back at the theater again.

"You don't have to answer me now. Think it over before you say no. I'll phone you in the morning."

"We're in church on Sunday morning."

"Then I'll call you in the afternoon." Giving her a smile, he pushed open the door then stepped back, allowing the two plenty of room to exit.

She huffed then rushed past him. "You needn't bother. I won't change my mind."

Megan tugged on her mother's hand as they walked to where they'd parked her neighbor's car. "Isn't five thousand dollars a lot of money, Mama?"

Sabrina sighed. "Yes, it is, baby. A lot of money."

Megan began to skip alongside her as if she didn't have a care in the world. "I think it'd be fun to act like I was Mr. Winsted's daughter. It would be like having a daddy."

Sabrina forced her mouth into a grin. "Mama has a lot to think about. We'll talk about it tomorrow. Don't forget, you and I are going to have to walk to Sunday school. That means we'll have to leave bright and early. Right now, young lady, we need to concentrate on heading for home and getting you into bed."

❦

Tadd sat at the table in the bedroom area of his master suite on the second floor of his restaurant, nibbling on the light breakfast one of the busboys had brought up to him and thinking over the quandary he'd gotten himself into, as well as the conversation he'd had with Sabrina at the theater. It was obvious she not only *claimed* to be a Christian but she had Christian principles. He hated it that so many troubles had hit her at once, and it seemed unfair for him to take advantage of her situation by talking her into something she didn't want to do, but he desperately needed her and Megan to act as his family. Too bad he hadn't asked her which church she attended. He could have been waiting for her when they came out. No, it was better that he call her at home like he'd said he would.

Maybe he should call and tell his parents the truth—that he'd not only lied to them, but he'd actually hired a woman and her daughter to pose for that wedding picture. He could just hear his mother crying, his father shouting in disgust, and his brother laughing at him, deriding him for his foolishness. Well, if he had a mind to, he could tell them a few things about good ol' Charles. Things his parents didn't know. But, even though it would probably sink Charles to rock bottom in their estimation, Tadd would never do such a thing. He'd go to his grave before he told them how his brother had been the one to break his mother's prized Ming vase and not the servant they'd fired over it. Nor would he tell them how Charles had changed figures in the company's computer to elevate the sales they thought he had made. Nor would he tell them how, on a number of after-hours occasions, he had caught Charles making out with his secretary in his locked office. Or about the time he discovered that the biggest part of Charles's business trips wasn't business trips at all, but gambling trips paid for by his father's company, his traveling companion and roommate a lovely brunette who just happened to work for his father as the promotions director. He'd kept his mouth shut rather than be the one to rat on Charles and burst his parents' bubble about their perfect son. Such revelations might cause Charles's wife to leave him and take his children, which would destroy his mother. If Charles's improper shenanigans were ever to be revealed, it wasn't going to be because Tadd had been the one to do it. He'd let Charles hang himself. His biggest concern was what a discovery like that would do to his parents.

Even with the amount of money I've offered her, I doubt Sabrina is going to change her mind. Which means, I have no other choice, he told himself sadly. *I have to tell my parents the truth. I have to put an end to this right now. It's not fair to Mom and Dad, and it's certainly not fair to Sabrina.* Dreading what he was about to do, he picked up the phone and dialed his parents' number. To his surprise, his father answered on the first ring.

"Dad? What are you doing answering the phone?"

"Oh, Tadd, I'm glad it's you. I was just about to call you. Your uncle Helmut passed away in his sleep last night. I'm helping take care of the details. Even though we've been expecting it, death is never easy. Your mother is upstairs lying down. She is really taking it hard."

Tadd's heart went out to her. He knew how close she'd been to her only brother. "Maybe I should try to come."

"No, don't come. Since Helmut has been ill for so long, he'd lost touch with all his friends. And, with so few relatives left on your mother's side, she decided on a small graveside service. It's going to be the day after tomorrow."

"I guess this means you'll have to delay your trip to Hannibal." Tadd felt a sudden guilty rush of relief at the thought.

"No, this hasn't changed our plans at all. In fact, we want to come now more than ever. Your mother said to me, not more than an hour ago, this trip is exactly what she needs to take her mind off her loss, and I agree. After all the hours she's spent at her brother's side these past two years, she needs some joy in her life, something to bring her out of her doldrums. I think a complete change of scenery and getting to see you and meet your new family is what we both need. I thought maybe the five of us could take that wonderful *Mark Twain* Mississippi riverboat dinner cruise. A friend of mine took it when he was in the States and said it was a marvelous experience. I'd also like to see Mark Twain's boyhood home. I can't tell you how much we're looking forward to this trip."

Tadd's free hand rubbed at his forehead. *I can't tell them I've lied now, not after Mom has just lost her brother.* They finished their conversation, with Tadd reminding his father to give his mother a big hug and convey his sorrow at her loss. He gazed at the phone as he severed the connection. *I have to find a way to talk Sabrina into posing as my wife. But how? What can I do to convince her that I haven't already done?*

An idea occurred to him. One that might work, although a risky one. One he hoped he wouldn't have to use.

Chapter 3

Sabrina gazed out the window at her broken-down car, then at the notice-to-vacate paper in her hand. Two monumental problems—and she had no idea how to solve either one. And, to add to her woes, her boss at the grocery store was furious with her and was probably going to fire her. She'd come to her wit's end. Her prayers seemed to go unanswered. It was as if God wasn't interested in her troubles. He'd never forsaken her before. Why now? Hadn't He supplied a roof over their heads, food for their table, clothing for their backs, and coats to keep them warm in the cold Hannibal winters? Surely God was aware of her plight.

Wearily, she sat down at the kitchen table and poured herself another cup of coffee. Even though it warmed her insides, it didn't warm her soul. Her thoughts went to Mr. Winsted's outlandish offer. Five thousand dollars for an acting job that would take no more than a few days, a job that would pay more than she could earn in several months' time. Would it be so wrong to take it? To accept his generous offer? Wasn't the burden of responsibility for deceiving his parents on his shoulders? All she and Megan would be doing was performing the acting jobs he had hired them to perform. Isn't that what they did at the theater? Play the roles of people they weren't?

Megan wandered in from the bedroom rubbing her eyes, her curly red hair in disarray from sleeping with the covers over her head as she was prone to do.

"Good morning, sleepyhead. I was about to waken you." She bent and kissed her child's forehead. "We need to hurry if we're going to make it to Sunday school on time. Don't forget. We have to walk."

Megan frowned. "Do we have to? It's a long way. Can't we call someone for a ride?"

Sabrina shook her head. "No, it's a beautiful day outside. The walk will be good for us. Now eat your breakfast so you can get dressed."

❖

Tadd checked the phone book and found Sabrina's number, along with her address. Even though he had said he would call, he much preferred to speak to her in person. That way she couldn't hang up on him. Aware that she and her daughter would be in church that morning, he waited until after one o'clock before arriving at the address he'd scribbled on a scratch pad.

This place is not only a dump, he thought as he rechecked the address, *it looks like a firetrap. No wonder they're turning the area into a parking lot.* He made his way up the front steps, found Sabrina's name and apartment number on the group of mailboxes inside the front door, then climbed the stairs to the third floor, mustering up his courage as he knocked. Almost immediately, Sabrina's beautiful face appeared.

"What are you doing here?"

"Do you mind if I come in?" He tilted his head to one side and peered around her. There was Megan, sitting on a worn sofa, smiling at him, a book in her hands.

She hesitated for a moment then motioned him inside.

Megan grinned at him. "Hi, Mr. Winsted. You want me to read you a story?"

"Actually, I came to speak with your mother." He sent a questioning glance toward Sabrina. "If—if that's okay with her."

"Why don't you take your book and go into the bedroom and read, sweetie? Later I'll fix you a bowl of ice cream."

Megan screwed up her face. "Do I have to?"

"I think Mr. Winsted is here to have grown-up talk. I'm sure you'd be bored."

"I wouldn't be bored. I—"

Sabrina pointed her finger toward one of only two doors in the room. "Megan. Now," she said in a soft but demanding voice. "And please close the door behind you." Without another word, the child picked up her book and walked into what he assumed was their bedroom and closed the door. Sabrina motioned toward the sofa then seated herself in the only chair in the room, a small faded blue club chair.

Tadd awkwardly sat down and folded his hands in his lap. Where should he begin? What could he say that would make her change her mind?

"May I get you a cup of coffee?"

"No, thank you. I just had lunch."

She straightened in her chair then leaned slightly forward. "Would you like to tell me why you've come instead of phoning?"

He couldn't help but stare. With the sunlight streaming in through the window, her curly red hair took on a flamelike glow, making the color of her eyes appear even greener than he remembered. And he loved her freckles. They suited her and, in his opinion, made her that much more attractive. "I—ah—thought it would be easier if we talked face-to-face. First, I need to apologize for lying to you—about the picture."

Her brows rose. "The picture you said was to be part of a joke."

He gave her a nervous smile. "Yes, that picture. I've already told you about the competition between my brother and myself, why I'm delaying getting married and having a family, as well as many other things I've never told anyone. You know my parents are coming for a visit, and how I'd lied about having a wife and daughter, and my warped, convoluted reasons for doing so."

"Go on."

Tadd raised his right hand to shoulder height and flattened his palm toward her. "I promise everything I am about to tell you is the absolute truth. No more lies. Okay?"

She nodded. "O–kay."

"I called my parents this morning. I know you'll find this hard to believe, but I had made up my mind I was going to tell them the truth—until my father told me my uncle Helmut passed away during the night."

"I'm so sorry," Sabrina said quickly, her face filled with concern.

"His death was expected. He's been in the Alzheimer's unit at a local nursing facility for a number of years, and even though he hasn't recognized my mother in a long time, she's still taking it pretty hard. She and my uncle were about the only members of her family left."

"Oh, your poor mother. How terrible for her. Are you going for the funeral?"

"No, Dad said I shouldn't come."

Her eyes widened. "I'd think they'd want you with them at a time like this."

"They're only having a simple graveside service the day after tomorrow and—"

"But surely you could book a flight and get there in time."

"Maybe. Getting there in time isn't the problem."

"Then what is? And what does all this have to do with me?"

"Dad thinks that since Mom has been spending so much time with Helmut at the nursing facility, getting away and having a complete change of scenery would be the best thing for her. They don't want me to come because they're still coming to Hannibal as originally planned." *Out with it. Tell her. You promised her the truth.* "Which means I need to have a wife and child to introduce them to, now, more than ever."

"Or—you could tell them the truth."

He shook his head. "Not now. Not after Mother has just lost her brother. Believe me. Telling them at a time like this is not even an option. Considering the delicate state my mother is in and the grief she is suffering over Helmut's death, I'm afraid it would be more than she could handle."

Sabrina leaned her head against the chair's back, closed her eyes, and let out a long sigh. "You *are* in a predicament but, unfortunately, you put yourself there."

On impulse, Tadd scooted to the end of the sofa nearest her, reached for her hand, and folded it in his. "Please, Ms. Stewart—Sabrina—I'm begging you. I can't hire anyone else. Mom and Dad have already seen your picture. Please say you'll help me out. You're the only one who can. You don't know my mom, but if you won't do it for me, do it for her."

"Look, Mr. Winsted, you're right. I don't know your parents, but to keep from adding to their burden, I'd like to go along with your scheme, but it's not possible. Even though I desperately need the money you've offered me, I can't do it. As a Christian, I refuse to lie to your parents and let them believe you and I are married, even for the few days they'll be here. I hope you understand, and I know this puts you in a real dilemma, but I just can't."

She made a feeble attempt to pull her hand away, but he held on and was pleased when he felt it relax. "That money would go a long way toward solving your problems."

"Yes, it would. I can't imagine what is going to happen to Megan and me without it. You have no idea how tempting it is to take it, but to tell a man's parents that I am his wife when I'm not—well, I just can't do it."

Tadd had never felt such desperation. How could he have

been so stupid as to think he could pull off something so foolish? "That's your final answer? You don't need time to reconsider?"

"No, that's my final answer."

He decided it might help if he sweetened his offer. "What if I not only gave you the money but loaned you one of my cars until you can find one you can afford?"

"It certainly would help if I had something to drive to work and get us to church and the theater. . .but. . .my answer is still no."

"It's a long way to the theater from here, and not a good idea for a beautiful woman and her young daughter to be out walking the streets alone at night."

"Maybe one of the other actors will bring us home after our performances."

Okay. He'd hoped he wouldn't have to use Plan B, but it looked as if it was going to be necessary. If that didn't work, he was all out of options. "Ms. Stewart—Sabrina—"

Chapter 4

Tadd sucked in a deep breath. He'd already made one mistake by not thinking through the ramifications. What if he made another one and it led to even more trouble than the first one? No, what he was about to propose was the only logical solution. Good for him and, he hoped, good enough for Sabrina that she would accept his offer. It would be a win/win situation for both of them.

He tightened his grip on her hand as he gazed into her troubled face. "Then marry me, Sabrina."

Her eyes widened as she stared at him. "How many times do I have to tell you I won't pretend to be your wife? Is there something about the word *no* that you don't understand?"

"I'm not talking about *pretending* to be my wife. I'm talking about the real thing. I want you to marry me—legally. Marriage license, justice of the peace, flowers, the whole wedding thing."

She tugged her hand away and glared at him. "You, Mr. Winsted, are out of your mind. You barely know me, and I certainly don't know you that well!"

He donned a gentle smile. He had to put her at ease, make her realize the sincerity of his words so she'd hear him out. "Look, you said you refused to *play* the part of my wife, but if we were truly and legally married, you wouldn't have to pretend. I'd have a wife and you'd have the money you need."

His words nearly knocked her off her feet. The last thing she'd expected when he'd walked through her front door was a legitimate proposal of marriage.

"This will be a marriage of convenience only," he added hastily. "As a Christian, you know your Bible. Isn't that the way they did it in Bible times? Marry people they didn't know because their parents set it up? Most of those marriages worked, even if the people weren't in love when they first married. Other than holding your hand, and maybe giving you a few hugs and affectionate-looking pecks on the cheek when my parents are with us, I promise not to touch you. We won't even be sharing the same room. You'll be staying with Megan. Think of it as a vacation. You won't have to cook or clean or do laundry. Mom and Dad will only be here for a few days. All you'll have to do is look beautiful, which will take no effort whatsoever on your part, be cordial to my parents, make a few wifely gestures toward me to convince them we're happy newlyweds—that's it."

Sabrina had to admit his revised offer sounded a bit more acceptable, and it would certainly go a long way toward helping her get back on her feet, but one extremely important question still needed an answer. "What happens after your parents go back to Germany? I wouldn't want us to stay married!"

"We'll get an annulment right away. People do it all the time. In a month or so, I'll tell my parents it just didn't work out as we'd hoped, and we decided to remain friends but go our separate ways."

"Won't that upset them?"

"Not as bad as being told I'd sent them a false wedding picture."

"What about your staff at the restaurant? What if they say something to them?"

"That's not likely. I get along well with my staff, but I keep my private life to myself. Besides, they've already seen us together at the restaurant and have probably assumed we're dating."

"I'm concerned about Megan. I'd hate her to become attached to you, even for a few days, and then suddenly lose you like she did her father." Sabrina's heart beat faster and faster. She could feel it quickening in her chest. What he was saying would make their marriage real—and legal, but definitely not consummated, and she wouldn't be lying to Mr. and Mrs. Winsted, she would be his wife. *Oh, I'm not sure what I should do. Tell me, God!*

"We'll handle it any way you deem best. Also, I doubt you will mind, but since I am a man of considerable means, I would prefer that we have a prenuptial agreement set up between us. Not that I think you'd take advantage of your legal rights as my wife during the time we're married, but like you said, I know very little about you, even less than you do about me. You don't mind, do you?"

"No, I don't mind." She could well understand his concern. "But, Mr. Winsted, since I don't really know you either, it seems only wise that I also have a safeguard. I'd like to have my money up front."

"I'll have it for you in the morning. But if you're going to be my wife, you have to stop calling me Mr. Winsted. My name is Tadd. Of course around my folks you can call me things like honey and darling, but only if you're comfortable doing it."

Sabrina felt herself blush.

"I'd like for you and Megan to move your personal things into the living quarters above the restaurant tomorrow; then we'll be married as soon as we get the marriage license."

"Tomorrow? I work tomorrow."

"The sooner you can move in, the better it will be for all of us. You and Megan need to get settled and the three of us need time to get acquainted and become comfortable with one another."

"You make it sound so easy."

"It will be easy."

"And you'll loan me a car?"

"Yes, and I'll pay all your expenses for you and your daughter's needs while you're with me."

She couldn't help but pull back when he reached for her hand again. The idea of being held in another man's arms and calling him by endearing names, even if they didn't come from the heart, was something she never expected to do again in her lifetime. Certainly not until Megan was grown and out on her own. But hadn't she done those very things with some of the men actors in their plays? Would it be so different? She watched as a shy grin crossed his face.

"Okay, I see you're not quite ready to say yes yet. Time is of the essence, Sabrina. Missouri has a three-day waiting period for marriage licenses. If we're going to do this, we need to do it right away, and we'll need to do it in Pike County so it won't come out in the local papers. Let me add one more thing to convince you to marry me as soon as possible. How about if I add another thousand dollars?"

"Another thousand?" Sabrina went into a state of shock. Five thousand would be wonderful, but six? That extra thousand would pay for several months' rent on the new apartment.

"I realize what I did was wrong, dear sweet Sabrina, and I had no right to drag you into my stupid scheme, but that's all hindsight now, and I'm begging for your forgiveness." His eyes pleaded with her. "Please try to find it in your heart to say yes. If you refuse, I have no other choice but to call my parents and add even more sorrow to my mother's grief by admitting I'd lied to them, and hope the shock isn't too much for her."

Sabrina gazed into his sad eyes. He did seem truly sorry on both counts. She certainly didn't want his mother to be more upset than she already was, and she couldn't stand to think how hurt—or angry—his father would be, not to mention the ridicule his brother would heap on him. She might be making the biggest mistake of her life by accepting his offer, but then, refusing his offer could mean she and her daughter would be cast out onto the streets, with nowhere to live, no transportation, and possibly no job. She could never let that happen. And hadn't she been praying to God to perform a miracle in their lives? So it appeared—the best thing for everyone would be to accept his offer.

"If I do what you're asking it won't be to get you out of the jam you got yourself into, it will be because of your parents. And also because we will legally be husband and wife, so we won't have to lie to them about that part. And, since you're being honest, I, too, have to be honest and admit Megan and I really need the money you're offering us. I've been praying God would provide a way for us to pay for a car and another apartment. Maybe this is His way of doing it."

"You're really into this God thing, aren't you?"

"My relationship with my Lord is the most important thing in my life." She lifted her face and looked directly into his eyes. "Have you ever accepted Christ as your Savior, Mr. Winsted?"

"Ah—well—not exactly," he stammered. "Like I told you, I've tried to be a good person, and occasionally I read my Bible. I know I should go to church, but I've been so busy with my business I haven't had time. But, honest, I am interested."

"So maybe we can talk about what it takes to become a Christian sometime?"

"Sometime? Does that mean you're saying yes? You'll do what I've asked?"

Somehow just knowing he was open to the gospel gave her hope for his salvation. "Yes, I'll do it."

Tadd let out a "Yee-haw," then swept her up in his arms,

twirling her about the tiny living room with an excited, "Thank you, thank you, thank you!"

Before she could demand he put her down, the bedroom door flew open and Megan appeared, her emerald eyes widened in surprise as she stared at them.

Sabrina pushed away from Tadd as he lowered her feet to the floor. "Everything is okay, Megan. We—Mr. Winsted and I—" How could she ever hope to explain things to her child and have her understand?

"Your mother and I are going to be married!"

Sabrina frowned at him. "If you don't mind, Mr.—Tadd. I'd prefer to discuss this with my daughter. In private."

Tadd sent a quick glance at Megan then back to Sabrina. "Oh, yeah, I get it." He pulled a set of keys from his pocket and handed them to her. "I'll get one of the busboys to help me deliver the car I'm loaning you later this afternoon. We'll park it as close as we can to your building. You can't miss it. It's red, and the license tag says WINSTED."

Her heart still pounding like a determined woodpecker on barn siding, she nodded. "Thank you, I'd appreciate it."

His smile reflected both relief and gratitude. "You won't be sorry, Sabrina. I'm going to make your stay at my home as comfortable and as happy as I can. Your wish will be my command." He glanced around the room thoughtfully. "Didn't you say the owner of this building wanted you out of here within the next few weeks?"

"Yes, why?"

"I was just thinking. You said you'd rented this place furnished.

Since you're going to be moving in with me for at least two weeks, why don't you let me take all your personal belongings to my place? There's plenty of storage there. That way you can save yourself a month's rent. You'll have the check for the money I owe you tomorrow, so you can start looking for a new apartment whenever you're ready."

She eyed him warily, but she had to admit his words made good sense. It was pretty stupid to be paying rent on her run-down apartment when she wasn't even living there. "Are you sure you don't mind?"

"Not in the least. It's the wise thing to do. It's about a forty-five minute drive to the Pike County courthouse. Let's plan on me picking you up at eight."

She ventured a smile. "Eight is fine but, remember, I have to report for work at noon and I can't be late."

"I'll make sure we're back in plenty of time."

"And I'll try to have all our things packed and boxed up by Tuesday morning so we can get them moved before I go to work."

"Good idea. See you in the morning at eight. Bye, Megan." He moved out the door then waved.

Sabrina followed him then leaned over the railing and watched as he climbed down the two flights of stairs and headed for his car. *Whoever said, "Oh what a tangled web we weave, when first we practice to deceive!" certainly knew what he was talking about.*

Megan grabbed onto her hand and stared at her with eyes full of confusion. "Are you really going to marry Mr. Winsted?"

Sabrina gazed down at her child's innocent face as she took her hand and led her back into the little apartment they called home. "Remember when he asked us to play the role of his wife and daughter? Kind of like we do in our plays at the theater when we act in the musicals?"

Megan nodded. "Like we did in *The Unsinkable Molly Brown*? That was my favorite."

"Yes, like that, only he wanted us to do it to play a joke on his parents. When we're acting in a play, the audience knows we're only acting—that what we are doing is not true but playing a part in a story someone made up to entertain people."

"But you told him we wouldn't do it, right?"

Sabrina nodded. What she was asking of an eight-year-old might be more than her daughter could give. "Right, that's exactly what I'd told him. But now Mr. Winsted has asked me to marry him in a *real* wedding ceremony. That way, I'll really be his wife and you'll really be his stepdaughter. Do you understand what I'm saying?"

Megan's eyes twinkled. "Does that mean he's going to be my daddy? I've always wanted a daddy."

Sabrina chose her words carefully. The last thing she wanted was to see her precious little girl hurt. "Yes, he'll be your daddy, but only for a little while then—"

"Are you going to wear a beautiful white dress like when you danced at the ball with the prince in *Cinderella*?"

"No, our wedding will be a small one. I'll probably wear one of my church dresses."

"Can I be the flower girl?"

"Maybe. We'll see. The day after tomorrow, the two of us will move into Mr. Winsted's house. He lives above the restaurant. You and I will have a lovely room together and we—"

"Aren't mommies and daddies supposed to stay in the same bedroom? That's what they do on TV."

Explaining this was even harder than Sabrina had imagined. "Some mommies and daddies do, but you and I are going to have a bedroom together, like we do now." She placed a reassuring hand on Megan's shoulder. "Trust me, honey, it'll be fine. We'll talk more about it tomorrow. Right now I need you to help me start boxing things up for our move."

❀

Tadd stood on the landing at the head of the restaurant's grand staircase and surveyed his options. There were five bedrooms on the second floor. His bedroom suite, which he understood had served as the bedroom of Captain Gregory Alan Royce, the man who had built the original house in 1898, was at the far left side. The corner suite sported magnificent views of the mighty Mississippi River. Next to his room was a wide hallway, then a smaller room alongside a walk-in linen closet. Directly behind where he was standing was a second bedroom with its own private bath, which he had added on to the bedroom when he had purchased the house. Though it was some distance from his master suite—the one that his parents would assume he and Sabrina were sharing—it would be the best place for her and Megan.

To the right of the staircase was another large bedroom—one he felt would be perfect for his parents. By placing them there, they, too, would have a glorious view of the Mississippi River but would be far enough away from his room, and from Sabrina's, that they would not be aware of the fact that the two of them were not actually living together.

Happy and relieved that he and Sabrina had finally come to an understanding and things were running on schedule, he smiled to himself with a small degree of satisfaction. The next morning, he and Sabrina would apply for their marriage license. Then, after they got back to Hannibal, he would phone the Pike County justice of the peace to reserve a time for their wedding. Next, he'd call his attorney.

Chapter 5

Since no one else was in line when they arrived at the Pike County Courthouse the next morning, it took only a few minutes for the clerk to get their marriage license application papers ready. Tadd read them over then signed his name and added the date before passing them to Sabrina along with his pen. "Read it thoroughly, sign it, and we'll be on our way." He pointed to the places the clerk had marked. "After the three-day waiting period, we'll be married by the justice of the peace and everything will be legal."

As she took the pen from his hand, she offered him a feeble smile. Though what she was about to do was simple and would only take a few seconds to complete, Sabrina found herself hesitating. What they were doing was legal, but was it right? Was it *really* the best thing for everyone? Especially his parents. Her breath caught in her throat as she felt a strong arm encircle her waist.

"Sabrina? Is there a problem?"

She looked up into Tadd's face and found nothing but kindness. The man had done a stupid, childish thing by lying to his parents, and now he was doing his best to cover that lie to avoid hurting them. It was obvious he never meant to harm them and was ashamed of his stupidity. Was what he had done so awful? By the time his parents arrived, the two of them would be married—husband and wife—just like he'd told them. "No, I—ah—was just thinking." Leaning over the counter, she filled in the remaining blanks, signed her name, and then handed the clipboard to the clerk.

Their charade had begun.

❖

The next day passed so rapidly Sabrina barely had time to catch her breath. Between working at her job, packing boxes, and helping Tadd move them to his home, she felt like a hamster on a giant runaround wheel—too tired to stay on, yet too excited to get off.

After they had placed the last box in her room, Tadd pulled off his gloves and wiped at his brow with his sleeve. "If you need it, I could have an extra bureau moved in from one of the other bedrooms."

She glanced around the spacious room, the nicest room she'd had in her entire life. "Thank you, but we have plenty of drawer space. We'll only be unpacking a few things."

"Then I'll get out of your way. I knew you'd be tired, so I've taken the liberty of ordering for you and have asked one of the busboys to bring your dinner to your room. I won't see you in the morning. I have to make an early run to Columbia to check on some new equipment for the kitchen, but I'll be back in plenty of time so the three of us can have dinner together." He snapped his fingers. "Oh, I nearly forgot. I placed the Bible my grandmother gave me on the bookshelf over the bed. I thought you might like to have it there."

"That was very thoughtful of you. Maybe the two of us can read it together sometime."

"I'd like that."

She thanked him for all he'd done then, feeling totally exhausted, closed the door behind him and leaned against it.

Giggling with childlike enthusiasm, Megan slipped her arms about Sabrina's waist and smiled up at her. "I like our room. It's pretty."

Sabrina drew her close. "I like it, too, honey. Living here is like stepping into a fairy tale, but we have to remember we'll only be here a short time, so we'd better not get used to this much luxury. I doubt our new apartment will be much nicer than our old one."

"But I thought he was going to be my daddy."

"I know this is hard to understand, Megan. He will be your daddy but only for a short time."

"Why?"

She wanted to cry as she gazed at her daughter's troubled face. "This isn't something you should worry about. Just trust Mama, okay? Everything is going to be fine." Her daughter deserved so much more than she was able to give her. How she longed to shower her with some of the niceties of life. Hopefully, with the extra money Mr. Winsted was paying her, she would be able to put enough money aside for school shoes and a decent warm coat for Megan, maybe even enough for a sweater or two.

"You know what, Mama? I really like Mr. Winsted. He's nice to me. Do you think if I pray and ask Him, God will let him be my daddy forever?"

What could she say? There was no way Megan could understand the complicated arrangement she had agreed to or why Tadd Winsted had gotten himself into such a mess. If she said no, it would be the same as discouraging the child from praying for the things important to her. If she said yes, it would be the same as telling her daughter there was a chance God might give her Tadd as her father. "You, my precious one," she said, feigning a laugh, "ask too many questions. Right now you need to take a quick shower and get to bed."

Later, after a long, hot soak in the tub and a tearful review of all that had happened to her in the past week, Sabrina crawled into bed.

When Sabrina and Megan walked down the stairs and into the restaurant area the next evening, the headwaiter greeted them and bowed low. "Good evening, Ms. Stewart. Tadd is waiting for you at your table in the main dining room."

She thanked him and then followed behind as they made their way through the tables of those already seated and enjoying their dinners. Tadd rose and took her hand. Then he kissed her on the cheek before turning to smile at Megan.

"I got to thinking about something after I went to my room last night. It would probably make more sense when we officially announce our marriage, if everyone thought we were already engaged." He reached into his pocket, pulled out a small drawstring bag, opened it, took something out, and handed it to her. "Maybe you'd better wear this."

Sabrina let out a gasp at the sheer beauty and brilliance of the single diamond set in a wide band of gold. "It's—beautiful!"

"Glad you like it. A number of years ago, before I decided to leave Germany, I met a girl and thought I was in love with her, so I bought that ring. Turned out, she jilted me for one of my close friends before I even had a chance to propose to her."

Not that she had expected him to rush out and buy a diamond ring specifically for her. She hadn't. But the fact that he had bought it for another somehow diminished the joy of being asked to wear it. She managed a smile then slipped the ring onto her finger. It was a bit snug, but that wouldn't matter since she would only be wearing it a short time. "It's a lovely ring, but are you sure you want me to wear something this expensive? What if I lost it? A zircon would work just as well."

He shrugged. "Naw, go ahead and wear it. It's insured. Besides, it looks great on you."

"Is that the real reason you've never married?"

He huffed. "Because of her jilting me? I've got to admit it hurt. But wanting to devote all my time to getting my business established was the real reason."

They ordered their meals then listened attentively as Megan told them, in animated fashion, about the new game she'd played that day with her babysitter. To Sabrina's surprise, the self-proclaimed bachelor actually seemed to enjoy being with her daughter. After the waiter had placed their salads before them, she once again asked Tadd if he minded if she prayed and thanked the Lord for their food. She almost felt like a hypocrite for even asking. Other than their mealtime prayers and the prayers she had with Megan each night before bedtime, her prayer life, since God had allowed her husband to die at a time when she needed him most, had been severely lacking. Sometimes she wondered if He cared or was even listening. But just in case God *did* care and *was* listening, she had continued to pray.

"Not a bit. Go ahead. In fact, I think praying before our meals would be a nice touch when my parents get here. It would make us seem more like a real family."

They enjoyed a wonderful, sumptuous dinner, laughing as Tadd shared some of his fondest childhood memories with them. After they had finished their dessert and the dishes were cleared from the table, he turned to her. "I've been talking way too much about myself. Tell me about you, Sabrina, about your life. I don't mean to pry, but if we're going to carry this thing off, I'll need to know as much about you and your background as you care to tell me."

She leaned back in her chair and appraised his face. "There's not a whole lot to tell. I was born in Arkansas to an exceedingly poor family. We lived in a small cabin way up in the hills and ate mostly what we could raise in our garden. My mom cleaned houses for some of the rich folks in town. My dad didn't do much of anything but drink beer and talk to his friends about how unfair life was. I didn't have any brothers or sisters, probably because Mama didn't want to bring any more children into the world and not have the money to properly care for them."

"But you seem well educated. How did that happen?"

"She reads lots of books," Megan inserted, looking up from the paper placemat the waiter had brought for her along with a box of crayons. "She still does."

"I didn't want to grow up and be poor like my mama and daddy, so as soon as I could read, I checked out every book I could from the book wagon that came by my school once a week and read every one of them. And I worked hard at spelling and learning to speak proper English. I even won first place in the local spelling bee four years in a row. I determined I wasn't going to end up being a poor, uneducated hillbilly like my folks." She shrugged. "But look at me. I'm nearly as bad off as they were. I can barely provide the daily necessities of life for my daughter and myself."

From the sad expression in her eyes, Tadd was afraid Sabrina was going to break down in tears. He'd known things had been hard for her, but he'd had no idea the amazingly beautiful, soft-spoken woman sitting beside him had come from such humble beginnings. Instinctively, he scooted his chair closer to hers and wrapped his arm about her. "Don't worry, Sabrina. Everything is going to be all right."

She lifted misty eyes and gazed into his face. "All right? How can you say such a thing? You, whose life has been handed to you on a silver platter? Do you have any idea what it's like to wonder where your next meal is coming from? If the next knock at the door will be the sheriff to evict you because you're behind in your rent? Have you ever had your child beg you for a new pair of shoes and you had to tell her no?" She slightly pulled away from his grasp. "Mr. Winsted—Tadd—I'm sorry. None of this is your fault. I'm the one who let you talk me into coming here. It's amazing what a person will do for money."

She tried to pull away, but he held her fast.

"Is everything all right, Mr. Winsted?"

Tadd looked up at the sound of his headwaiter's voice. "Sabrina isn't feeling well. I'm going to take her to her room." Releasing his hold and taking her arm, Tadd eased her from the chair, motioned a wide-eyed Megan to follow, then led her toward the stairs, to the room she and Megan shared. "Is there anything I can get for you?" he asked after Megan had closed the door. "A glass of water? An aspirin, maybe?" Feeling totally inept, he watched as she sank onto the velvet-upholstered love-seat beside the fireplace.

"No, thank you." With a sigh, she reached for a tissue from the box on the end table then dabbed at her eyes. "I'm sorry, Mr. Winsted. I don't know what got into me. I had no right to speak to you that way. It's just that sometimes my life is overwhelming, and I don't seem to know what to do about it. It's not me I'm concerned about, it's—" Without finishing her sentence she made a slight gesture toward her child. "I want so many things for her. Things I never had. If you were a parent, you'd understand."

"I want to understand, honest I do, and I'm trying. But you're right, my life *has* been handed to me on a silver platter. I've never had to want for anything. I can't imagine living the way you have."

"It wasn't so bad the first year of our marriage. Mike and I both worked, but then I got pregnant with Megan, and the doctor made me quit. That's when the bills began piling up. Then, just a few months after she was born, Mike died suddenly of a heart attack. Since then, I've done nothing but make a mess of things."

"Surely he had life insurance."

"Life insurance? No, I even had to borrow money to pay for his funeral."

"His parents couldn't help?"

"He didn't have a dad, and his mom was worse off than we were. We married quite young and thought we were in good health. Purchasing life insurance on the little salary my husband was able to bring in was the last thing on our list of priorities."

He dropped to one knee beside her and took her hands in his. "No wonder it has been so difficult for you. I'm amazed you've done as well as you have."

"I should have done better."

"Oh, Sabrina, you've had to do it all alone, without anyone's help."

"Hopefully, things will get better when Megan is old enough to be left alone and I won't have to pay a babysitter." She lowered her head, avoiding his eyes. "I can't believe I've told you all of this. I'm normally a very private person."

His heart ached for her. "I'm glad you've told me. I want to know everything about you. Your sorrows, hopes, fears, your dreams."

"You still want me to go through with this? After the way I behaved? Made a scene in your restaurant?"

"Yes, more than ever. I know we are just getting acquainted, but from all I've seen so far, you're a wonderful person. If I were to list the attributes I'd want in a wife, I'd be describing you."

"Me?"

"Yes, you. I'd want my wife to be kind, loving, caring, sincere. Compassionate toward others, willing to step in and help where needed. You're all of those things. I'd want her to be beautiful, with gorgeous red hair and lovely green eyes. I'd want a woman with godly morals and principles, who would wholly devote herself to me and any children we may have. One who would make our home a haven, a place where we would feel loved, but I'd also want her to be her own person and take a stand for the things in which she believes."

Tadd paused and gave his head a shake to clear it. Where had those things come from? How had he let himself get so carried away? He'd never said anything like that to a woman before. Why was he saying it now? To boost her spirits? Help her self-esteem? Make her feel better and realize her life had value? He turned loose of her hands and rose. He had to get out of there before he said something even more foolish and maybe even started quoting poetry. "I'd better go. You need to try to get some rest." He stopped at the door long enough to say good night to Megan then turned to catch one last glimpse of his wife-to-be. "Remember, call if you need anything."

She nodded. "I will—and, Tadd, thanks for being so understanding."

As he lay in bed that night, all he could think about was the beautiful woman down the hall and the things he'd said to her. And he wondered, was she laying awake thinking of him, too?

Tadd's first thought when he arose the next morning was of Sabrina. Had she slept well? Was she feeling better? As soon as he was dressed, he hurried to Sabrina's room and gently tapped on the door. When she didn't respond, he tapped again. Then again. Deciding she was probably still sleeping, he headed downstairs to begin his day at the restaurant. "Have you seen Ms. Stewart?" he asked one of the busboys who was standing at a counter folding freshly laundered napkins.

"Yes, sir. She and her daughter left over an hour ago."

"I don't suppose she said where she was going."

"No, sir, she didn't. She came out of the kitchen with a bucket then left in your car."

A bucket? What use could she have for a bucket? And where was she taking it?

He began his usual tasks of checking over the reservation list, going over supply invoices, and doing the myriad of other jobs that needed to be accomplished to keep a restaurant the size of the House on Cranberry Hill running smoothly and profitably, but his mind kept wandering to Sabrina. *Why?* he wondered as he stared at the database on the computer. Why did her lovely image keep appearing before his eyes, blanketing out the headings and numbers on the screen? Was it because he felt sorry for her? Is that why he couldn't get his mind off her plight? Or maybe it was because of the guilt he felt for being born to parents who could give him anything he wanted when Sabrina had so little. Why should he feel guilty for that? He'd had no choice as to whom he should be born, any more than anyone else did.

In frustration, he hit the computer monitor's OFF button then leaned back in his chair, his hands locked behind his head. *I have to get over this—whatever it is. I can't let this woman and her problems dominate my every thought. I have a business to run.*

"Did Ms. Stewart find the scrubbing pads she asked for?" Tadd glanced at the waitress.

"She asked me where they were, but I told her I didn't know. By the time I was able to find them, she was gone."

"I—I don't know," Tadd confessed, trying to appear casual. "She left before I came downstairs." He watched until the woman had gone back to her duties, then grabbed his jacket and rushed toward the door. There was only one place Sabrina could be.

Sabrina emptied the bucketful of dirty water down the bathtub drain then rinsed and refilled the bucket with clean water before carrying it into the living room. She had already wiped down the walls, scrubbed the shelves in the kitchen cabinets, cleaned out the refrigerator and washed the wire shelves, and scoured the range top and oven as best she could without scrubbing pads. After that, she had swept and mopped the bedroom and closet floors. The living room would be next, then the kitchen floor, with the bathroom last. Her back was tired from all the bending and stooping, but she couldn't stop until the job was finished.

She had barely dropped to her knees and wrung out her rag when the door flew open and Tadd's frowning face appeared. "What do you think you're doing, Sabrina? You don't have to leave this apartment spick-and-span. They're going to bulldoze it!"

"I know, but I always like to leave a place better than I found it."

He reached out his hand and assisted her to her feet. "You scared me when you didn't answer your door this morning. I—I thought maybe you'd changed your mind and run off."

She turned her head away as if to avoid his gaze. "I probably should have. After the way I behaved last night, I wouldn't have blamed you if you asked me to leave."

"I wouldn't do that. I'm glad you told me the things you did. It makes me understand you better. If I'd gone through what you have, I probably wouldn't have done half as well. You're quite a woman, Sabrina Stewart, and Megan is lucky to have you as a mother." He glanced around. "Where is Megan? She did come with you, didn't she?"

She nodded. "She's downstairs playing with one of our neighbors' daughters."

Tadd suddenly realized this was the first time he'd had Sabrina all to himself. He wondered what it would be like to hold her in his arms. Not as he'd done before, when he'd been trying to comfort her, but hold her close, nestle his chin in her hair, feel her cheek against his. He gave his head a shake. *Am I going bonkers? This woman is working for me. Doing a job. That's all. Once my parents leave, she'll be gone, and I'll probably never see her again.* For some reason, he found that thought unsettling. He couldn't imagine Sabrina walking out of his life. "What if I don't want you to go?" The words slipped out before he could stop them.

She turned to stare at him. "Don't want me to go where?"

"Ah—to—to—ah—to put gas in my car." He felt like a dork but that was the first thing that popped into his head.

Her stare turned into one of confusion. "Your car had a full tank of gas when you gave it to me. I've barely driven it."

He backed toward the door. "Oh, that's right. I forgot. I'd better be going. And you'd better give up cleaning a place that will soon be hit with a wrecking ball."

"I have to be at work by eleven. Megan and I won't be back at your place until around six."

"We'll plan on having dinner together, okay?"

"Yes, that would be nice. Thank you."

Tadd was waiting in the lobby that evening when Sabrina and Megan arrived. After telling Megan to go on in and sit at their usual table, he grabbed hold of Sabrina's arm and pulled her to one side. "I've been thinking. Since it would be best if folks think we're engaged, maybe we should act more like—you know—lovers, instead of two people who just met and barely know one another."

"Like how? What do you mean?"

He offered a slight shrug. "You know. Hold hands, smile tenderly at one another. I should put my arm around you, and maybe even kiss you now and then."

She answered with a slow, "O–kay. If that's what you think we should do."

"Good, I'm glad we have that settled. Now give me your hand." He couldn't believe how good it felt to hold hands with Sabrina. Once seated, he leaned toward her and wrapped one arm about her shoulders then, drawing her close, whispered, "I'm going to kiss you. Try to act like you're enjoying it." With that, he slowly placed his lips on hers and held them there, with plans to withdraw them after a moment or two, but he found he couldn't. Instead, he lingered, his lips tasting the sweetness of hers, his heart pounding with irregular beats. When he was finally able to pull away, he caught sight of Sabrina's green eyes, her lovely ivory skin, and the gorgeous halo of red hair that surrounded her face, and he realized he was falling in love. "Wow, that was nice!"

"I thought so, too." Sabrina's diminutive voice quavered so close to his face he could feel her breath on his cheeks.

Suddenly he remembered Megan was at the table. In his haste to kiss Sabrina, he'd forgotten all about her presence. He turned to her, unsure how she would react to him kissing her mother as he had.

Megan looked first at him, then her mother, then back to him. "Can we eat now? I'm hungry."

Though he was tempted to take her in his arms and kiss her

good night when he walked Sabrina and Megan to their room, he didn't. As much as he would like to have done it, without an audience to see them, he had no excuse for kissing her, and the last thing he wanted was to get her upset with him. "Tomorrow is the last day of our waiting period," he reminded her as he backed out the door. "One more day then we can be married. You and Megan looked so beautiful in the things you wore in that wedding picture I sent to my parents, I called the rental agent and told him I'd be picking up the same items tomorrow so we could wear them for our actual wedding. We can put them on when we reach the courthouse. Our ceremony with the justice of the peace is set for ten o'clock, so we should leave here by nine."

Megan clapped her hands. "Oh, goodie, Mama. Now you won't have to wear your church dress!"

He frowned. "Church dress?"

"Megan had asked me if I was going to wear a white gown. I told her no, I'd probably be wearing my church dress. But," she added quickly, "I'll be happy to wear whatever you think I should."

After a wink toward Megan, Tadd cupped her hand in his. "I think Megan and I would both prefer the white gown."

Sabrina gave him a bashful smile. "Then white it is."

Sabrina was almost giddy as she lay in her bed that night, with feelings and emotions she hadn't experienced since that special day when Mike had held her in his strong arms and asked her to marry him. Surely she wasn't in love with Tadd Winsted! What a ridiculous thought that was. Yet what else could explain the joy she felt at his smile, the thundering of her heart when he was around, the thrill that coursed through her when he held her in his arms, the way her lips craved the touch of his? *Get hold of yourself, girl. You're talking about Tadd Winsted. There is no way a prosperous man like him would fall in love with you. He could have his pick of women. This is a business arrangement. He's not interested in you! What do you have to offer? Nothing—but a ready-made family. He's simply using you to cover up a mistake he made. The minute his parents are on that plane headed back to Germany, he'll forget all about you. If you were smart you'd put aside any thoughts of love, forget about him, use the money he's giving you, and get on with your life.*

Sabrina flipped onto her side and buried her face in her pillow. *I can't forget. I'm already in love with him!*

Chapter 6

To Sabrina's surprise, Tadd barely said a word on the way to the courthouse. He'd seemed fine the night before. Complimentary. He even seemed excited about their ceremony. Had she said something to upset him? Was he having second thoughts about having a real wedding instead of lying about one? She'd already signed the prenuptial agreement, so that couldn't be the reason for his solemn mood.

"Oh, Megan," he said with a quick glance toward the back-seat. "I almost forgot. See that big white box next to you?"

"Yes, I see it."

"Since you're going to be our flower girl, I had the florist make up a basket of rose petals for you, and I had him put together a pink corsage for you to wear on your dress."

Megan squealed with delight as she opened the box. "They're so pretty! Thank you, Tadd."

"See the green box next to it?" he asked, sending her another glance. "Give that one to your mother." Megan reached for the box and passed it over the front seat to Sabrina.

Sabrina frowned. "This is for me?"

He nodded. "Yes."

Her gasp nearly equaled that of her daughter as she lifted the lid. "Oh, Tadd, a bridal bouquet. It's lovely, but I didn't think to get you a boutonniere."

A faint grin tilted at his lips. "That's okay. I got my own."

"It's fun having you for a daddy, Tadd," Megan offered from the backseat. "I've been asking Jesus for a daddy for a long time."

Tadd swallowed hard. "Until you came along, Megan, I never thought I'd want a daughter, but being with you has changed my mind. You deserve the best daddy ever."

Sabrina wanted to cry. It was obvious her daughter was in awe of Tadd. There was no way Megan could come out of this unscathed. But it was too late to do anything about it. Tadd's car was turning into the courthouse parking lot.

"We're here," he said, giving the key a twist in the ignition. "I'll help you girls carry your things to the women's restroom; then I'll go get dressed and meet you in the hallway.

His businesslike manner was almost more than Sabrina could bear. Aside from their exchange of a few pleasantries, to him this wedding was a business. To her, it was the beginning and ending of a love she had never expected to happen again. When she and Megan were finally dressed, disillusioned and with a heavy heart, she took her daughter's hand, and the two of them walked out into the corridor, ready to take part in a wedding that should never happen.

Decked in his tuxedo and looking more handsome that Sabrina had ever seen him, Tadd, his face wearing such a somber expression it almost frightened her, was leaning against a doorway waiting for them. "Megan," he said, taking her daughter by the hand and leading her into the courtroom, "I need to speak with your mother. Could you sit here for a few minutes and wait for us? We'll be right outside in the hall. Can you do that for me?"

When Megan nodded, Tadd reached for Sabrina's hand and led her back out into the hallway. "I have something important to tell you."

Chapter 7

Sabrina's heart raced. She'd never seen him like this. Was he going to tell her he'd decided to tell his parents the truth after all and wanted his money back? After she'd given up her apartment and moved into his place? Fear seized her and held her mercilessly in its clutches. What would she do? Where would she go? *Oh, God, is this my punishment for doubting You and Your will? I might deserve this but not Megan. She's the innocent party here. Please, please don't let her be hurt because of me and my foolishness.*

The look on Tadd's face as his gaze locked with hers made her dizzy with worry. He apparently noticed because he reached out his hand and pulled her toward him.

"Sabrina, dear, sweet Sabrina. Through my stupidity and desire to cover a lie, I've involved you in a scheme of which you should never have been a part, and for that I apologize. I'll never forgive myself for what I've done to you." He pursed his lips, as if giving serious thought to his next words before speaking.

"I—I have something I must tell you. I wasn't going to tell you until after we'd legally become husband and wife, but I know I must tell you now. It isn't fair that you become legally tied to me without knowing."

She pulled her hand from his and backed away. "Knowing what? Please don't tell me there are more lies."

"No, no more lies. Ever again." He paused and rubbed at his temples. "I got a phone call last night, long after you'd gone to bed. It was my father."

She gasped. "They found out you were lying to them?"

He shook his head. "No, they still believe that lie."

"Then what? Why did he call?"

"Mom tripped as she was going up the stairs to bed and broke her ankle in several places. They're operating on her this morning."

"Oh, Tadd, I'm so sorry. No wonder you've been so quiet. Now they'll have to delay their trip."

"Not *delay* their trip, Sabrina. They're not even coming. The doctor says it's going to take time for her to recover, and she'll be involved in several months of physical therapy once she is able to handle it."

"So if they're not coming, you don't even need us. You'll be able to go ahead with your plans of telling them in a few months that we've decided to divorce and you'll be off the hook. But I don't understand. Why drive us all the way to the courthouse and wait until we got into these clothes before telling me?" Suddenly she wanted to scream at him. His bizarre actions really upset her. Maybe this was fun and games to him, but to her it was serious.

"Because I was afraid if I told you *before* we were married, you'd run off and I'd never see you again. I know you've hated this plan right from the start."

Before Sabrina knew what was happening, Tadd pulled her into his arms and held her close. "That's why I had to tell you now, even at the risk of losing you. The lying had to stop, and not telling you my parents weren't coming until after the wedding would be the same as lying to you. I want whatever relationship we have to be based on honesty." He stroked her cheek with the back of his finger. "Because, Sabrina, as crazy as it sounds, considering what a short time we've known each other, I'm falling in love with you."

"In love—with me? But I..."

He pressed his finger to her lips, silencing her. "Yes, my sweet Sabrina, in love with you. I was hoping after our ceremony, given time, you could love me, too. I'm asking you, pleading with you, to be my wife, my real wife. I'm hoping we can be a real family. You, me, *and* Megan."

She felt faint. His words had come as a total shock. "You mean—marry you for real? Not just for a few days?"

"Yes, for real, and forever and ever."

She wanted so much to say yes. His proposal was more than she'd ever dared dream. What he was offering was all she'd ever hoped for, except for one very important thing. He was a good man, but he didn't know her Lord. She'd heard horror stories of Christian women who had been so in love they had ignored God's warnings and their lives had been miserable. She couldn't let that happen to her, or to Megan. A house divided could never stand. She was about to give him a firm *no* when Tadd smiled down at her with a smile she'd remember forever.

"I want our marriage to last a lifetime, sweetheart. I'm not sure exactly what it takes to become a Christian, but I've listened to you and Megan pray, and watched how important God and your church is to you, and I want the same thing in my life. I'm smart enough to know being a Christian isn't simply being a good person, it's a relationship with God, but I'm not sure how to go about asking Him to be my God like He is yours." He wrapped his arms about her waist and pulled her close, locking his gaze with hers. "But, Sabrina, I'm willing to learn. I love what you are, and I want it for me—for us. I never thought I could love someone this much, but I love you more than words can express. Please, my darling, say you'll marry me."

His words, not only saying he loved her but that he wanted to know God, were the words she'd longed to hear, but she had to be sure. She couldn't take a chance on him saying the words she wanted to hear without knowing, for sure, he meant them. Lifting her face toward his, she cupped his cheeks in her hands and gently kissed his lips. "I—I do love you, Tadd, but. . ."

"You do?"

"I've loved you since that first night you walked into the theater, and I want to marry you, but—don't you think we should wait a few weeks? Get to know each other a little better, since there is no longer any hurry to be married for your parents' sake? I'm sure neither of us wants to make a mistake." *And I have to make sure you're serious about accepting my Lord before I commit my life to you.*

"Do you think Megan will be all right with this? That she'll be willing to accept me as her father?"

Remembering how her daughter had asked, if she prayed, would God give her a daddy just like him, Sabrina blinked back tears of joy. "Oh, yes. I'm sure she will."

"Then we'll have a real wedding, my love, in a church, with a real pastor performing our ceremony, one with all the pomp and circumstance a wedding deserves, witnessed by our loved ones and friends." Releasing his hold on her, Tadd grabbed onto her hand and tugged her toward the courtroom. "Let's go tell the judge this wedding is off."

"Maybe, since we're planning on delaying it for a while, your mother will be feeling better and your parents can come."

"That, or we could have our wedding in Heidelberg."

Sabrina's eyes widened. "Heidelberg?"

"That way my parents could attend. Heidelberg is a beautiful city. You'd like it."

"But—I don't speak German."

He threw back his head with a laugh. "That's okay. I'm sure we can find a church and a minister who speak English."

A good Bible-believing church, I hope. Nothing else would do.

The two of them turned as Megan came running into the hall. "That guy in there wants to know if you're ready yet."

Tadd quickly knelt before Megan and clasped her hands in his. "Megan, I've fallen in love with your mother. While you were waiting in the courtroom, she and I had a serious talk and I've asked her to marry me. Not here at the courthouse, but in a real wedding in a church. And I've fallen in love with you, too. I want you to be my daughter. I want us to be a family. A real family."

Megan gazed at him for a moment, as if trying to digest all he was saying.

"I'll do everything I can to make the two of you happy," Tadd added. "I want to be your daddy, Megan."

"You—" Megan paused long enough to send an unsure glance toward her mother. "You promise you won't leave us?"

Tadd slipped his arm about her. "I promise, Megan. You have to believe that."

Megan threw her arms about Tadd's neck and kissed his cheek. "I love you, Tadd."

"I love you, too, Megan." As Tadd rose he reached out his hand to Sabrina. "And I love your mother."

Her feet barely touching the floor, with tears of happiness, Sabrina rushed into his arms. "And I love you, Tadd." *Please, God, speak to this man's heart. I so want to marry him, but I can't— I won't unless he shares my faith. Make him realize his need to confess his sins, ask Your forgiveness, and accept You as his Lord and Savior.*

The three turned as the courtroom door opened and a dignified, nearly bald man in a long black robe appeared, a miffed expression creasing his brow. "It's well past ten. I have other duties to perform. Are you two going to be married today or not?"

Tadd circled his arms about Sabrina and Megan then grinned at the man. "Sorry, sir, we've changed our minds. We're going to have a church wedding with all the trimmings."

The man's scowl morphed into a smile. "Wise idea, son. I wish you both success." Then turning to Megan he asked, "What do you think about all of this, young lady?"

Megan slipped her hand into Tadd's. "I think it's fine. I've always wanted a daddy."

The man's smile broadened. He lifted his hand, nodding first to Tadd, then Sabrina, then Megan. "Take it from an old man who knows, put God first in your lives and everything else will fall into place."

Tadd reached out his hand. "Thank you, sir. I intend to do exactly that."

"Then go in peace and may God's blessings be upon your little family."

Sabrina lifted misty eyes heavenward, and in her heart said, *Thank You, God.*

"Let's go home, girls." Tadd motioned toward the stairway leading to the parking lot. "We have a wedding to plan."

"When we're a real family, are we going to live at the House on Cranberry Hill?" Megan asked as she skipped merrily alongside them.

Tadd bent and gave Sabrina a quick peck on the cheek. "If that's where you and your mother want to live."

Sabrina sighed with happiness. "Sounds wonderful to me. I love that house."

"I was hoping that's what you would say. I think it's about time the House on Cranberry Hill became a real home again—the way Captain Gregory Alan Royce had intended it to be. At least the second floor." He gave Sabrina a shy grin. "Maybe, eventually, we'll add the pitter-patter of little feet."

She smiled up at him. "Maybe."

Looking mystified, Megan tugged on Tadd's hand. "What does the pitter-patter of little feet mean?"

Sabrina couldn't hold back a laugh. "Don't worry about it, honey. It's more grown-up talk."

Tadd grinned at Sabrina. "I couldn't have answered that question better myself. You're a great mom."

Reveling in his compliment she returned his grin. "And you're going to make a terrific dad."

"Ya think so?"

"I know so."

Arm in arm, the three walked out of the courthouse.

❀

The next few weeks were pure bliss for Sabrina as she and Tadd spent every possible waking moment together, many times including Megan. Each day, they found themselves more in love than the day before—and more convinced than ever that they belonged together. Tadd made a real effort to include Megan in as many things as possible and found he loved taking on the role of daddy. In addition to riding the Hannibal Trolley around town, visiting the Mark Twain cave complex, the Unsinkable Molly Brown home, and the Sawyer Creek Family Fun Park, he also treated them to the *Mark Twain* riverboat cruise, which was something Sabrina had always hoped to do but could never afford.

"You really don't need to entertain us, Tadd," Sabrina told

him as the three made their way up the staircase after an exceptionally busy day. "Megan and I just enjoy being with you."

He slipped his arm around her shoulders and pulled her close. "I know, but I love the way Megan smiles and gets excited when she does something she's never done before. I enjoy spoiling the two of you."

She reached up and cupped her hand over his. "And we love being spoiled but, really, it's not necessary. The best gift you could give us is yourself. Promise me we'll always have time for one another, okay?"

"You don't have to ask me twice. Every minute I'm away from you is torture. And I love being with Megan, too. I think it has helped all three of us to have these few weeks to get better acquainted. Our time together has made me realize how important family really is."

When they reached the landing, Sabrina turned to Tadd and slipped her arms about his neck. "I'm glad we didn't get married by that justice of the peace. Having a real wedding, the way we both want it, is going to be so much better."

"You're not sorry we decided to have it in Heidelberg instead of here in Hannibal?"

"Heidelberg is the perfect place for it. That way your parents and your brother and his family can be there, and I'm hoping your sister will come, too. I want to meet the whole family."

Lovingly, he pushed a lock of hair from her forehead then kissed her cheek. "They're going to be your family, too."

"I know. I can hardly wait."

"They're going to love both you and Megan."

"And we're going to love them. She's so excited about having grandparents."

Tadd glanced around. "Where'd she go? She was here a minute ago."

"Megan?" Sabrina called out. "Where are you?"

A red-haired ball of curls appeared in the doorway of the room the mother and daughter shared. "I'm right here."

Tadd frowned. "You didn't even say good night."

Megan rolled her eyes. "I know. You two take too long kissing. I'm tired. I want to go to bed."

Tadd threw back his head with an exaggerated laugh. "In that case—you'd better go and get your pajamas on, 'cause I'm a long way from being finished kissing your mom. Good night, Megan."

"Good night, Tadd."

He gave her a mischievous wink. "Good night who?"

Megan grinned. "Good night—Daddy."

He grinned back. "That's better. Good night, sweetheart."

"Good night, Mama."

"Good night, precious. I'll be in—in a few minutes—to pray with you and tuck you in. Don't forget to brush your teeth." Sabrina dreamily leaned her head against Tadd's shoulder.

Megan rolled her eyes. "Mom, I'm eight years old. I always remember to brush my teeth." With that, she blew them each a kiss and disappeared.

"Do you think Megan will let me pray with her and tuck her in sometimes once we're married?"

Her heart filled to overflowing with love for this man whom

God had sent so unexpectedly into her life, Sabrina smiled up at him. "I'm sure she will. She's already mentioned it."

"Good. I was hoping she would."

She suddenly frowned as a thought that had been plaguing her surfaced. "Do you think your parents will like me? I'm sure I'm nothing like the woman they would have picked out for you."

"I think they learned their lesson with Charles and my sister. Both of their spouses were the ones my parents had picked out. My sister's marriage ended in divorce, and if my brother doesn't get his act straightened up, his probably will, too. Believe me, they're going to love you." Lifting her face to his, he kissed her. "Just think, sweetheart. One week from today and you'll be all mine."

Sabrina tapped the tip of his nose playfully. "And you'll be all mine."

"You're not worried about the long flight to Germany and meeting my parents, are you?"

She closed her eyes and swallowed hard. "A little, I guess. I've never flown before."

He cuffed her chin playfully. "Have faith, Sabrina. The Lord will take care of you."

A spirit of peace and calmness came over her as his words penetrated her heart. "I know. He always has and He always will. I just need to trust Him more."

Chapter 8

One week later

The day of the wedding arrived more quickly than either Sabrina or Tadd could have imagined. Dressed in black tuxedos, white shirts, and pink cummerbunds, the two Winsted brothers made their way to the front of the sanctuary, to where a white flower-laden wrought iron arch had been set up for the wedding that would soon take place. Once Tadd and Sabrina had toured the little Bible church near the intersection of Julius-Becker-Strabe and Kralsruher Strabe and met with the pastor, they had been certain it was the perfect place for them to be united as husband and wife. Though the church itself was small, in comparison to many of the grand Heidelberg cathedrals, the congregation spoke English and the pastor preached the Word of God.

Charles gave Tadd a good-natured slap on the back. "Well, bro, it's your wedding day. You sure caught yourself a beautiful bride, even if you did have to lie to Mom and Dad about it."

Choosing to ignore his brother's snide comment, Tadd grinned. He wasn't about to let anything ruin his wedding day. "I wish I could take the credit for catching her, but God is the one who brought us together."

Charles sat down on the front pew, spread his long arms across the back, then stared at Tadd. "What's with you? You're— different. Has living in the States all these years changed you that much?"

Tadd had been hoping for an opportunity to witness to Charles. "God changed me. Thanks to Him and His mercy, I'm not the same person I used to be."

Charles huffed. "What'd God do? Snap His fingers and *voilà*! You became a new man?"

"Nope, it didn't happen that way. God has laid out very specific plans in His Word about the way a man can become a Christian and have eternal life. I did it His way. I confessed my sins, asked His forgiveness, and then turned my life over to Him."

Again his brother huffed. "Confessed your sins, huh? That must have taken awhile."

"We've all sinned, Charles. Every one of us. The only way we can know that we're going to go to heaven and spend eternity with the Father is by doing it the way He demands. There's no other way."

Charles lifted his head and squared his chin defensively. "Speak for yourself, bro. I'm a good person, so God would never. . ."

"Hey, this is me you're talking to. I know about your little indiscretions, the travel trips you didn't take alone, the illegal changes you made to the books. Don't tell me those aren't sins."

When his brother didn't respond, Tadd sat down beside him and went on. "I'm not pointing any fingers. I've done more than my share of sinning. But God forgave me, Charles, and He'll forgive you. But you have to ask Him."

"I take it this miraculous transformation of yours came about because of that goody-goody fiancé of yours."

"She didn't pressure me into it, but she definitely had a part in it. Sabrina is different than any woman I'd ever met before. I was fascinated by her and the closeness she had to God, and I asked her to show me how to become a Christian, too, and she did. I wanted that closeness and that assurance for myself." He scooted closer to Charles. "Remember how Grandmother Ingaborg used to talk to us about the Bible and pray with us when we were little kids?"

Charles nodded. "I always thought that old lady was a bit off her rocker."

"I have to admit at times I did, too. But since I've become a Christian and have been reading my Bible, I've come across many scriptures I remember her quoting to me, like John 3:16."

His brother quickly stood to his feet. "Can we not talk about this? All this religious stuff may be okay for you, but not for me. Besides, I want to go outside and have a smoke before the ceremony starts."

A sadness filled Tadd's heart as he watched his brother head for the side door. "Go, if you want, but I'll be praying for you. You can't ignore God. Take it from me, I know. I tried."

"You're beautiful, Mommy."

Being careful not to muss her train, Sabrina carefully swiveled to face her daughter. "Thank you, sweetie. You look beautiful, too." They both turned as a rap sounded on the door and a wheelchair rolled into the little room the church had designated as the bride's room.

"I hope you don't mind. . ." Mother Winsted's German accent gave her English a regal tenor. She paused as she carefully maneuvered her chair up close to Sabrina. "But I wanted to tell you how excited I am that you are marrying my son. I've never seen him this happy. And I'm glad the two of you decided to be married here in Heidelberg. Since it looks like I'm going to be in this chair for quite a while, I doubt we would have been able to attend if you'd had your wedding in Hannibal. It would have broken my heart to miss it." She smiled at Sabrina then reached out her hand to Megan. "And I'm delighted to have such a lovely granddaughter."

Megan slipped her small hand into Mrs. Winsted's. "I'm going to call you grandma."

Sabrina winced. Grandma was a very undignified name for such a dignified lady.

The elderly woman lips tilted up in a shy smile. "I'd love to have you call me grandma."

"Maybe she should call you grandmother," Sabrina inserted quickly.

Mrs. Winsted gave Megan's hand an affectionate squeeze.

"No, that's far too stuffy. I'd much prefer grandma."

"I hope you realize how much your son loves you," Sabrina told her, feeling it was important that she know.

"I have to admit I had my doubts when he insisted on moving to America, but I shouldn't have been surprised. Tadd has always walked to his own beat. I'm very proud of what he has accomplished. So is Mr. Winsted."

"You're really not upset that we wanted to be married in this small evangelic church instead of the large cathedral where you attend?"

"Not in the slightest. All I care about is that I am able to be here for it." She glanced toward the door.

"Thank you, Mother Winsted. You have no idea how happy it makes me to hear those words. Tadd and I both wanted to have our wedding in Heidelberg. You will come and visit us when you get well, won't you? He has so wanted you to see the House on Cranberry Hill restaurant and the way he has turned the second floor into a comfortable home."

"Oh, yes. I'm excited about coming to visit you and your wonderful Hannibal, Missouri. I can't tell you how many times my husband and I have visited Hannibal's Web site. It looks like a wonderful place to raise a family." She glanced at her watch. "I'd better get back to the sanctuary. I'm sure my husband is wondering what happened to me."

Megan leaned in and kissed her new grandmother's wrinkled cheek. "I love you, Grandma Winsted."

With tears in her eyes, the woman smiled at her. "I love you, too, Megan."

After reaching out to give her new mother-in-law a hug, Sabrina wrapped her arms about her daughter's shoulders and the two watched as Mrs. Winsted rolled her chair through the door and disappear down the hallway. "I really like her, Megan, and I think we're going to love being a part of the Winsted family, don't you?"

Before Megan could answer, the door opened and the woman from the church who had been assisting with the setting up of their wedding appeared. "The music has started. We're ready for Megan. I'll come back for you in a moment."

Sabrina handed her daughter the little basket of rose petals. "I love you, baby."

"I love you, too, Mommy." Megan took it then followed the woman out the door, leaving Sabrina alone.

Blinking back tears of joy, she lifted her face and hands heavenward. *You are truly an awesome God. How can I ever thank You for what You have done in our lives? We want to live for You, God. Bless Tadd and me as we, along with Megan, become a real family. May our lives, our thoughts, and our love always be centered on You, the giver of real life.*

As the music swelled and the strains of "Here Comes the Bride" filled the church, Sabrina picked up her bouquet and moved quickly out the door and into the hallway toward Tadd, the man she loved, the man with whom she would spend the rest of her life.

JOYCE LIVINGSTON

Widowed in 2004, Joyce moved from their lake cabin back to their home city to be nearer to hers and Don's big family. Most of her days are spent in front of her computer writing stories of love and laugher, tears and victory—her all-time favorite thing to do, especially since Joyce feels writing is her God-given ministry. The rest of her time is spent with the many members of her family or at her church where she actively serves as a part of the Volunteer Ministry Team. As time allows, she speaks to women's groups and also teaches the Motivator's Sunday school class. Currently, thirty-five of her books have been published with more on the way. She has been voted by Heartsong readers as their Favorite Author of the Year three times and four of her books have been voted Favorite Contemporary Book of the Year, honors she is thrilled and humbled to have received. Although she enjoys writing Heartsong-length novels, she has also branched out into the longer women's fiction and plans to write more. Her personal creed is, "Life is good, God is good. What more could I want?"

A Letter to Our Readers

Dear Readers:

In order that we might better contribute to your reading enjoyment, we would appreciate your taking a few minutes to respond to the following questions. When completed, please return to the following: Fiction Editor, Barbour Publishing, Inc., P.O. Box 719, Uhrichsville, OH 44683.

1. Did you enjoy reading *Missouri Memories*?
    ❑ Very much—I would like to see more books like this.
    ❑ Moderately—I would have enjoyed it more if _____
    _____
    _____

2. What influenced your decision to purchase this book?
    (Check those that apply.)
    ❑ Cover   ❑ Back cover copy   ❑ Title   ❑ Price
    ❑ Friends   ❑ Publicity   ❑ Other

3. Which story was your favorite?
    ❑ *Finishing Touches*   ❑ *Finally Home*
    ❑ *Beyond the Memories*   ❑ *The Pretend Family*

4. Please check your age range:
    ❑ Under 18   ❑ 18–24   ❑ 25–34
    ❑ 35–45   ❑ 46–55   ❑ Over 55

5. How many hours per week do you read? _____

Name _____

Occupation _____

Address _____

City_____ State _____ Zip _____

E-mail_____